THE LEAPING FLAME

*

Mona, after five years abroad, comes back home from America. Penniless, all she has left are the memories of an ecstatic but clandestine love affair. In the quiet of her ancestral home in the country, her past comes back to her in poignant, agonizing memories.

Despite her unhappiness Mona affects everyone with whom she comes into contact. The lives of the parson, the doctor, the landgirl and Michael the local Squire, are all changed as if ignited by a living flame.

How a woman from the past threatens to destroy Mona's precarious security and how through physical suffering she has a final chance of real happiness, is told in this passionate, sensitive and dramatic story by Barbara Cartland.

Also in Arrow Books by Barbara Cartland

Autobiography

I Search for Rainbows
We Danced All Night

Polly: the Story of My Wonderful Mother

Josephine, Empress of France

Romantic Novels

Barbara Cartland

The Leaping Flame

ARROW BOOKS

ARROW BOOKS LTD

3 Fitzroy Square, London W1

AN IMPRINT OF THE HUTCHINSON GROUP

London Melbourne Sydney Auckland
Wellington Johannesburg Cape Town
and agencies throughout the world

First published by
Robert Hale & Co 1942
Revised edition 1973
Arrow edition 1973

*Made and printed in Great Britain
by The Anchor Press Ltd.,
Tiptree, Essex*

ISBN 0 09 908130 X

'And there are those
Through whom the stream flows slowly,
Often dim and grey, but never still.
Its flow unceasing, ceaseless,
Till—as dawn breaks in a sable sky—
The purpose of its moving stands revealed,
The path of God—the leaping flame of life.'

I

'Hell, I look awful!'

Mona knelt on the seat of the railway carriage and stared at herself in the looking-glass. She was too thin and there were dark lines heavily scored under her eyes.

'Over-dressed, too,' she thought, and reaching up, she unclasped the diamond brooch from her shoulder.

Then she stared at it for some moments. The diamonds were exquisitely set in platinum—French workmanship, of course, no one could design or set jewels like the French.

But it wasn't of its beauty that Mona was thinking as she turned it over in her hands then hurriedly, as if she could not bear to look at it any longer, put it away in her handbag.

How vividly she could remember Lionel giving her that brooch! They had been in Naples; they had dined together, and just before midnight they had walked out on to a wide marble balcony.

Beneath them lay the city, its golden lights glittering and flashing; in the distance was Vesuvius, silhouetted against the velvet sky, and not far away a young voice of haunting beauty was singing a serenade.

It was a night of stars which the sea reflected on its smooth surface—smooth, yet moving gently and rhythmically, like a woman's sleeping form.

Mona had leant forward with her arms on the cool stone of the balustrade; she could feel the soft night breeze on her face, smell the fragrance of flowers, and hear, above the murmur of the city, Lionel's voice ask softly:

'Are you happy, darling?'

She had turned towards him. No need for words—he could read the answer in her eyes, in the expectant parting of her lips.

Then, breaking in upon the enchantment of the moment midnight had struck and the tinkling chimes from many parts of the city came clear and melodious on the night air.

'Many happy returns of the day, my darling.'

Lionel had kissed her and for a moment they had clung together, a moment so ecstatic, so pulsating with wonder and loveliness that Mona shut her eyes, wanting it to last until eternity.

Then he had released her and drawn a small pink leather case from his pocket.

'For you, my sweet.'

She had opened her eyes to thank him but it was difficult not to look at the man she loved rather than the present he offered. She had opened the box and drawn in her breath.

'Oh, it's too marvellous! Put it on for me.'

He had pinned it where her dress ended low between her breasts.

'It suits you,' he said.

Thinking more of the touch of his fingers than of his gift she had whispered—

'I wish it could stay there for ever. I wish we could stay here for ever.'

'Darling, I can think of better places—not so public,' he laughed, and had broken the intensity of her mood so that she had laughed too.

How wonderful Lionel had been that night! How old had she been? Nineteen? No, twenty. Five years ago! How far away it seemed now! How lost—that quivering, breathless happiness . . .

Mona was suddenly conscious that she was still kneeling and staring with unseeing eyes at her reflection in the railway carriage mirror. She stood up, steadying herself against the swaying movement of the train.

Again she looked at herself in the glass. The brooch was gone but it made little difference. She could not alter the cut of her clothes, the richness of silver foxes, the elegance with which the curls of her red-gold hair lay against her ears.

Every inch of her screamed sophistication, polished poise, 'a woman of the world'—and she knew just how flamboyant she would appear in Little Cobble.

She made a slight grimace at her reflection. Oh well, what did it matter? But she unpinned a spray of orchids from the furs lying across her shoulder—purple orchids, fragile, exotic, and romantic.

How long, she wondered, would it be before she was given such flowers again? That nice man had scoured Lisbon for these.

'To bring you luck,' he murmured as he said goodbye.

She had let him kiss her hand and then her cheek. What did it matter? She would never see him again and he had been kind this last month while she had waited for a seat in an aeroplane to bring her home.

'You were made for orchids,' someone had once told her.

She had forgotten now who it was but she could recall the tone of voice in which the nameless one had spoken. Perhaps it was true. Orchids were useless, beautiful flowers without any scent.

'That's me,' Mona thought. 'Something decorative without a soul.'

Then she laughed out loud at her own theatricalism.

'How serious I am becoming—and what a bore!'

She glanced out of the window. She would arrive in another five minutes.

The train was passing through a well-remembered bit of flat, dismal country and the weather might have chosen its mood specially to greet her—a grey day, a mist on the horizon, the fields wet and muddy from recent rains.

'Typical English weather,' she told herself, 'I might as well get used to it.'

Funny to think how long it was since she had last seen the dreary dampness of an English winter. Four or was it five—years since she had been home? It was difficult to be sure, but her mother would be able to tell her exactly.

At the thought of her mother Mona made an impatient gesture. Here was really the reason for her self criticism. Darling Mummy—how eagerly she would be waiting—killing the fatted calf, of course, for the return of the prodigal daughter.

'And what shall I say to her?' Mona asked herself. 'Mother, I have sinned against heaven and before thee?'

That, at least, would be appropriate and truthful. Yet was she going to tell the truth? Hadn't she planned in her own mind to announce that she had come back to help her country?

'I understand there is work for every English-woman however unskilled.'

How easily, how convincingly she would say it! No!—she was sick of lies, sick of subterfuge. Hadn't she had enough of them these last years? She'd tell the truth—she'd say—

'I've come home because I'm broke.'

That was the truth, anyway, even if it wasn't the whole truth. And supposing Mummy asked :

'But darling—what did you do with the salaries you told me you were getting all these years?—the sums you got as secretary to that American millionaire?—as companion to that delightful Frenchwoman?—for running that little dress shop in Cairo?'

Or was it Cannes? Why hadn't she kept a list of the things she was supposed to have done? She had forgotten them now—forgotten the lies she had invented, the convincing answers she had given to the questions from home.

She couldn't even remember the names of the people with whom she was supposed to have been. They had been clever names, too.

Sometimes Lionel and she would amuse themselves by inventing them. Sometimes she would take them from the character in a play or from the gossip columns of some local paper, and then she would go on to describe the person wittily and in detail.

Having written them down, across the world her lies would wend their way by aeroplane, by train, by ship, until finally they reached their destination at the Priory.

Now they would be waiting for her, those pages and pages of lies, preening themselves like the white pigeons on the grey gables. That was a good simile, because they were white lies after all . . . 'Yes, white,' Mona told herself fiercely, as if someone had contradicted her.

And if white lies had kept Mummy happy and free from worry wasn't she justified in telling them?

How could she have told the truth?—how could she have begun to explain? Now, perhaps, she might have to! Not if she could avoid it, but there was always the possibility that she would not be able to go on lying. What was it Nanny used to say when she was a child?

'Be sure your sins will find you out.'

Dear old Nanny! She would be waiting too, getting excited now at the thought of seeing her.

The train was slowing up. Mona threw the spray of orchids under the seat and started collecting her things—the crocodile dressing-case, the soft pale-blue cashmere travelling rug, the mink coat of dark, specially selected skins—they all seemed incongruous in her present situation with a third-class ticket in her handbag.

When she had tipped the porter that would leave her exactly ten shillings in the world. Of course, when she got to the bank she might find that some of Ned's ridiculous shares had paid at last, but it seemed unlikely in war-time.

Oh well, she was lucky to get home at all. There were many English women abroad in a far worse position than herself—left completely penniless without even the price of their ticket home.

Now the train had stopped. She opened the door and saw Dixon standing on the station. How old he looked! Of course he must be over seventy—why, she had thought him an old man when he had first taught her to ride a pony!

'Here I am, Dixon.'

She held out her hand.

'It's fine to see you, Miss Mona.'

Dixon never could remember that she had another name. 'I've got a mass of luggage in the van. Is there a porter?'

'There's one of them women about somewhere,' Dixon replied. 'Ted was called up last week. Reckon us'll have to move it ourselves.'

'I'm afraid that's impossible,' Mona said. 'The cabin trunks are very heavy.'

'Maybe someone will give us a hand,' Dixon said laconically as they walked down the platform together.

His optimism was justified. A couple of soldiers assisted and soon all Mona's numerous pieces of luggage were piled on the platform, their foreign labels looking like a flight of butterflies, she thought, a gay, frivolous touch on the otherwise dreary station.

She thanked the soldiers graciously. 'It's a pleasure,' one of them told her.

People always found it a pleasure to do things for Mona, there was something appealingly feminine about her and if she needed help men appeared as if by magic.

'Reckon us won't get all this in the trap,' Dixon said, scratching his head.

'Dixon, you don't mean to say you've brought the little governess cart?'

'It's that or nothing nowadays,' Dixon replied. 'Us put up the car at the beginning of the war.'

'Well, we certainly can't get even half these in on one journey,' Mona said. 'What are you going to do?'

'Robinson will bring 'em up when he brings the coal,' Dixon said. 'It'll be all right.'

Mona looked slightly apprehensive at the idea of her luggage resting cheek by jowl with the sacks of coal, but there was nothing for it, and soon, with only her dressing-case beside her, she was being driven away from the station in the old governess cart in which she had driven round the countryside as a child.

'How is my mother?' she asked.

'Her seems well enough,' the old man replied. 'Don't alter much.'

'Nor do you, Dixon,' Mona said, but he shook his head.

'I be getting on,' he replied, 'but I mustn't grumble. I ain't fared too badly this winter, one way and another, and there's been a lot to do. I be the only man left at the Priory nowadays.'

'Your son's gone, then?' Mona asked, remembering vaguely, although she could not recall his name, a middle-aged man who used to work in the garden.

'Yes, Jack be in the Pioneers,' Dixon said. 'He were in Crete but he got away and the last the wife heard from him he were somewhere in Egypt.'

'Somewhere in Egypt!' That brought back memories—memories of palm trees and sand, of moving slowly up the Nile, of Luxor, of a moon shining on the enigmatic mystery of the Sphinx, of driving out into the vast waste of empty desert, and of the hot, weary nights when she had lain in loneliness longing for Lionel. . . .

No use thinking of that now. She gave herself a little shake—she must keep her mind on the present.

They had reached the bottom of the hill, the pony began to climb slowly up it. She could see the squat tower of the church, the thatched cottages and the ugly red brick of the school.

'The village hasn't changed much,' she remarked.

'No, things don't alter in Little Cobble,' Dixon answered.

'Is everyone the same? Are the Gunthers still at the Vicarage?'

'Yes, they be here right enough.'

'And Doctor Howlett and his wife?'

'Yes, the doctor be here, too.'

They reached the top of the hill. Mona looked back. That was the view which always meant home and England to her—the valley, green and flat, stretching away into a blue distance, broken only by the winding of the river and a line of poplars pointing like startled fingers towards the sky.

Now they were driving past the church—a few very white gravestones—and here were the gates. The gates of the Priory just as they always had been, dilapidated and still in need of a coat of paint; but what did that matter when they always stood open invitingly?

The overgrown drive, the rhododendron bushes interspersed among the green and red holly, the oak trees which had once formed an avenue but which were now irregular and ragged, their orderliness destroyed by age, by tempest and by lightning.

And there was the house, the clinging ivy green against the weathered beauty of Elizabethan brick, the delicate tracery of stone-mullioned windows, and the nail-studded oak door under its pointed arch.

'Home!' Mona thought, and saw her mother standing in the doorway, a smile of eager welcome on her face. . . .

Upstairs, Mona drew her hat slowly from her head. Her room seemed very small and yet she was ridiculously glad to be in it again. She had been half-afraid that her mother would insist on her sleeping in the spare room. But it had been stupid of her to think for one moment that such an idea would occur to her mother.

Custom and tradition were the ruling factors at the Priory and, even though she had been away for years, nothing had changed, everything was just the same. Even the ornaments were in their accustomed places.

She looked round her bedroom. Yes, it was identically as she had left it, even to the pig with Brighton's coat-of-arms across its back standing on the mantelpiece! The chintz four-poster, the blue casement curtains—a little more faded perhaps—the dressing-table with its flounced petti-coats to match, and the silver candlesticks by the bed—nothing was forgotten, nothing was changed.

'I've come home,' Mona thought, 'and now that first moment of arrival is over I'm glad.'

It was a relief to be able to relax, to know that she need not be amusing or clever, to know that there were no cold, calculating eyes waiting to criticise, no bitter, spiteful tongues moving relentlessly.

Suddenly she wanted to identify herself with the house, to be part of its quiet, cosy shabbiness, to shut away in a cupboard with her mink that other smart, sophisticated self she hated—and regretted.

'I must find something suitable to wear,' she reflected, visualising those piles of chiffons and satins, ermine-trimmed velvets, brocades and lambs, all waiting at the station for the privilege of coming up in the coal cart.

How utterly incongruous they would be here! No need even to unpack them, she would never need them. All she would want would be an old tweed skirt, a jumper or two, and a pair of thick shoes.

'I don't believe I possess such a thing,' Mona said out loud.

'Possess what, dearie?' a voice asked from the doorway, and she saw that Nanny had come in.

'The right clothes.'

'Haven't you brought any with you?' Nanny inquired. 'Because if you haven't I've got some of your old things put away in the wardrobe.'

'What things?'

'The tweeds you had before you married and that tea-gown of yours that you used to be so fond of—the black velvet with the little lace collar.'

'Oh, Nanny, you haven't really kept them?'

'Indeed I have, and perhaps you will be glad of them now. What with coupons and high prices there's nothing that doesn't come in useful.'

'I shall be thrilled to see them again—they're exactly what I want.'

'They'll have to be taken in then,' Nanny said reproach-fully. 'You've got so thin there's nothing of you. What have you been doing with yourself, child, all these years? Burning the candle at both ends, I shouldn't wonder.'

'That's exactly what I have been doing,' Mona replied, half-seriously, 'but, oh Nanny!—it gave a lovely light!'

Nanny sniffed.

'You always were one for doing too much. Restless—tearing about, wearing yourself out. But now we've got you home again we'll soon fatten you up, though goodness knows what with ! So little butter and so little sugar ! As I said to your mother, it's a puzzle nowadays to know what you can eat, and no mistake.'

Mona suddenly put out her arms and giving the old woman a hug she kissed her wrinkled cheek.

'I am glad to be home, Nanny—really glad.'

'And so I should hope. It's about time you did come home—five years next April it will be since we last saw you.'

'As long as that ?'

'As long as that,' Nanny echoed sharply. 'Disgraceful, I've always thought it, the way you neglected your mother —but there, she wouldn't listen to me.

' "Write and tell her to come back," I've said to her so often, but she wouldn't listen.

' "She's having a lovely time, Nanny," she'd answer, "and she's meeting nice people. That's what I want for my daughter—nice friendships with the right sort of people." '

Mona turned away sharply. If Mummy only knew ! But thank God she didn't ! 'Nice people !' she almost laughed aloud.

What would Mummy have thought of . . . ? But no—she wouldn't even think about them now; they had passed, they had all gone from her life, they all belonged to a chapter that was closed. She had tried to forget their names; she had tried to forget all they had said and all that they had meant over the passing years.

Some things she could never forget—those things that were hers and Lionel's—secretly, exquisitely their own—but the rest could be swept away into the limbo of the unwanted and forgotten.

'You look sad, pet.' It was Nanny speaking.

'Do I ?' Mona asked. 'I'm not.'

No, she wasn't sad. How could anyone speak of sadness

when their whole life had collapsed, had crashed into pieces? That didn't make one sad, that just shattered one's whole being, left one dazed and broken and too utterly forsaken even for misery.

'No, I'm not sad,' she repeated. 'I am happy—happy to be home. Let's go downstairs. Where's Mother?'

'She's getting the tea ready for you.'

'Haven't we any servants?'

'We have a woman who comes in in the mornings, a married woman, of course—all the others have been called up—and then your mother and I manage in the afternoon.'

'Good heavens!—but what about the housework?'

'We've shut up most of the rooms,' Nanny explained. 'We had evacuees in them at the beginning of the war but they all went back to London. They found it too dull here.

' "I'd rather be bombed than bored," one of them said to me—a pert young bit she was.

'Complained because she couldn't get her hair waved once a week! If they start bombing again I suppose we may get some children, but at the moment the rooms are empty. I give them an airing once a month, but otherwise we keep them shut up.'

'Perhaps it's a good thing,' Mona said. 'The house always was too large for us, or rather, too large for our income.'

'And your Mother's let the Lodge. Did she tell you?'

'No I haven't heard any of the gossip yet. Who has she let it to?'

'A writing woman of some sort,' Nanny answered. 'She got her house bombed in London and has three small children. Her husband is there, too; he's an adjutant at the aerodrome. They manage all right, but how, I can't think. The Lodge was always too small even for old Hodge and his wife.'

'What's happened to them?'

'Dead some time now. Both carried off the same winter from pneumonia.'

'I thought I saw some new gravestones in the churchyard as I passed.'

'They're not the only ones,' Nanny said.

'Well, don't be gloomy, darling,' Mona admonished. 'I think I had better hear about the births first and come to the deaths slowly, although I know there's nothing Little Cobble enjoys more than a funeral.'

She left her room and walked down the wide oak staircase with its heavy carving, which had been there since Elizabeth's reign.

The stained glass in the hall windows cast a strange, iridescent light and the heraldic leopards on the newels stood out in relief against the sombre darkness of the panelling.

Mona opened the door of the sitting-room. It was a long, low room and over the open fireplace was the one treasure in the house, the portrait of the first Vale to own the Priory, painted by Van Dyck.

Mrs Vale, small, grey-haired, and indefatigably energetic, was sitting by the fire pouring out tea. She looked up as her daughter entered and smiled. There was a faint, faded echo of Mona's loveliness, combined with the charm of a sweet personality.

'Come along, darling,' she said. 'I've made some hot buttered toast for you. You must be hungry after that long journey. I wish I could offer you an egg, but just because Nanny and I particularly hoped they'd do their best for your arrival, the hens have all refused to lay for three days.'

'I couldn't eat one even if it was there.'

'All the same, I'd like to have been able to offer you one. You have got so thin, darling, you really must try to eat a lot now you are home again.'

'At least I'm fashionable,' Mona said lightly.

'But I don't think it's pretty,' her mother replied. 'You never were fat, but your face has got quite haggard.'

'Tell me I'm looking a fright and have done with it.'

Her mother smiled at her affectionately.

'You were always pretty, you silly child, but I like to see you looking your best. After all, you've been away so long I want to show you off.'

'Good heavens!—who to?'

'All our friends,' Mrs Vale replied. 'I can't tell you how excited everyone is at the thought of your return.'

Mona helped herself to hot buttered toast.

'It gives them something to talk about, I suppose. They must have been hard up for scandal since I went away.'

'Now, darling,' her mother admonished, 'you mustn't talk like that. You know that little trouble has been completely forgotten—completely. Besides, a lot of people down here really knew nothing about it. It was only the more sensational London papers that made such a fuss. And since then you've been married.'

'And widowed,' Mona added.

'Yes, dear. Poor Ned! Do you ever hear anything from his relations?'

'Not a word.'

'I did see something in the paper about his mother the other day,' Mrs. Vale went on. 'I think she was opening a bazaar or something like that.'

'She would be. A tiresome woman—I never liked her.'

'Poor thing, I was sorry for her. Such an unsatisfactory way to lose one's only son. But I never thought that was an excuse for the letter she wrote to you. Why, you might have thought that you'd encouraged him to go dashing about in that idiotic manner!'

'Perhaps I did,' Mona said reflectively

'Now, darling, don't talk like that,' her mother pleaded. 'You always make yourself out worse than you are.'

'That would be difficult.'

'Mona!'

'I'm sorry, Mother. Go on telling me how delighted everyone will be to see me and who you want to show me off to. How do you suggest I dress for the occasion?—in sackcloth and ashes as the repentant sinner?'

'Darling, you are being very unkind.'

'I'm sorry, Mummy, I really am.' Mona got up, and putting an arm across her mother's shoulder, kissed her gently. 'It's just embarrassment that's making me stupid.'

'Embarrassment?'

'Well, shyness, if you like. It's so long since I have been home.'

'But it is your home and it has always been there waiting for when you were ready to come back.'

'Yes, I suppose that's true, it's always been here waiting for me. I've thought about that—yes I have. I have really, and though I've been afraid, it's been a heavenly feeling to know it was there.'

'Afraid? Why should you be afraid of coming home?'

'Did I say afraid?' Mona asked quickly. 'That's a silly word. Don't listen to me, Mummy. Go on talking, tell me what you were going to about your friends. Who is there to see I'm back?'

'Well, Michael for one.'

'Michael! Of course, I had forgotten him. Is he still here?'

'Of course he is, my dear, where else would he be?'

'I didn't think about it really. Isn't he in the Army or something?'

'Now, Mona, I told you in my letters how he was wounded at Dunkirk. He has been invalided out of the Army now and I'm afraid he'll always have a permanently stiff leg. He did everything he could to make them keep him, but it was no use and so he's back again farming. And a very good thing too, really, the estate got into a terrible way when he was in the Army.'

'Michael!' Mona spoke his name softly. 'Do you know, Mother, I hadn't thought about him all these years and yet I suppose Cobble wouldn't be Cobble without Michael at the Park.'

'Indeed it wouldn't,' Mrs Vale said. 'I always hoped . . .' She stopped.

'That I would marry Michael,' Mona finished. 'But, darling, of course we all knew that. Why, I was thrown at his head ever since I could sit up in my pram. I remember at a children's party when you insisted on us dancing together that I pinched him and in retaliation he pulled my hair.'

'Michael was always very fond of you.'

'Yes, that's true. When I first came out he did like me in a condescending sort of way. Now, Mother, don't argue. Michael was very condescending, so dark and so superior, and the Merrill nose gave him a supercilious air.'

'He couldn't help that.'

'No, I know he couldn't. There have been Merrills with that sort of nose at Cobble Park ever since there have been Vales with noses turned the other way like mine at the Priory. Well, it's no use—those sort of noses don't mix well together despite all your schemings, my darling.'

'You're a ridiculous child. I shall ask Michael to dinner in spite of all you say.'

'And I shall be delighted to see him,' Mona replied.

She got up from the table and stretched herself.

'Oh, it's good to be back. You make me feel young again, I feel as if I was seventeen, leaving school and coming out into a big exciting world full of drama and romance and young men and excitements. What fun I had!

'Do you remember that first Christmas—the party here, and how we danced even after breakfast, and how we skated on that lake and tobogganed down the hill to the station? How shocked everyone was at the way we went on—and what glorious, perfect fun it all was!'

'I remember,' Mrs Vale said. 'And Lionel was one of our guests. You knew, of course, darling, that poor Lionel had died in America?'

Mona stood still. She felt suddenly paralysed. The one question she dreaded had come.

2

She waited for the agony she had anticipated to stab her, but it didn't come. Instead, she heard her voice, quite steady and impersonal—the voice of a stranger—say :

'Yes. I knew.'

'Such a tragedy!' her mother said sadly. 'After all, he was only thirty-nine and with such a brilliant career ahead of him. Everyone said he was certain to be given an Ambassadorship soon. I suppose you didn't see anything of him just before he died?'

'No.'

That was true too, those three days had seemed like centuries—centuries of frantic, agonising waiting.

Mrs Vale was still talking.

'I expect his wife will stay on in America. It would be the wise thing to do with those two small children. Senseless to come back to England and risk both the journey and the bombing. I'm afraid she will be broken-hearted, poor girl. The whole thing was so sudden and unexpected. Did you like her, darling?'

'I didn't know her.'

Must they go on talking like this? Was there no way to stop these questions?

'I should have thought you might have run across Ann in your travels, but then I suppose diplomatic parties weren't much in your line. You always did hate ceremonial occasions. But I'm sorry about Lionel. How excited he was about his first appointment! He heard about it when he was staying here. Do you remember?—the Christmas you came out.'

'Yes.'

'I can see him now coming down to breakfast wearing an eyeglass instead of his horn-rimmed spectacles. You all teased him and someone—I'm not certain it wasn't you,

darling—said, "Lionel, you look the perfect diplomat,"
"I am one—at last," he replied.

'Then he told us about his appointment. He wasn't to go
at once but to remain in London for some months and then
go to Paris—that's right isn't it?'

'Yes, that's right.'

'Of course—it all comes back to me now. And you saw
quite a lot of him in Paris when you were living over there,
didn't you, darling?'

'Yes, quite a lot.'

'You know, Mona, at one time I'd an idea that you and
Lionel were fond of each other. Of course you had so many
young men that I didn't pay any particular attention to
those that were in love with you, but I rather fancied that
you had a soft spot in your heart for Lionel.

'I shouldn't have minded you marrying him, for, although
you were cousins, it wasn't really near enough to make any
difference to your children, and I always liked Lionel. He
had great charm and he was so ambitious that one felt he
was bound to go far. Still, as things have turned out, perhaps it's all for the best.'

'Stop! Stop!' a voice inside her was shrieking. 'I can't
hear any more. . . . I can't bear it!'

Now the pain for which she had been waiting was twist-
ing her heart. She couldn't bear it—no, she couldn't. And
yet that strange, impersonal voice, which didn't seem to
belong to her, was speaking quite casually.

'It's raining.'

'Oh, is it?' her mother exclaimed. 'It isn't surprising. I've
been expecting it all day. I'm thankful it's held off till now.
And perhaps it's a blessing; it will mean there's no chance
of Mrs Skeffington-Browne coming here this evening.'

'Who is she?'

'Oh, my dear, the most tiresome woman! She's taken
The Towers.'

'Why, what's happened to the Colonel?'

'Darling, you know he died two years ago. I wrote and
told you.'

'Yes, of course.'

'Funny,' Mona thought, 'I can't remember a thing about it. Did I merely forget to read Mummy's letters or was it that they meant nothing to me, that I was too busy thinking of other things, too busy living and—loving?'

'Well, these Skeffington-Brownes,' Mrs Vale was saying, 'bought The Towers. I don't want to be a snob, but really the Skeffington-Brownes are almost unbearable.

'They are rude to all the nicest people, and toady to all those whom they think are important. A title, of course, is Mrs Skeffington-Browne's idea of bliss. You should have seen her eyes glisten when she heard you were coming to stay.

' "I shall take the first opportunity, Mrs Vale," she said to me, "of coming to call on your daughter, but I'm afraid Lady Carsdale will find it very dull here after her exciting life abroad." '

Mona turned away from the window.

'She sounds terrible,' she said indifferently.

Then added earnestly :

'Mother, I want to ask you something. Do you think I must use my title now I'm home again? I'd forgotten about it abroad, as I told you, I preferred not to use it. I like being Miss Vale. Don't you think I can go on calling myself what is, after all, my own name?'

'No, I don't think you can,' Mrs Vale exclaimed. 'It will look so odd. After all, what will people think?'

'I'd much rather not use it,' Mona insisted.

'Well, darling, you can't help it. You are a married woman, or rather a widow, in the eyes of the law as well as in the eyes of the world, you can't call yourself Mrs Vale —that would be too confusing—and I don't see how you can be a "Miss".'

'No, I suppose it's a silly idea. I just felt that perhaps I could start again.'

'That's easy,' Mrs Vale said lightly. 'You can start again by getting married to somebody really nice.'

'That's one thing I shall never do,' Mona replied. 'Never! Never!'

She spoke with a sudden passion, her voice vibrating through the room. Her mother looked startled.

'But why . . .' she began, and then Mona stopped her.

'I'm sorry, Mummy. Don't take any notice of me, I'm tired.'

'Of course you are, darling, and I mustn't worry you with plans for the future the moment you arrive home. There's only one thing I want at the moment and that is to have you to myself. Goodness knows I haven't seen much of you these past years.'

Mrs Vale put her hand on her daughter's arm.

'I am so terribly glad to have you back.'

'Bless you!' Mona bent and kissed her mother on the cheek.

'There now,' Mrs Vale said, putting her handkerchief to her eyes, 'I feel quite absurdly sentimental. Mona, dear child, sit down in front of the fire and be cosy. I am going to help Nanny do the black-out. We had to have boards made for the hall windows and it takes two of us to lift them up. Such a nuisance and expense!'

'Shall I come and help you?'

'Certainly not. This is your first night home and you've got to rest and let us look after you. I shan't be long; just look and see if you can find a khaki scarf somewhere in the room. I can't think where I've left it and I've got to get it finished by tomorrow.'

'Is it so important?' Mona asked, looking round her.

She knew of old her mother's habit of leaving things in the most unlikely places.

'Well, we have our Knitting Party here tomorrow; or is it the W.V.S.? I can never remember.'

'Is there any difference?'

'Difference!' Mrs Vale ejaculated. 'I should think there is! I can't begin to tell you the trouble there is in the village over the war services. Really we seem to have had a little war of our own about it. It's all been very unfortunate but I've managed to compromise the best way I can.'

'We have the Knitting Party here one afternoon a week and the W.V.S. another. I'm afraid you'll find them rather a nuisance, except that the W.V.S. sit in the dining-room. We have the Knitting Party in here.'

'Why must they have different rooms if they don't come on the same day?' Mona asked.

'I really don't know,' Mrs Vale replied vaguely, 'except the feeling has been so intense between them that I think Nanny and I felt that even the atmosphere might be charged with hostility.'

'How ridiculous!' Mona laughed.

'It is, isn't it? But after all, when one has to live in the place I do dislike having to fight with anyone and so I belong to both. The only trouble is I keep muddling them up and taking the socks I've knitted for the W.V.S. to the Knitting Party and vice versa. My gifts are then received in stony silence.'

'As I can't knit,' Mona said, 'I shan't have to join either, thank goodness!'

'Don't you be too sure,' Mrs Vale retorted. 'There are some very determined women in both parties. Well, do find my scarf, darling, I must have it by tomorrow.'

Mrs Vale went out of the room and closed the door, but when she was alone Mona made no effort to look for the lost scarf. Instead, she stood staring into the heart of the fire.

Then, as if suddenly stirred into action, she raised her hands to the portrait of Sir Francis Vale above the fireplace. She pressed a hidden spring at the corner of the finely carved frame and, as she did so, a piece of panelling on the other side of the fireplace swung slowly open.

Mona hesitated a moment, took a deep breath, and entered the tiny, secret room where Sir Francis had once hidden with the Prior of the monastery while Queen Elizabeth's men searched the building.

The room where another Vale had been concealed while Oliver Cromwell's men looted and sacked the house; the room where Lionel had first kissed her at that Christmas party long ago.

The room was square and oak-panelled. It contained two old high-backed chairs and a *prie-Dieu*. It was nearly dusk, for it was dusk outside and the light came through skilfully concealed openings in the bricks.

Mona closed the panel which opened into the sitting-room and stood still in the twilight. There was the musty smell of age and dust and yet it seemed to her that the atmosphere was steeped in happiness—that ecstatic happiness which had been hers here in this secret place.

It had been snowing outside—snowing too hard for the party to go out. Someone had suggested playing 'Sardines', and Mona and Lionel had chosen to go and hide. It was Lionel who had thought of the hidden room.

'It wouldn't be fair,' Mona had protested, 'the others don't know about it. After all, it is supposed to be a family secret. They'll never find us.'

'Never mind,' Lionel had replied. 'We'll go in there for a bit to give them a real run for their money; then, when they think they have looked everywhere, we'll creep out and surprise them in some quite obvious place. Come on.'

Mona had agreed. She had found it easy ever since he had arrived in the house to agree with her good-looking older cousin. They had pressed the spring in Sir Francis's picture, the oak panelling had swung back, and they had crept through, closing the narrow door behind them.

There had been a faint, eerie light in the secret room, they could just see the expression on each other's faces, and they seemed to stand in a No-Man's-Land between the centuries, knowing neither age nor period but only a disconnected present.

They had been silent and Mona was conscious of some strange tension, of a breathlessness she had never known before. Leionel was looking down at her, and the laughter which had come so easily to her lips all day was stilled.

'Mona!' He spoke her name, hardly above a whisper.

She did not answer and he said it again. 'Mona!—Why are you trembling?'

'I don't know,' she replied, her voice as low as his.

And yet she did know. It was his nearness, the feeling of being softly and steadily overwhelmed, of watching him come nearer, of feeling his arms go round her and her head fall back against his shoulder. . . . With his lips close to hers he had waited just a second longer.

'You're lovely,' he said. 'Oh, God, Mona, how lovely!'

Then he had kissed her. Her first kiss—and the whole world was throbbing, pulsating, trembling and quivering, until she did not know whether she was more happy or afraid.

He had kissed her eyes, her hair, and the softness of her neck; he was gentle and experienced, aware that she was as tremulous as any captured bird.

His lips were on her fingers and the palms of her hands and again he sought her mouth.

'Oh, my lovely . . . my lovely!'

His words were broken now—Lionel, the sophisticated, the assured, the poised young diplomat was incoherent with emotion. Mona thrilled at the first awareness of her power even while she still trembled.

So this was love?—this restless, breathless beauty, this beating of heart and pulse, this unsatisfied seeking of lips and hands?

How long they stood in the secret room she had no idea. In sentences which were half-lost in kisses, they planned their future. . . . They must wait, of course, they'd tell no one as yet. . . .

It was unthinkable for a young diplomat seeking his first job to arrive with a wife. . . . But later it would be easy. . . . He'd go ahead very fast, be so successful that it would only be a year or two at the very most before they were together for always, when he could know that she was his—could hold her like this . . . could kiss her like this. . . .

'Oh, darling, darling!'

She heard her own voice warm and caressing, and it

sounded to her like the murmur of the silver stream as it reached the fall above the lake. At last, she knew what living meant, this plunge—exciting, thrilling and exhilarating—into the unknown and unexplored depths of love.

'We must go back.'

It was Lionel who remembered that they had been away a long time. The others would have got tired of looking for them, would be playing something else—cards, perhaps, or toasting chestnuts in the open fireplace of the Long Gallery.

'We must go back,' Mona echoed; yet, as the panel opened and they emerged from the secrecy of the hidden chamber, she had felt as if she left behind something that was infinitely precious.

Perhaps never again would there be such a moment of exquisite wonder, such a moment when time would stand still beyond any reckoning of hours or days or centuries. She was back in the dear familiarity of the sitting-room.

Only an hour had passed since she left, yet with its passing Mona had merged into womanhood—she had grown up.

Standing now in the darkness with her eyes closed, Mona, the woman, felt again the sweet, pulsating madness of it. . . . Lionel's voice . . . Lionel's hands . . . Lionel's lips. . . . She could feel them—and then blindly she groped her way back to the door.

She could not bear the echo of that perfect moment. She had opened up the past and now it was too poignant for her.

She closed the oak panel behind her and then sank down on to the hearth-rug before the fire. Her eyes were dry and so were her lips.

She could only stare ahead and experience what it felt like to be old, to have only memories on which to exist—only memories and no hope for the future.

3

The door opened and Mrs Vale came in.

'There, we've finished the rest of the house,' she said, 'now there's only this room to do. Thank goodness we've got blinds in here!'

She pulled them down as she spoke.

'You'll find it difficult to remember the black-out at first,' she went on. 'How funny it would seem now to see bright street lighting and know that one could leave the curtains undrawn without having an irate warden hammering on the door within a few minutes!

'Nanny and I have often thought about you in the "Lights of Broadway". Well, as things are at the moment, it seems to me it will be a long time before we talk about the "Lights of Picadilly" again.

'And talking of New York reminds me,' Mrs Vale went on, pulling the last curtain and coming towards the fire-place. 'I want to show you the scrapbook into which I've put all your post cards.'

'My post cards?' Mona questioned.

'Yes, darling, the ones you have sent me over these last years. So interesting, I thought, they are like a kind of pictorial diary. You remember how I used to keep all the cuttings and photographs which appeared about you in the newspapers?

'Well, I stuck those into a book and then when you went away it seemed rather sad to have a gap of years. Of course, I didn't know you were going to be away so long, but still I started then and there to stick in the post cards you sent me and now I have nearly completed a whole book. Would you like to see it?'

'I'd love to, of course,' Mona replied. 'What an old hoarder you are, Mother! I don't believe you've ever thrown away anything.'

'Not very much, I must admit,' Mrs Vale replied. 'Do

you know, Nanny and I were looking through things in the attic the other day and we found a petticoat that my mother wore at her wedding, and the tie your father wore at his.

'Oh dear!—such memories they brought back—and a satin belt that I wore at my coming-out ball. I had an eighteen-inch waist in those days—it seems unbelievable now to think it ever went round me.'

'I suppose you think if you keep it long enough,' Mona said, 'it will come back into fashion again.'

'No, darling, I don't think that. I don't believe we could ever be so ridiculous as to tight-lace ourselves again. But you never know, it may come in useful as a head-band, or you may even want it yourself as a collar or something these days of rationing. Now let me think—where did I put your book?'

Mrs Vale opened several drawers in a Queen Anne bureau and finally found what she wanted on the lower shelf of the bookcase.

'Here it is,' she said. 'It's really a record of your whole life. "The Mona Book" Nanny and I call it and it starts off with you being born.'

Mrs Vale opened the first page to show the cutting from the front page of *The Times* announcing the birth of a daughter 'to Mary, wife of Stephen Thornton Vale, of The Priory, Little Cobble, Bedfordshire'. Then she rapidly turned over the pages to where the post cards were stuck in neat orderly rows.

'They are all here,' she said, 'and I have put the dates above each one. There—that's delightful, that lovely one of the Seine at twilight, and I love that view of the Bay of Naples. I remember your father and I went there on our honeymoon. And here we start the Egyptian page—you sent me quite a lot from there. Did you like Egypt?'

'No, I hated it.'

Mona's voice was muffled, but Mrs Vale didn't seem to notice.

'Well, I often think these beauty spots are overrated,' she said. 'And here's one from Vienna—a place I always

31

loved—and now I suppose it will never be the same with those awful Nazis there.

'New York was rather disappointing really, you didn't send many and the ones you did are very conventional. Surely, there must be other aspects of America besides the Statue of Liberty and the Empire State Building?'

'It's what you are expected to admire,' Mona said. 'I must look at this book properly, Mummy.'

She picked up the book and moved away from her mother to the other side of the fireplace. She sat down and tilted it on her knee, swiftly turning the pages backwards.

'I'm so glad you are pleased with my idea,' Mrs Vale said, delightedly. 'I used to say to Nanny—"I wonder how long it will be before Miss Mona comes home and we can show her the book instead of just sticking things in it?" Ah!—here's my knitting.'

She moved a cushion on the sofa and pulled out her scarf.

'Now where was I . . . two purl, two plain. I had to undo three rows last night.'

She chattered on, unaware that her daughter was not listening.

Mona had turned the pages swiftly, past a photograph from *The Tatler* captioned 'the beautiful representative of an old Bedfordshire family', past snapshots of herself at a point-to-point, in the finals at a tennis tournament, winning the first prize at a local gymkhana, past all these until she came to what she sought—headlines from the more sensational papers—photographs—long, long columns of interrogation.

There were several pages of them; Mrs Vale had faithfully cut out from every newspaper the bits that referred to her daughter.

'Here is my history,' Mona thought, 'and here is where everything went wrong in the story of Mona Vale.'

It could so easily have been told in another way. How ridiculously trivial fate was!

It allowed the lives of several people to hinge on one unimportant action, one unpremeditated decision in which a

'Yes' might so easily have a 'No', and the pathway taken would have been a broad and happy one instead of tortuous and stony.

She had been in London, unhappy, wanting Lionel and angry because he was staying longer in the country than she thought necessary.

After all, his holiday was so short, soon he would be going back to Paris and then goodness knows when she would see him again. It was this secrecy over their engagement which made things so difficult. Surely he was well enough established now to announce publicly that he was engaged?

They might have to wait to get married, that Mona could understand, but not this wearing, unnecessary subterfuge —this pretending a casual friendship when really there was something very different. Yet Lionel was so insistent.

'I must think of my career, darling,' he said over and over again. 'You want me to succeed and a false step at the beginning can do one immeasurable harm—in fact, it can cripple one's whole future. You know I love you and if you love me what does a short time of waiting matter when we have our whole lives together afterwards? You aren't jealous?—you know there's no reason for you to be.'

No, Mona wasn't jealous, not of other women—but she was jealous of a career which took Lionel away from her; jealous of the time they must spend apart, of the days and hours when they ached for each other, of the months when they couldn't meet—when she was in England and Lionel in France.

And now he was back in London and she had come up from the country ostensibly to stay with a friend, but really to spend every available moment with the man she loved. But Lionel had gone home for the week-end.

'I can't help it, darling,' he said. 'My mother's got a house-party—you know the type of thing—"young people". How I abominate them!'

'And a collection of nice girls who would all make good

ambassadors' wives, I suppose?' Mona had teased—half jokingly.

'As a matter of fact, you are right,' Lionel replied. 'She's invited Ann Welwyn, a pretty little thing, daughter of the Elstrees. Mother always was a snob, she can't help it, poor darling, and the Elstrees are looking for a nice rich son-in-law.'

'They can't have you,' Mona said possessively.

'Of course they can't, my sweet,' Lionel agreed, 'but I can't tell them so openly, can I? I've got to be polite but make it very obvious that I don't like the shape of Ann's nose.'

'How do you know you won't when you see her?'

'Shall I tell you?' Lionel asked. 'Shall I tell you why no other woman can possibly attract me—possibly interest me in any way?'

Mona had raised her mouth to his.

'Yes, tell me,' she whispered. . . .

Lionel had travelled down to Wiltshire on the Friday night and promised to be back in London first thing on Monday morning.

Mona had spent a boring week-end in London, annoyed with herself that she had not gone home, yet feeling it might be difficult to make an excuse to get away again.

On Sunday she had walked in the park, lunched with a school friend and gone to an Albert Hall Concert in the afternoon. It was all rather dreary and she went to bed on Sunday evening thinking—

'I must go to sleep quickly and then morning will be here and with it Lionel.'

Monday morning had brought her, not Lionel, but a letter. He was terribly sorry, he couldn't get away until Tuesday. His mother had arranged a tennis party on Monday afternoon and they were all going to a dance in the evening. Would she please understand and remember that he loved her?

Mona knew that, but it didn't take away the sense of frustration or lessen the conviction that Lionel's mother would not consider a penniless second cousin a good match for her clever and wealthy son.

The hours of Monday dragged by slowly and Mona was thinking of dining alone in the flat which had been lent her by a friend who was in Scotland, when the telephone rang.

It was Judy Cohenn speaking, a voluptuous, middle-aged Jewess, whom Mona had met on one or two occasions and had seen the day before at the Albert Hall. Judy was so glad to catch Mona.

'Will you come to dine this evening?' she asked. 'I have two young men coming, and it will be much more fun if we make it a *parti carré*.'

Mona hesitated. She did not like Lady Cohenn and she knew that Lionel would think her both ostentatious and vulgar. Still, it was something to do. Better have a good dinner at the Café de Paris than sit at home feeling miserable.

Besides Lionel would be dancing—why shouldn't she do likewise? She hesitated a fraction longer.

'Is it worth it?' she asked herself. 'Wouldn't I be happier going to bed early so that I can look my best for Lionel in the morning? I'll have a light supper and read a book in bed.'

Then she remembered that she had not changed her library book for a fortnight.

It was the lack of something to read that sent Mona out with Judy Cohenn that night. She accepted the invitation and putting on a frock that Lionel had never liked, went to the Café de Paris.

The two men in the Party were exactly what she had anticipated. They were the type one always saw about with Judy Cohenn. One was rather an effeminate young man, wearing sapphire and platinum studs and links of which he was obviously inordinately proud; the other was a Rumanian with a blue shadowed chin and somewhat limited possession of the English language.

This, however, did not prevent him making love to every

35

pretty woman very effectively. Mona felt his knee against hers before they had finished the first course at dinner.

The Café de Paris was full. There was the usual glitter of jewels and glistening of white shirt fronts, the usual chatter of voices and laughter which seemed to lack spontaneity, and the usual soft crooning music which soothed one into a sense of unreality.

Halfway through the evening Ned Carsdale, a blond young baronet, whom Mona had met three weeks earlier, came down the stairs. When he saw her he hurried across the floor.

'I'm so delighted to find you again,' he said, taking both her hands in his. 'Do you know, I've scoured the telephone directory, I've asked everyone I knew, and very nearly had detectives out looking for you. Where do you live?'

'In the country,' Mona answered.

'Damn it!—why did I never think of that? What a fool I am! But you don't look country, somehow.'

'I can't help my looks.'

'Thank goodness you can't,' he said meaningly. 'Listen, Mona—I've got to see you again. Dine with me tomorrow night?'

'Quite impossible.'

'The next night then? . . . the night after . . . the night after that?'

Mona shook her head. Poor young man, he was obviously very smitten with her charms, but she could promise him nothing. Every second, every moment must be left free in case Lionel wanted her.

'Ring me up,' she prevaricated, and gave him the number of the flat where she was staying.

'You'll hear from me tomorrow morning,' Ned Carsdale promised.

'Not too early then,' Mona admonished him.

'And not too late in case you've gone out. I'm not going to lose you again.'

'Don't be too sure,' Mona replied provocatively, but she was amused with the encounter.

36

'That's a very silly young man,' Judy Cohenn said when he had left the table.

'Why?' Mona asked.

'He's spending a very large fortune in a very short time.'

'Why not—if it's his?'

'It won't be for long.'

Some hours later they went on to a night-club. Again Mona hesitated, wanting to go home and yet feeling it would be disagreeable to break up the party.

In the night-club they joined up with a whole crowd of Judy Cohenn's friends—raffish, hilarious, and slightly absurd in their eagerness to snatch pleasure where it seemed to Mona no pleasure was to be found.

Yet, weary and indifferent, she lacked the initiative to make an effort and go home alone.

Finally, in the early hours of the morning, they ended up in a studio in Chelsea, drinking gin and beer out of pewter tankards. Once or twice Mona made a movement to leave, but every time there had been such an outcry that good-humouredly she had given in.

She hated asserting herself and it was easier to stay than to escape. But she was getting tired and she hoped soon that the whole party would break up and she could go to bed and dream of Lionel.

It was about three in the morning that the tragedy happened.

The effeminate young man had been drinking a great deal during the evening. Mona had thought him rather unpleasant and had noted that most of the evening he seemed to be quarrelling with Judy Cohenn.

Now the quarrel was getting noisy. The young man was almost in tears—protesting, arguing, waving his hands, his sleeve links flashing ostentatiously with every gesture.

'What's the trouble?' someone asked the man sitting on the sofa next to Mona.

He shrugged his shoulders.

'The usual ending to a dull story,' he said. 'Judy always does take up the most impossible people, gives them ideas above their station and then pushes them back where they belong. Occasionally, they don't like going. That's all there is to it.'

'Who is the young man?' Mona asked.

'I haven't the slightest idea,' was the reply. 'The last one Judy picked up was a motor salesman. He lived *en prince* for about six months and then she tired of him. When I last saw him he was on the dole.'

'I had no idea that she ...' Mona stopped.

She was going to say—'was as bad as that', but she changed her mind, saying it mentally and adding to herself—

'She's a horrible woman and I won't see her again.'

Then there was a sudden cry—a shriek of rage and horror. The young man of the sapphire sleeve links suddenly hit Judy Cohenn in the face, pushed her backwards against a chair, and with a scream, which was like that of a frantic animal, rushed towards the open window.

They saw him disappear ... they heard the thud of his body on the pavement four floors below....

The scream was echoed from several startled, horrified throats. Mona, silent with terror, thought swiftly—

'What will Lionel say?'

4

Mona leant against the old stone wall which bordered one end of the lake.

It was a favourite spot of hers, for here, where the lake curved, she was out of sight of the house and sheltered by a bakground of young silver birches which marked the boundary between the Priory estate and that the Merrills.

There was a glimmer of pale winter sunshine forcing its way through the moving clouds.

Involuntarily, Mona's lips moved, and she said aloud :

> *'A blue sky of spring*
> *White clouds on the wing.*
> *What a little thing*
> *To remember for years—*
> *To remember with tears.'*

'Why with tears?' a voice asked and, startled, she turned quickly.

'Michael!' she exclaimed.

'Hello, Mona. Welcome home.'

He held out his hand and she put hers into it, looking up at him in surprise. She had forgotten how tall he was, how dark and good-looking.

'You must have crept up behind me,' she said accusingly. 'You've given me quite a fright.'

'You're trespassing,' he said, smiling.

'Nonsense!' she replied. 'This part of the lake has been hotly contested for years. Do you remember when your father put up a board—"Trespassers will be prosecuted"— and mine retorted with one saying—"If you can catch them"?'

'Of course I remember,' Michael answered gravely.

Mona realised that he knew she was talking at random— talking quickly and nonsensically to give herself time to recover, to blink away the tears which had glittered in her eyes when he had found her.

She was half angry with him for catching her unawares.

'Well,' she said, feeling she had regained control of herself, 'the old place and the old people don't seem to have changed much.'

'You've changed.'

'I expect so. Grown older for one thing, and if you tell me I am thinner I shall scream. Mummy and Nanny have talked of nothing else since I got back.'

'I wasn't thinking of your figure or your age, as it happened,' Michael said slowly, 'but of your looks. They've improved.'

Mona stared at him.

'A compliment! Good gracious, Michael, I feel my ears must deceive me!'

She spoke provocatively, but somehow she found it difficult to meet his eyes. There was something penetrating in the way Michael was looking at her.

He was always disconcerting, she thought.

There was a feeling of force and of strength about him which was overpowering. One always felt he was determinately making for some secret objective, and that he would sweep any opposition, however formidable, from his path.

'It is silly, really,' Mona told herself—'this capacity Michael has for making one feel small and shy.'

After all, what had he accomplished or what, indeed, was he likely to accomplish here in Little Cobble? Yet, nevertheless, she found it difficult to talk to him—she always had.

'Are you glad to be home?'

Michael was questioning her abruptly yet intently—another characteristic she remembered.

'In some ways. It's a change, at any rate.'

'And for us, too. It's been dull without you.'

'You've had nothing to talk about, I suppose,' Mona said. 'Well, you're all going to be disappointed now. I'm going to settle down and look at the cabbages and behave so discreetly that even Mrs Gunther will take me to her skinny bosom.'

Michael's lips twitched and then he laughed.

'Mona, you're incorrigible. I'm glad you're back—really glad.'

There was a ring of sincerity in his voice and Mona looked at him with raised eyebrows.

'I really believe you are. What a moment of triumph that is for me! The ancient feuds are buried. Shall we smoke a pipe of peace?'

'I'm sorry—I forgot that you smoke.'

Michael pulled a rather battered packet of cigarettes from his pocket. Mona took one and he held a match for her between his cupped hands.

'Thank you,' she said, 'and after this there shall never be a cross word between us.'

'Were there many in the past?'

'A few; but it was not only what you said. Michael, have you any idea how disapproving you can look?'

'I've never meant to.'

'Nonsense! You know that you thought me terrible—you made it quite obvious.'

'That's not true,' Michael protested.

For a moment Mona fancied he looked embarrassed.

'I have never disapproved of you, but, shall I say, I didn't care for your friends.'

'Or the life I was living. Be honest, Michael.'

'If you will have it,' he agreed, 'or the life you were living. And being an old friend, I dared to tell you so.'

'Dare!' Mona ejaculated. 'You positively bellowed at me. You were so self-righteous, smug, and utterly detestable —how I hated you! Michael, I suppose it never struck you that I might have been unhappy about what had happened, that I might have regretted some of the things myself.'

'I was a bungling fool,' Michael said. 'I did think of all that—but afterwards.'

'Oh well, it doesn't matter now, but at the time it struck me as rather unnecessarily brutal. If you want a cliché, it "got me on the raw".'

'I'm sorry, Mona. Will you forgive me?'

'Of course, Michael, there's nothing to forgive. It is what I might have expected of you.'

'That's the cruellest thing you've ever said to me.'

'Is it? Well, I'll take it back. I don't want to be cruel, I want to be kind and pleasant to everyone. I'm going to settle down, I'm going to forget that somewhere some people are concerned only with enjoying themselves and spending as much money as they can.'

'You sound bitter,' Michael said.

'That's the last thing I am.'

'Well, we'll take it at its face value. And how long do you think this idyllic state of mind will last?'

'Until they carry me feet first into the graveyard. So now, Michael, you know what to expect. You can help instruct me if you like. I long to know what you plant after cabbages and how many tons of manure you use during the year.'

'It's no use, Mona,' Michael replied. 'I refuse to be made angry by your teasing. You've always been the same, you know, making me out a dull sort of fellow.'

'Dull! Why, Michael dear, I've always thought you positively sinister, sitting there in that huge house all by yourself looking disdainfully down the Merrill nose at the importunate at your gate.'

'One day, Mona,' Michael said slowly, 'I shall forget myself and give you the spanking you so richly deserve. As it is, I shall leave you—I hope with dignity—as I have to go into Bedford, but we shall meet for dinner. I am dining at the Priory, in case you don't know.'

'I'm not likely to forget it,' Mona retorted. 'Mummy and Nanny are clucking round the place like a couple of old hens, wondering how they can tempt your fastidious appetite, and the whole place will be *en fête* tonight. I assure you.'

'I'm flattered.'

'So you should be. I've even been told to get out one of my best dresses for you.'

'Quite right. Your mother has the appropriate idea of the importance of the occasion.'

'Mummy has only one idea,' Mona replied, 'and she's had it ever since I was born.'

'What is that?'

'To see her little daughter chatelaine of the Park. You know that, Michael. Poor darling Mummy, she still goes on hoping.'

Mona smiled provocatively but Michael seemed at a loss for words. Then he laughed.

42

'Did I tell you,' he asked, 'that I'm glad you are back? We've been taking ourselves and the war very seriously in Little Cobble. We need a light relief.'

'Light is a tactless word to have chosen,' Mona exclaimed. 'After that, Michael Merrill, I hope your dinner this evening is burnt to a cinder.'

'I shall be with you punctually at eight o'clock,' he replied. 'Until then, Mona, let the village sample you in small doses. We've lived a sedentary existence up till now.'

'Good-bye,' she said with a small grimace. 'You always were the rudest man I ever knew!'

Michael turned away. Mona sat on the broken wall and watched him walk across the field to where his car was waiting in the lower lane.

He must have seen her as he drove by and come towards her while she was looking the other way so that she had not heard his approach.

He walked with a bad limp, she noticed, and it gave him a jerky, slightly raffish look, out of keeping with his usual staid dignity.

Dear Michael, she thought with a smile, how funny he was, although he didn't mean to be. He had always been the same, conventional and conservative in everything he thought and did.

She had always liked teasing him, in fact she had made it her business when they were young to rag him unmercifully. As a schoolboy she thought he had hated her; she had played all sorts of tricks and pranks on him in the holidays.

Then, when she had grown older, it had seemed Michael was becoming interested in her. He had certainly made himself useful by taking her to dances, and being at her disposal whenever she wanted an escort.

His car had been an invariable method of conveyance, she had ridden his horses, and made him fetch and carry as did all the other young men in the neighbourhood. Mrs Vale had been delighted and had not tried to disguise her feelings.

Michael had always seemed to her the ideal husband for her pretty, irresponsible daughter.

But the first Christmas she was grown up Lionel had come to stay and from that moment Michael had ceased to exist, save as a butt for her wit.

He had been extraordinarily good-humoured about it on the whole, she reflected now. Perhaps in a way he had enjoyed it.

No one else in the county would dare to have spoken in such a way to a young man who was actually of some importance, as things went. The Merrills were a very distinguished family, and Michael was also extraordinarily rich.

'It's funny,' Mona thought, 'how I always attract wealthy men.'

But it was difficult to know if Michael had really been attracted by her. He had never proposed to her, never spoken a word of love. He had scolded her more often than not.

Never would she forget how horrid he had been during that miserable time when she had fled home, frightened and shaken by what was happening and unable to stem the relentless avalanche of events.

She had been like a child—bewildered, terrified, and yet determined not to show it—determined to keep her head high—to brazen things out.

Her defiance was the direct result of an agonising fear beyond anything she had ever experienced before; but no one could be expected to understand that.

To an older and more staid world, Mona Vale was proving that the newspapers' vituperative phrases of disgust and horror at the modern manner of living were not unjustified.

Those who condemned her did not know that she read the reports of the tragedy with the tears pouring down her face, that she knelt night after night by her bed praying that it was untrue, that nothing more would be discovered, that by some miracle these facts could all be contradicted.

'Oh God . . . stop . . . please stop it . . . save me . . . dear God save me !'

But her prayers went unanswered and every morning the headlines screamed :

New Disclosures in Chelsea Suicide Case. Noted Jockey's Son Victim of Passion
Titled Hostess's Expensive Presents
Dope Gang Suspected in Connection with Chelsea Suicide
Famous Actress's Disclosure at Inquest
The Secrets of Society Unveiled

There was no ending to the discoveries, to the dramas, to the unsavoury sordid details which appeared one after another in every edition of the papers.

It was no use for Mona to protest that, until he died, she had no idea of the identity of the young man with whom she had spent the evening.

Who wanted to hear that she knew nothing of the dope gang with whom the owner of the studio had been associated? That, in fact, she had never seen cocaine or heroin or any of the drugs which were found in large quantities by the police?

Useless to repeat that she hardly knew Judy Cohenn, to aver that she had no idea that the young Rumanian with whom she had dined and danced was the illegitimate son of a famous actress and a reigning monarch.

Nothing she said made any difference, people believed what they wanted to believe and Mona tried to laugh at a world who would not listen to the truth.

It was the wrong attitude and one which an older and more experienced woman would not have assumed, but Mona was neither wise nor old.

So she lunched and dined at smart restaurants, she allowed herself to be photographed in the street, in the flat, eating, drinking and dancing.

She was interviewed and gave her views not only on the sensational tragedy which continued to monopolise the

45

front pages of the newspapers but also on current events —on the modern girl—on Mayfair parties—on the morals of the aristocracy.

She generalised on things she knew nothing about. She was sweeping, caustic, and extremely ridiculous.

There was one reason for everything she did, one reason which drove her further and further on the reckless path to destruction, but a reason which she could explain to no one—Lionel had not returned to London.

Instead he had telegraphed to her that he had been recalled to Paris. He had gone without saying good-bye; without coming up, even for an evening, so that they could be together.

Mona understood.

She had known deep within herself that it was inevitable from the moment when that scream like an animal's had vibrated across the studio. Lionel had a career—love, for him, must always take second place to his ambition.

No breath of scandal must be allowed to mar his advancement.

And so she had driven in deeper the nails of her crucifixion and, laughing, had gone out to dance while her real self was weeping brokenly and bitterly for the future which could never be, for the dreams of happiness which had died over-night as surely as if they, too, had thrown themselves out of a fourth-floor window.

At last the letter she had expected, the letter for which she had been waiting, came.

Lionel admitted quite frankly that he was horrified at what had occurred, and went on to tell her that in a few weeks his engagement would be announced to Lady Ann Welwyn.

'*After my leave was cut short,*' he wrote, '*Ann and her mother came over here to stay with some friends and I have seen a good deal of her. Try to understand, Mona darling, and wish me happiness. I shall always remember the joyful*

*hours we have spent together. Please remember them—
and me—kindly.'*

Remember them! Was it likely that she could ever forget?

The morning his letter arrived she had felt as if something had snapped within her, and at last she had done
what she should have done a fortnight earlier. She went
home to the Priory.

She had crept back like a wounded animal, wanting only
to hide her hurt—to lie with closed eyes and let the world
drift by.

But she had gone too far. There could be no obscurity
for her now. Mona was not the type of person that people
forget easily, and the papers had taken her up as 'news'.

She was written up as 'the modern girl', and a famous
artist had been inveigled into saying that her beauty reminded him of one of the pagan goddesses in Greek mytho-
logy.

Has Paganism Returned? one headline ran, and added
beneath' Mona's photograph—*Well-known Beauty Resem-
bles Pagan Goddess.*

She had gone to London a pretty country girl who was
admired within the narrow radius of her friends. She came
back a notorious beauty and her features were known to
every newspaper reader over the whole country.

If she had looked sad and crushed at what had occurred
it might have been better, but her loveliness had never been
of the wistful sort. When Mona smiled, even though it was
an effort, everyone who saw her smiled back.

She gave an impression of natural gaiety, her voice had a
lilt, her eyes sparkled. Mona, at eighteen, was as lovely and
as joyous with buoyant flaming youth as the sun glinting
on a playing fountain.

Mrs Vale had said very little. She was deeply perturbed
but she alone understood that Mona's part in the tragedy
had been that of an innocent spectator.

She realised, too, that those who rightly criticised and

47

condemned the tragedy did not want to believe in the innocence of anyone who had taken part in it.

They wanted, perversely, to believe that beautiful things and beautiful women were easily besmirched; that beneath a decorative exterior there was nothing but vice and rottenness.

The public were passing through what was known as a 'Debunking' period. They had been disillusioned by world events; they had lost their jobs, their stability, and their savings in the depression. They were down and they wanted to drag people and personalities down with them.

'The Secrets of Society' made good reading—it revealed that those who flaunted themselves as being important, aristocratic, famous, or merely sensational were all the same —susceptible to temptation, rotten at the core.

Mona crept home, but she couldn't shut herself away in seclusion.

The world was waiting on her doorstep; the telephone rang, photographers, reporters, advertising agents, theatrical managers besieged her; all were hopeful of gaining something from her; of using her newly-acquired publicity to their own advantage.

Mrs Vale kept them at bay for a few days while Mona lay on her bed upstairs crying over a letter which would have told them a story far more human and pathetic than anything they wanted to hear.

But such a commonplace story would hardly have interested them—it was as old as the story of the creation—a girl with a broken heart, a girl who loved a man who no longer wanted her.

Youth is resilient. After several days, during which she longed to die, Mona stopped crying. She tore Lionel's letter into tiny fragments and in a dramatic mood carried them up to the ancient ruined tower.

There she threw out her arms in a gesture of renunciation and watched the little white pieces of paper float away, like fallen, fading blossoms of a flower which had once been fragrant and very lovely.

Then she had slashed the lipstick on her mouth and gone downstairs with her chin in the air.

Michael was one of the first people she had seen.

He had misunderstood—as everyone else did—her laughter, the courage which made her talk carelessly and indifferently about what had occurred, and the smooth beauty of a face which did not betray the shrinking misery of her heart.

His words of disapproval had made Mona feel as if she were being whipped naked when already she had been tried beyond her strength.

She had mocked at Michael, answering him defiantly, and all the time something inside her was holding out its hands for sympathy, crying out for understanding, for compassion.

Michael failed her and there was no one else to whom she could turn for comfort.

And so when Ned Carsdale came rushing down in his long shining racing car, tearing noisily up the drive, the exhaust frightening the pigeons from the gables, the birds from the lawn, she had run out eagerly to meet him.

Here, at last, was a friend, someone who had taken the trouble to seek her out, to be kind.

'Come back to London,' he had said. 'What are you staying down here for?'

'I don't know,' she had replied, and wondered why she had stayed so long.

Why she had let herself cry over the letter which had now been carried away on the wings of the wind—why she had listened to Michael or let his cruelty hurt her.

'Come back,' Ned had cried, and she had gone with him.

He had told her there were parties waiting for her; there were friends longing to see her, and she had listened neither to her mother's pleadings nor to Nanny's reproachful protests.

She had packed her bags and they had set off that very

evening, Ned looking like some fair young Viking, she thought. They had both been hatless in the open car as they had swept, too fast and too noisily, down the village street.

Many eyes had watched them go, but they saw only each other. They were the spirit of youth defying the fates, denying the possibility of retribution and risking the future for the thrill of the present.

Their car might have been a chariot carrying them from the gloomy strongholds of rules and regulations to a palace of glittering, sunlit tinsel.

Ned was proud of his car.

'I'll let her out when we get on the Great North Road,' he shouted above the roar of the engine.

'Yes, do,' Mona replied.

They had skidded on two wheels round the sharp corners of the twisty country lanes.

Once Mona had looked back. Silhouetted against the red sky she had seen the Park and the roofs and chimneys of Michael's great house looked dark and disapproving against the warm glow of sunset.

'Why should I care what he thinks?' she asked herself.

Yet she knew that Michael had stood for something in her life—if only for childhood memories of clear, untainted laughter; of clean, spontaneous fun, and of easy, undemanding companionship.

Well, he was an enemy now—as, in reality, were the people waiting for her in London.

That crowd—already she felt she knew them well—who liked sensationalism, were interested in her because she had achieved notoriety. She was alone, except, perhaps, for Ned ... Ned, who really seemed to like her.

She snuggled down in the rugs he had wrapped round her legs, she smelt the heady scent of the big bunch of tuberoses which he had given her on his arrival.

They were pinned incongruously against the collar of her tweed coat and they seduced her with their strange, exotic fragrance.

They were a part of the life towards which she was heading; a life of excitement, gaiety, and surprise; of thrills, music, and champagne.

A life where nothing mattered except enjoyment, where the croakings of the old and the respectable did not count and were not listened to—where men like Michael were considered boring.

A world where the only ambition was to go to a bigger and better party tonight than the one enjoyed until the dawn this morning.

Lionel would disapprove, she thought suddenly—but then Lionel's opinion no longer mattered.

He was going to be married, his arms would be round Ann Welwyn, his hands—those thin, sensitive hands she had loved—would never touch her again.

For a moment Mona shut her eyes against the rushing wind—Lionel's lips were on hers, Lionel's voice was calling her 'darling', telling her how lovely she was.

Lionel was touching her throat with his fingers, pushing back her curls so that he could find her ears. . . .

Lionel loving her and her love for him growing in intensity beyond all words, beyond all expression. . . .

What was the use of thinking of it? She opened her eyes and moved nearer to Ned, nestling her shoulder against his, putting her hand on his knee. He turned to laugh down at her, his eyes alight.

'Now we'll let her go,' he cried. 'I can get ninety out of her if the road's clear.'

'Good,' Mona replied, the force of the wind snatching the word from her mouth even as she spoke.

'You're sweet,' Ned told her, 'so sweet. . . . You're going to marry me . . . aren't you, Mona?'

His voice was jerky, coming in gasps. The landscape was rushing past them—houses—trees—a horse and cart—some children on bicycles . . .

'Say, yes,' he called to her, his eyes on the road ahead.

He was smiling and the last rays of the sun turned his hair to gold.

'Why not?' Mona asked.

Suddenly she began to cry silently, the tears running swiftly down her cheeks as they raced faster and faster towards London.

5

Mona left the lake and walked along the right-of-way which came into the village at the back of the churchyard.

As she reached the stile she sat still for a moment looking down the sloping pastureland to where the River Ouse, in flood, had overflowed into the green meadows, turning them into smooth lakes reflecting the pale sunshine and blue and grey sky.

'How quiet and peaceful it all is,' she thought. 'Perhaps I, too, shall become like that.'

As she lingered a sharp March wind caught her shining curls, blowing them across her forehead, and to the man coming up the church walk she looked at that moment the incarnation of vivid, living beauty.

She heard his footsteps, turned her head swiftly, then jumped down from the stile and walked to meet him.

'How are you, Vicar?' she said, holding out her hand.

'I heard you were home,' he replied, 'and I was coming up to the Priory this afternoon hoping to be one of the first to welcome you.'

'Thank you,' Mona said. 'How are you?—and how's the world been treating Little Cobble since I have been away?'

'Things are much the same,' he answered, but he smiled and that smile transformed his lined, melancholy countenance, giving it a fleeting impression of youth.

Stanley Gunther had been a very good-looking young man, he had thin, clear-cut features and the broad shoulders and narrow hips of an athlete.

He had been exceedingly popular at Oxford, and several people had thought that he would go far. But he had made a fatal mistake—in the second year of his curacy he had married his vicar's daughter.

Mavis Gunther was the type of woman who, in medieval times, would doubtless have been easily disposed of by one of her enemies. In the twentieth century she could not, unfortunately, be exterminated.

She was warped and frustrated; a nature twisted and contorted out of any semblance to real humanity. She had married her father's curate because his virility had attracted her.

She had wanted him, and with the cunning and determination of a strong character she had made it impossible for him to escape her.

Stanley Gunther never could remember quite clearly how he had become engaged to Mavis. She could have told him; for she had planned every movement, every moment, almost every word of what would be said and what would happen.

Having captured her man she was not content to accept his half-blooming affection for her; she wanted to bludgeon him into love.

Because she had no real knowledge of what love meant and not even a faint reflection of it within herself, she killed the first groping tenderness with which her husband approached her.

Being shrewd, she realised what she had done, and then, disappointed, took her revenge cruelly and relentlessly.

A year after they were married Mavis was delivered of a still-born child. She was desperately ill and the doctors told her that she could never have another. It was then that she

53

began to persecute her husband for being unable to give her the love she craved, the love she believed was her due.

She told him that she believed that marriage in the eyes of the Church was instituted only for the procreation of children.

As God had denied them that blessing, they must work together in His service, they must live together as man and wife, but their marriage must be above physical delights, beyond the uniting of their material bodies.

It was a monstrous cruelty to inflict on any young man of twenty-five, let alone one of Stanley Gunther's temperament, who, strong and healthy, had been made to breed children, to live, love and be happy.

He was too much of a gentleman to force himself upon his wife or to treat her as she should have been treated; instead, slowly, perceptibly, his abnormal private life took its toll.

Something withered and died within him so that he lacked sympathy and sometimes understanding with those who turned to him in trouble.

The fire was lost from his preaching, the spring from his step, far too soon he became an old man—a man who went through life like an automaton finding contact with few people, hardly conscious of what he missed, only a shell of what he once had been.

Everything seemed uninteresting to him, drab and dull, as flat as the county in which he now lived, as unchanging as the fields and the slow, turbid waters of the river.

There was only one goal, one horizon—death. Between that and the present there were but grey days, grey hours, and his own grey thoughts to keep him company.

Yet now, looking down into Mona's face, he felt a sudden stirring within himself.

She had always been to him the most beautiful woman he had ever seen; but now her small, oval face held a new beauty, seeming spiritualised, as if her loveliness had grown transparent, and through it one could see the springing, leaping flame of unquenchable life within.

'I am so glad you are back.'

He spoke simply, but it was as if he had stretched out his hands towards a fire.

'Thank you for saying so,' Mona answered. 'I've been half afraid that I should not be welcome.'

'How could you doubt that?' he asked. 'We have been very dull and some of us very lonely without you. Your mother, for instance—she has been counting the days until you returned.'

'Poor Mummy. I'm feeling guilty so don't scold me too much. Nanny's already had "her say" and you know what that means.'

Stanley Gunther laughed.

'I do. Your Nanny always makes me feel as if I were a little boy. She came down to the Vicarage last week to speak about some dead flowers that had been left on the graves, and I expected at any moment she'd put me in the corner for having forgotten to have them removed.'

'Dear Nanny. I think we are all children to her. Perhaps Nannies, as a clan, fear neither God nor man. How delightful that must be.'

'But, surely, you are not afraid of anyone?' Stanley Gunther asked.

'Oh, yes I am!' Mona exclaimed. 'I'm terrified of hundreds of people—women mostly, I must admit.'

She did not add 'and your wife is one of them,' but she thought it.

'Where are you going?' she asked.

'I was going up to the Park to ask Major Merrill if I might arrange a party there for all the land girls in the neighbourhood.

Stanley Gunther had been going to do nothing of the sort. It had been vaguely, very vaguely, on his conscience for some time that nothing had been done for the influx of land girls into the neighbourhood, but he had felt apathetic and lazy.

What did it matter what he did?—things eventually got done even if he did nothing about them.

But now, suddenly, he felt an infusion of interest, a new desire to be energetic, to do all those things which wanted doing and which had been neglected for so long.

It was Mona who made him feel like this. He remembered now that she had always had that strange quality of galvanising himself, and he supposed others, into activity.

She suggested nothing, she made no demands, and yet she inspired each man she met with the desire to shine in his own particular little world.

'A party! What a good idea!' Mona cried. 'And I shall come to it, so don't forget to invite me. I'd like to see Michael surrounded by land girls.'

'He's employing a good number of them himself,' Stanley Gunther answered. 'We are glad to have him back, but I know he is sorry that he had to leave the Army.'

'He's very lame.'

'Yes, I'm afraid he will be always,' the Vicar replied, 'but it was a gallant action and I'm glad that it was recognised.'

'What do you mean?' Mona asked.

'Haven't you been told? He got the D.S.O.'

'No, I hadn't heard. What did he do?'

'Although he was wounded, he dragged himself nearly a quarter of a mile to a deserted machine-gun post. With the help of a sergeant—who was killed later—he kept the enemy at bay for nearly twenty minutes until reinforcements could be brought up and the position saved.'

'It sounds like Michael somehow,' Mona said. 'He'd hate to give in. He gives one the impression of being invincible.'

'I don't know that I have ever thought that about him,' Stanley Gunther said, 'but then I am very bad at dissecting the characters of those I know well.'

'Perhaps that is a good thing for some of us,' Mona said with a smile, but the Vicar noticed that the expression of her eyes was sombre.

'I wonder if she is afraid of what people say?' he thought.

He was so used, like everyone else, to thinking of Mona dancing through life unaware of what lay beneath her feet, deaf either to the applause or reproaches of those who only watched her.

He felt suddenly ineffectual. He wanted to say something comforting and reassuring and yet he could not find the words.

'What a failure I am!' he thought angrily. 'There's something here—a tragedy perhaps—and yet I cannot understand it.'

A suffocating sense of his own inadequacy to cope even with the little insignificant community in which he lived made Stanley Gunther suddenly clench his hands and swear deep within himself that he would try again.

'I won't let it get me down,' he told himself, and knew that to be truthful he might have put the pronoun in the feminine gender.

Feebly, he sought for words and chose the wrong ones:

'I so often think of your wedding and what a beautiful little service it was.'

'Was it?' Mona asked.

The smile that moved her lips was a cynical one.

It had not been a beautiful little service, and in reality Stanley Gunther did not think so. It had been a riot of insincerity, of reporters, photographers and newsreels.

They tried to keep it quiet, she and Ned, for he had agreed with her that after all the publicity over the case, a quiet wedding, with only her mother and his present, would be the wisest and best arrangement.

But Ned could do nothing quietly.

Of course, he talked—of course, he told a few chosen friends and asked them to come down to Little Cobble.

When Mona arrived at the church, in the simple satin dress that she had bought in a hurry and the ancient lace veil which was a family heirloom, she had found the narrow aisles packed out.

The villagers were there, of course, but there were also women wearing orchids whose sleek shining cars were parked along the village street, and there were Ned's men friends—some of them dashing and reckless as himself, others from race-courses, bars and night-clubs.

Ned was rich; Ned was generous; Ned was open-handed —they were all very eager to prove their friendship and make themselves as indispensable to Ned's wife as they had been to Ned in his bachelor days.

And to the reporters it was a heaven-sent piece of news :

Secret Wedding of Wealthy Baronet and Pagan Goddess

The name had stuck. Now, everywhere she went the absurd caption was tacked on to her photographs.

'Lady Carsdale, whose pagan beauty has set a new standard of modern loveliness.' . . . *'Lady Carsdale, who is known as the Pagan Goddess.'* . . . *'Ancient beauty in modern dress—Lady Carsdale in. . . .'*

Oh, how tired she grew of it all !

It was hopeless to escape it and, to a fire that was already burning fiercely, Ned provided an unending supply of fuel.

'Sir Edward and Lady Carsdale have a forced landing in their private aeroplane.' . . . *'Sir Edward and Lady Carsdale give a racing car picnic on the top of Snowdon.'* . . . *'Ned Carsdale's filly, Pagan Goddess, loses the Silver Cup at Goodwood by a nose.'* . . . *'Ned Carsdale's speed-boat capsizes in Monte Carlo harbour . . . Pagan Goddess escapes death by inches.'*

No, there was no ending to the things Ned could attempt, and always, whatever the result, they were good newspaper stories. And Ned liked the publicity, or else he was too good-humoured ever to refuse a reporter.

'Come round and have a drink, old boy, and I'll tell you all about it,' he'd say when they telephoned him.

In fact it was a joke among the gossip-writers that if they

were a hundred words short they rang up the Carsdales for a paragraph.

'My wedding was symbolic of what was to come,' Mona thought.

Stanley Gunther, she remembered, had been nervous. She had felt his hand tremble as he had joined hers and Ned's. But she had been quite calm.

Why should anything upset her now?—all her emotions had gone, had disappeared, leaving only indifference and a sense of detachment as if she saw the world and everyone in it from behind a glass-paned window.

Lionel was to be married in a week's time. Well, she had beaten him to the post.

He should hear about her marriage first, he should think of her lying in Ned Carsdale's arms before she must think of Ann Welwyn and—him.

The papers had carried the news of his engagement, they also put in photographs of Ann. Mona had studied them —a pretty face; pretty, but ordinary; wide honest eyes and a sensible, good-natured little mouth.

'The perfect Girl-Guide,' Mona thought, 'the right type of woman to uphold the dignity of the Court of St. James. She'll look her best when she's fifty. By that time she will be slightly stout and carry off a tiara with an air of distinction.

'And I hope Lionel likes that!' she added savagely. 'I hope he likes being married to a bread-and-butter miss.

'Will she be able to kiss him as I have kissed him? Will she be able to make him breathless and incoherent?

'Will she be able to fire him so that he loses the thread of what he is saying and reaches out blindly for her lips . . . the softness of her neck . . . the shadowy slant of her eyelashes against her cheek?'

Once she had torn Ann's photograph out of *The Tatler* and thrown it into the fire, but it didn't help.

The feeling of blankness, of being past suffering, of being only a doll which was dressed up for a wedding which had no reality, remained with her.

Yet, a leaden heart and nerves which had been anaesthatised into an unnatural quiet could not dim the radiance of her appearance as she had walked up the aisle to slip her hand confidently into Ned's.

To Stanley Gunther, as to many other people in the church, she had been almost unreal in her beauty.

The soft veil, parchment-coloured with age, had framed her face, and the slim curves of her body to fall into delicate cobweb-like folds to the floor in the semblance of a train.

She had carried the conventional bouquet of lilies; and yet in Mona's arms they, too, seemed to have an exotic beauty belying the symbolic simplicity of their blossoms.

When the service had ended and Mendelssohn's Wedding March—played rather badly and jerkily on the organ by Mrs Gunther—had heralded their procession down the aisle, Mona had noticed that her mother and some of the villagers were wiping the tears from their eyes.

She thought them ridiculously sentimental; she had not understood then that her loveliness and Ned's good looks stirred them to a tenderness which made the tears spring.

There was something so vulnerable and yet so triumphant in the bride and bridegroom's appearance—it seemed to those with simple minds that it was the real life ending to a fairy story—the prince and princess who lived 'happily ever afterwards'.

Ned was happy. He loved Mona as much as he was capable of loving anyone; he was enjoying every moment of the excitement, the thrill and the drama of getting married.

It was how he liked to live, perpetually giving a theatrical performance of which he was the hero.

He said the right thing to everyone; he shook hands with the villagers; he kissed Nanny and told Mrs Vale he was the luckiest man in the world.

He had sent down cases of champagne from London so that everyone had a lot to drink and became flushed and excited.

It was, Mona thought, a very successful wedding, judged by the standard of a stage show.

When they had been driven away on their honeymoon in Ned's car they had been pelted with rose petals and rice and at least half a dozen horse-shoes and old boots had been tied on the back.

They had roared off down the road, but when Mona had suggested stopping and removing the evidences of their newly married state, Ned had laughed at her.

'What does it matter?' he asked. 'I don't want to hide the fact that we are married, darling, I'm proud of it.'

They had arrived on the aerodrome from which they were flying to Paris to find, not only a crowd of Ned's friends waiting to see them off, but also a second and even larger collection of reporters and photographers.

'What a farce it was,' Mona thought.

Yet Ned had been pleased and everyone else had thought it an ideal match.

She had tried not to remember, when they reached the Ritz in Paris, that only a few streets away Lionel also might be going to bed.

'Is he thinking of Ann?' she wondered.

Was he writing to her the sort of letter she herself had so often received in the past? Little snatched notes of love scribbled as he had undressed.

'*Mona, my beloved, a dull day. The sun was shining on the Seine and it made me think of you; the way your eyes light up when I come upon you unexpectedly. I kiss your hair, my sweetheart, and perhaps now it won't be many weeks before I kiss your lips.*'

Notes like that, a few sentences of love, of a love which could not really be expressed because it was so deep, so overwhelming, so wonderful.

She was in Paris at last! How often had she wanted to be here! Now that her dream had come true it was like all dreams, distorted and unreal.

She had looked out of her window. The roofs of the city had been silhouetted against a sky that was not dark but rather a warm purple. There was a new moon, a few tender shimmering stars; there was the high toot of the taxis, the continuous murmur of distant traffic.

Paris! How much she had longed to be here!

Yet now that her wish had been granted she was only tortured by a gaiety and beauty which could mean nothing without the man she loved.

'A honeymoon—without the honey!' Mona thought bitterly.

She had laughed out loud defiantly and without humour at her own absurdity.

Ned, coming through the bedroom door, had seen her standing at the window, the faint breeze blowing her chiffon nightgown close to her body, her head flung back in laughter like some joyous Bacchante.

He had caught her up in his arms, saying over and over again:

'You're lovely! . . . You're lovely! . . .'

And he had not understood when she had cried out in pain because his words were but an echo of those spoken by another man.

6

Mrs Gunther, arranging the knitted scarves and khaki socks on the table by the sitting-room window, glanced through the thick Nottingham lace curtains from time to time, anxious not to miss anything that was happening in the village street.

She noted Wade, the gardener from The Towers, slipping in by the side door of the Crown and Anchor, she saw little Tommy Newall fighting with another choir-boy as they came out of school and made a note to speak to them about it the following Sunday.

At the same time she was measuring the scarves, checking them to see they were the right official length. One was two inches short and something like a smile of satisfaction curved her thin lips.

That was Mrs Abbot's effort, a quiet, rather nervous little woman who lived by herself at the end of the village. She'd have to speak to her about it tomorrow afternoon when they met at the Priory.

Mrs Gunther rehearsed to herself what she would say.

'I'm afraid you have not been quite accurate, Mrs Abbot, in the measurement of your scarf. However busy we are, we must try to do our best for the brave boys who are fighting for us. If they were slipshod in their methods, goodness knows where we'd all be !'

She knew that Mrs Abbot would be flustered by her words and upset because she had made a mistake. Her sight wasn't as good as it had been, but that was no excuse, Mrs Gunther told herself.

It seemed to her that she must spend her time correcting the faults of others and keeping them up to the mark.

'No one realises,' she thought, 'what a life of sacrifice mine is.'

There was Stanley, for instance, a man who was always prepared to let things slide—it was terrible to think what the parish would be like if she weren't continually at his elbow, jogging his memory and insisting on him doing his duty.

And then the maid they had now—Winnie. A more feckless, lakadaisical girl she had never had to handle; and inclined to be impertinent, too.

'Soon she'll have to go,' she said to herself. 'They always get impertinent sooner or later.'

She tied the scarves together with string and, looking through the window again, saw Mrs Howlett, the doctor's wife, come down the street on her bicycle.

Every line in Mrs Gunther's thin face seemed to tighten, her lips pursed themselves together, her eyes narrowed.

Dorothy Howlett—how she hated her!

And to think that she—that colourless, insignificant little person—had dared to set herself up as head of the W.V.S. in Little Cobble. The impertinence of it! The daring and —what was more—the stupidity!

Mrs Gunther almost laughed out loud as she thought with satisfaction how easily she had been able to prevent large numbers of people joining the W.V.S.

Many of those who had allowed themselves to be persuaded by Dorothy Howlett because of their affection or gratitude for her husband were now shamefacedly asking if they might join the Knitting Party as well.

Mrs Gunther made it too uncomfortable for them in many ways, and the village found that while Mrs Howlett was good-natured, Mrs Gunther was not.

It was better to keep in with the more dangerous of the two ladies, they felt—helpless pawns between two mighty queens.

Mrs Howlett disappeared out of sight on her bicycle and Mavis Gunther was just turning from the window when, at the end of the village, she saw her husband approaching the gate of the church with someone by his side.

She leant forward eagerly, peering through her spectacles, her nose almost touching the window-pane in her curiosity. Yes, it was . . . Mona Carsdale!

She had heard they were expecting her back and there she was, as large as life and as bold as brass, laughing up at Stanley as if she had seen him only the day before yesterday.

A nice thing to be away from one's home for over four years—but doubtless there were many good reasons for such a lengthy exile. Mavis Gunther made a mental note to find out those reasons if she could.

Her husband was opening the gate into the churchyard. She supposed Mona was going to look at the tablet that had been erected to that reprobate young man she had married so hastily.

It was very queer that she had not come over from Paris for the unveiling.

Mrs Vale had made excuses for her daughter, but then she always did; and very plausible excuses they were, too. Some people might be stupid enough to believe such stories, Mrs Gunther thought, but she was not one of them.

One had only to look at Mona Carsdale to realise that there were things in her life which could not bear too close a scrutiny. Besides, hadn't there been that scandal when she was only eighteen?

Mrs Gunther had not forgotten about that, and she made it her business to see that few other people in the neighbourhood did, either.

Disgraceful!—going about with dope fiends and taking it herself, she shouldn't wonder.

Not that Mona ever looked as if she doped, but still one never could tell, and if it wasn't dope that was because she found other vices which were more interesting, no doubt.

Now they were entering the church porch. Mavis Gunther leant forward so far that she rapped her nose sharply against the edge of the window.

She gave an exclamation of annoyance, then scowled angrily as she realised that the baker's boy coming up to the side door had seen her.

She didn't like young Johnny Weekes anyway, always whistling noisily about the place and giving her what she suspected was a cheeky answer on more than one occasion.

Well, she'd remember to speak to Holford next time she went into the shop.

She'd suggest that Johnny wasn't as conscientious on his rounds as he might be and that there were several other boys in the village who would be more satisfactory.

Mrs Gunther piled the khaki garments into the old suitcase in which she habitually kept them, then turned towards the door. She had not dusted the drawing-room yet, and she had the notes for her Sunday School class to prepare.

She wondered how long her husband and Lady Carsdale would be in the church and hoped Stanley was having the sense to ask her some questions about her plans for the future.

It would be nice to know before anyone else what she intended to do and how long she was staying at home.

In the church Mona stood looking at the white marble slab let into the grey wall beside the entrance to the Vale vault.

It was a very simple tablet in memory of Ned, saying briefly that he had lost his life accidentally at the age of twenty-two.

She remembered how shocked his mother and hers had been when she had refused to allow the letters 'R.I.P.' to be included on the memorial.

Now she felt that perhaps her insistence on their omission had been unnecessary. What did it matter what anyone put, either on a grave or a memorial stone?

But at the time, when Ned's eager, handsome youth had been so vivid in her mind, she had protested against what had seemed to her a ridiculous and hypocritical convention.

'It's absurd!' she had said. 'Ned wanted to live. He certainly didn't wish either to rest or be at peace. He loved life—to him it was always an exciting, joyous adventure.'

'If Ned still wants anything in another world, it will be neither inactivity nor peace—he will be living in it and living dangerously.'

She had gained her point despite protests; and sweeping aside all religious texts, had substituted two words: 'Another Adventure'.

Now she wondered why she had felt so strongly about it. After seven years it was hard to re-create Ned with any clearness in her mind. He was like laughter—a flashing, transitory emotion, delightful but without anything static or fundamental behind it.

He had flashed into her life and out of it again. Now the

memory of those ten months of restless excitement had become blurred—almost obliterated.

She realised that Stanley Gunther was waiting for her approval.

'It's very nice,' she said gently. 'I like it very much.'

'I am so glad,' he said. 'I was afraid you might be disappointed.'

'No, it is just what I wanted,' Mona said, 'simple and unpretentious. Memorials should always be like that, don't you think?'

'I like your inscription,' he said. 'At first it surprised me. I suppose the truth of the words took a little time to sink into my mind, but now I often find myself thinking of them and looking on death as an escape into a wider and more intense existence.'

Mona didn't show the surprise she felt that a man whose whole mission in life was to teach the evidences of the Resurrection should speak in such a way; instead, she stopped thinking of herself and thought of Stanley Gunther.

'Poor man! Death will be an escape for him,' she thought —'an escape from that wicked little monster of a wife who, like a black spider, spins her evil webs from the security of the Vicarage.'

Mona looked up at his lined, care-worn face, at his broad shoulders which were bowed as if he perpetually carried a load upon them.

'Perhaps we can never quite escape,' she said softly. 'If we go on we also take ourselves on with us. But, surely, the nearer we get to God the more intensified everything becomes?'

Life, not changed, not toned down to rest, sleep, and peace, but undiluted—vivid, pulsating, ecstatic—both glorious and radiant when it is released from the thraldom of a body through which it has filtered sluggishly.'

Mona had no idea why she said this—it was as if the words came through her mind and not from it, and only as she said them did she realise their significance.

A flashing stream pouring through this body . . . continuous, passing on unbroken and undivided . . . finally leaping like a flame towards its origin—towards the Creator who had given it birth.

Stanley Gunther had raised his eyes to the Chancel window. The sun was pouring through the stained glass, falling in an iridescent rainbow on the steps rising to the altar.

'Is that what is wrong with us?' he asked, speaking more to himself than to Mona. 'That we do not live fully—that we do not appreciate that life is . . . God?'

Mona did not answer; she knew that no words of hers could help him further. She had started a train of thought. He must find the answer for himself; even as eventually she must find the answer to her own problems, must discover the cure for the misery within her own heart.

How easy it was to know the right answers, she thought, and how impossible to apply them!

She moved away from the Vicar, who was still gazing abstractedly at the window. Slipping into the high-backed oak pew, which had belonged to the Vale family since the church was built, she knelt down.

It was a long time since she had formulated any direct prayer to God—a sense of shame had held her back all these years from approaching Him.

She had known that she was sinning and yet was determined to keep to the path she had chosen wherever it led, her love at once an excuse and a vindication.

But all the time, in the background of her mind, there had stood accusingly the Faith in which she had been brought up.

'Is it too late now,' she wondered, 'to go back?—to ask forgiveness?'

Surely, despite all the Bible teaching, God must require a very great sense of humour to put up with such twistings and foibles of the human mind?

Here was she, who had flaunted Him and all His teaching, while Lionel was alive, wanting to be taken back now that the temptation was no longer there to entice her away.

It was funny really. Poor God! What a lot he had to

stand from these hopeless, incredible men and women he had created!

She knelt, she folded her hands and closed her eyes, but instead of praying she merely asked a favour.

'I don't suppose you will grant it, God, but let me forget Lionel—let me stop missing him so terribly.'

She felt rather mean, rather greedy, to ask even that from the God she had neglected; but perhaps he would understand, she thought, and count it a virtue if only an infinitesimal one that she was humble and prepared to admit her own shortcomings even while she did not regret them.

She walked out into the porch and the Vicar followed her. As they reached the sunshine he said:

'I am so glad you are back.'

She felt warmed, for she knew he meant it and that she had at least one friend in the village.

'Where are you going now?' he asked.

'I'm going home. And, by the way, I forgot to tell you, it's no use your going up to the Park to see Michael—he's gone into Bedford.'

'I will tackle him this afternoon, then,' Mr Gunther said, 'and don't forget you've promised to come to the party.'

'I won't forget. Good-bye, and remember me to your wife.'

'I will,' he promised.

She fancied that a shadow passed over his face.

'Poor devil!' she thought. 'What a price to pay for purity and respectability!—having to live with a woman like that!'

Mona turned towards the Priory, and by walking swiftly arrived home only ten minutes late for lunch.

'It doesn't matter, I'm afraid it's only a cold meal today,' her mother said as she apologised. 'Nanny will have such a lot of cooking to do tonight. I've got Ellen coming back to help, of course—she always does when we have a dinner party—but she's not much of a cook, while Nanny is really good.'

'What a lot of trouble you are giving yourself,' Mona

said. 'I should feel guilty if I didn't know that no one enjoyed entertaining more than you, darling.'

'That's true,' Mrs Vale said. 'I wish I could do more of
it. I often think of the lovely parties your father and I
gave here when we were first married. We always complained then that the house was too small—there wasn't
enough room to accommodate all our guests. Now I should
be grateful if it was half the size.'

'You'd hate it altered,' Mona replied. 'Besides, when
you do give a party think how you appreciate being able
to use the big dining-room, with all our ancestors smiling
down at you from the walls! By the way, who's coming
tonight?'

'Michael, for one.'

'Of course, that's obvious. I saw him when I was out. I
told him you still hoped that we'd get married.'

'My dear child, I hope you said nothing of the sort!' Mrs
Vale exclaimed.

'Oh, yes, I did. He looked rather startled. I don't think
the idea had ever occurred to him.'

'Really, darling, how ridiculous you are,' her mother
expostulated. 'I do wish you'd be sensible for once. I want
you to like Michael and I am sure Michael likes you—but,
of course, if you're going to frighten him . . .'

'Frighten him!' Mona exclaimed. 'He wasn't very frightened of me this morning, I can assure you. I think, Mummy,
that Michael can well look after himself. He always was
disgustingly self-sufficient, which I have never been. But
never mind, don't let's talk about him. Who else is coming?'

'Dr and Mrs Howlett.'

'Oh, good. I like both of them, they are quite the nicest
people in the village.'

'And General Featherstone,' Mrs Vale finished.

'Your young man, in fact. Oh, darling, how gay we're
being. You talk about me looking nice—I hope you are
going to look your best?'

'What nonsense you talk!' her mother exclaimed, but all
the same she was pleased.

It was an understood thing that General Featherstone had loved Mary Vale ever since she was first widowed.

He was a courtly, handsome old man of over seventy and his courtship, if it was one—for Mrs Vale made no confidantes—had the old-world charm and the gentle, lingering fragrance of lavender.

'Well, we do see life in Little Cobble,' Mona said that evening as she was changing for dinner. 'Fancy Mummy giving a dinner party the night after I arrive home!'

'Your mother's been thinking about it ever since she heard you were returning,' Nanny, who had come up to help her dress replied. 'Now look your best, dearie, and be a credit to her. Don't go saying those things that upset her. You know the sort—nasty, unkind things about yourself. I've often said to your mother:

' "The child's her own worst enemy. If she had been born dumb there'd never have been a word spoken against her." '

'Nanny, darling, you're as full of theories as there are plums in a plum-pudding,' Mona said. 'Here, do me up at the back and then I mustn't keep you or your precious chicken will be burnt to a cinder.'

'Not it,' Nanny said stoutly. 'I do know my oven if I know nothing else.'

But all the same she hooked Mona's dress and hurried downstairs.

'I'm much too smart,' Mona thought, looking at herself in the glass. 'My old black velvet, with its lace collar, would have been far more appropriate. Ah, well! it will give Michael something to think about. I'd like to know his real opinion of me.'

Her reflection told her that she was lovely.

Her dress of sunshine yellow chiffon picked up in some magical fashion the lights in her hair; it was startling and slightly daring, both in its colour and cut, and yet it had a grace and a glamour which only a Hollywood dressmaker could have imparted.

She wore emeralds in her ears and a great carved cabochon emerald weighed down the third finger of her left hand.

Lionel had bought it for her in Cairo. He had paid a fabulous price for it and, when she remonstrated with him for extravagance, he had laughed and kissed the palm of her hand.

'I wanted to see it on your finger,' he said. 'I am still in two minds as to which is the most beautiful—your hand or the jewels with which I try to decorate it.'

Lionel had loved giving her beautiful things. He had been fastidious to an amazing degree; only the most perfect jewels, the most exquisite and expensive clothes were good enough.

He did not mind how much he paid—dressing her seemed to be one of his hobbies. Sometimes she asked herself if she was nothing more than a doll for which Lionel must search the world for exquisite trappings—sables from Russia, silver foxes from Canada, jade from China, and rubies from Ceylon.

He would spend hours choosing her a present and yet sometimes she had a feeling that he chose it as much for himself—as a connoisseur adds to a collection in a cabinet. He aimed at perfection and yet Mona knew that perfection was important only as long as it affected him personally.

She must look lovely for him; she must wear wonderful clothes, sensational jewels and unique furs.

But she must put up with tawdry, dingy lodgings when he could not be with her; she must travel alone; she must invite curiosity and gossip; she must associate with the riff-raff that thronged the second-rate hotels and the second-rate restaurants.

She must never approach the best, the most amusing, or the most distinguished people in any city for fear in that way her life might overlap Lionel's career and damage it.

No, Lionel demanded perfection, but only where that perfection was a part of their joint existence.

'Stop thinking about him,' she told herself, and smiled at her reflection in the glass.

'Mona Carsdale, ready to make her entrance into a new life,' she said mockingly, 'a brave new world of cabbages and cows—of furrows and farmers!'

She swept out of her tiny bedroom, along the passage and down the wide oak stairway.

Michael had just arrived and was standing in the hall below her. She called to him from the top of the stairs and he watched her coming down to him as warm and golden as the hot sun on some sandy beach.

'Well,' she asked as she reached the bottom step, 'do I grace the occasion or would you prefer a gentle little woman in grey?'

'I don't believe you'd be subdued even in that,' he answered. 'But before we start fighting, let me tell you—as I have already done once—that your looks have improved.'

'Before we start fighting!' Mona echoed with raised eyebrows. 'Why should you suppose we're going to do anything of the sort?'

'A foregone conclusion. I saw the glint of battle in your eyes as you came downstairs.'

'You're quite wrong. Nanny's been giving me a good talking to and I'm on my best behaviour tonight. I'm going to sit beside you, lisping prettily—"Oh, yes, Michael," "Quite right, Michael!" "But how wonderful of you, Michael!" How will you like that for a change?'

'I shall love it. Don't forget to keep it up.'

'I won't. Now watch me do my part gracefully.'

Mona opened the sitting-room door and swept in. The doctor, his wife, and General Featherstone were standing in front of the fire and Mrs Vale was handing them glasses of sherry.

Mona was certainly at her best, Michael thought, as he watched her gratify the Howletts with her apparent joy at seeing them and delight the General by kissing his cheek and asking him if he had been faithful to her while she had been away.

During dinner she kept the party amused, she was viva-

73

cious and witty, raising the whole tempo of the conversation by her gaiety.

Watching Mrs Vale at the end of the table, Michael thought that her delight was almost pathetic. She was so proud of her daughter—so anxious to show her off and to have everyone think how wonderful.

When the small but well-cooked meal was over, Mrs Vale shepherded the women into the sitting-room.

'Don't be long,' she told the men, 'and Michael—see that the General remembers to pass the port; when he is telling his best story he often forgets.'

Mona, leaving the dining-room, linked her arm through Dorothy Howlett's.

'And how have you been getting on?' she asked.

The doctor's wife was the one person in the village with whom she had been on confidential terms before she married. She was a small, rather insignificant little woman who had once been pretty.

She had a face which was as frank and open as a child's, and so simple in outline that at times it was difficult to remember that she had the same number of features as anyone else. She had, too, what was commonly known as 'a heart of gold'.

Dorothy Howlett's good nature was proverbial, with the result that she was continually doing twice as much as she ought to do. She had a busy, clever husband to look after, she had four small children of her own, and at the moment three evacuees in the house.

Yet she had undertaken not only the organisation of the W.V.S. but also the job of billeting officer for two villages —a task which required tremendous diplomacy and tact besides a certain amount of steely determination.

Dorothy Howlett did not complain; she never had a moment to herself, a holiday or a day off from domestic troubles, but she appeared happy and her adoration of her husband was very obvious.

'Is this what a happy marriage means?' Mona wondered. She looked at Dorothy's five-year-old evening-dress, which was beginning to split at the seam, and noted the grey growing in profusion in the brown hair which badly needed a set.

Dorothy was a little flushed now from the dinner and the glass of port which Mrs Vale had insisted she should have. She was talking with an almost pathetic eagerness, anxious to be pleasant and to respond to Mona's vivacity.

'Oh, I am so glad you are back!' she exclaimed.

'Everyone's being very kind,' Mona answered. 'Do you know, quite a lot of people have said they are glad to see me and somehow I didn't expect it.'

'But why not?' Dorothy asked. 'We have all been longing for your return. I know I have.'

'Why?' Mona asked curiously.

Dorothy looked at her in surprise, then saw she really wanted to know.

'Can't you understand?' she said. 'We all want waking up. We all want to be told that there's a big world outside Little Cobble. You're like a glimpse of some other life, even of another sort of civilisation, you're like . . . oh, how can I put it? You're like going to the cinema.'

Mona laughed.

'Oh, Dot, how lovely! I've never heard a better description—I only wish it were all true, instead of which I have come back dull and weary to lay my bones among you.'

There was a ring of emotion in Mona's voice, but before Dorothy could question her they were joined by Mrs Vale.

'How did you think my daughter's looking?' she asked proudly.

'Don't tell her,' Mona said quickly. 'She takes it as a compliment to herself, not to me. Poor mummy!—she still believes that her ugly duckling has turned into a swan!'

'You were never an ugly duckling,' Mrs Vale protested. 'Although you were my own, I thought you were one of the prettiest babies I'd ever seen.'

'But, Mummy darling,' Mona expostulated. 'Don't you

know that every mother thinks her baby is the prettiest in the world. Why, even the black mammies in San Francisco used to hold up their little chocolate-coloured piccaninnies for me to admire and you could see that they thought them prettier than any pink and white blue-eyed angel has ever appeared to us!'

'Quite right, too,' Mrs Vale approved. 'I've always said that there's nothing like children for giving one a sense of pride and a thrill of possession. Don't you agree with me, Dorothy?'

'Indeed I do,' Dorothy Howlett replied.

'You will understand what we mean one day, darling,' Mrs Vale said complacently.

The door opened as she spoke and the men came in. Mona got to her feet.

'You've come just at the right moment,' she cried. 'I'm sadly in need of help and support. Not content with wanting to find me a husband, Mummy now wants me to have a baby, and I can't really make out which comes first.'

'Really, darling,' her mother exclaimed. 'How you do twist my words! Don't listen to her, General, she's a very naughty girl.'

'But a very pretty one,' the General replied. 'I don't know what treatment they give you for looks in America, but if we could sell it in bottles over here we'd all make a fortune.'

'What a good idea,' Mona laughed. 'You shall be chairman of the company and I will be the managing director.'

'And what part am I to play?' Michael asked.

Mona looked at him provocatively.

'Financier, of course,' she said. 'I don't think you'd be useful as anything else, do you?'

She was delighted to notice a glint in Michael's eyes and know that her shaft had gone home.

It amused her to annoy him and she knew that in some ways he was sensitive about his money. He hated references to it and the fact that people, especially his friends, might care for him only because of his generosity.

Mrs Vale was pulling out the bridge table.

'Now stop talking nonsense, children,' she commanded. 'We older people are going to play bridge. Mona, I can't have you and Michael chattering and disturbing our game. Why don't you go up to the Long Gallery and roast chestnuts? I told Dixon to bring in some this afternoon.'

'What a lovely idea, Mummy,' Mona said demurely.

But when she had left the room with Michael she burst out laughing.

'Isn't Mummy divine?' she asked. 'Did you ever see anything so obvious? This is what is called "letting the young people get to know each other." Now, Michael, the next move is up to you.'

'What do you suggest I do?' Michael asked heavily.

'I'll tell you,' Mona replied.

They reached the Long Gallery and found the fire burning brightly and a big basket of chestnuts beside it.

'I'm awaiting instructions.'

'Well, you sit in the arm-chair,' Mona told him, 'and I sit gracefully on the rug at your feet. That gives a cosy atmosphere, you see, and while I put the chestnuts in the fire you ask me questions. "What do you think about life?" is a good one which inevitably leads us, sooner or later, to sex.'

She suited her actions to her words and sank down upon the hearthrug, her skirts billowing out round her so that she looked like a lake of golden light.

But Michael was silent, and after a moment she glanced up at him under her eyelashes.

'Well,' she asked, 'aren't you going to begin?'

'I think it is for you to do that,' Michael replied. 'They tell me "confession is good for the soul." '

'Confession!' Mona exclaimed. 'I'm not likely to confess to you, Michael Merrill, you wouldn't be a good person to choose. You would be too hard, too set in your ways —you wouldn't understand the waverings and defects of weak people like myself. You're strong—you stride through life going straight towards your objective.'

'There's still no reason why I shouldn't be understanding. Suppose you try me.'

'Confide in you! Not on your life. For one thing, I'd hate to ask you for comfort—I've had a taste of your disapproval once.'

'I've said I'm sorry for that.'

'What's the good of words? It's deeds that count. If you had been sweet to me then, if you'd played the big brother, which was what I wanted, well—things might have been different.'

'What things?' Michael asked sharply.

'Oh, I don't know,' Mona said impatiently. 'Perhaps it was all inevitable—everything, including your attitude.'

She turned towards the fire.

'This chestnut's done. Shall I give it to you?'

'No, thank you, I'm not hungry at the moment.'

'You sound peevish,' Mona teased him. 'Poor Michael! —I believe you're quite annoyed because I won't tell you the story of my life. One day I'll put it all in a book and then you will be able to read it and make caustic remarks about my behaviour to your friends.'

'Do you think that's likely?'

'I shouldn't know. I've come to the conclusion I know very little about anyone. People always behave unexpectedly in my life. Perhaps, like you, I am not a good judge of character.'

'Who said I wasn't a good judge?'

'I did. But that's only sour grapes. I always wanted you to admire me, to think I was clever and brilliant, even when I was a little girl. Instead, you just looked superior, with a "girl's don't count" sort of attitude.'

'Listening to you I begin to believe I'm a rotten sort of fellow.'

'Listening to me,' Mona retorted, 'you'll learn that you're just a little bit smug.'

'How do you know. You've been away a long time. I might have altered.'

'So you might,' she agreed reflectively. 'I never thought

of that. Have you altered, Michael? What have you been doing? Having dashing, romantic love affairs?'

'Perhaps.'

'Oh, how thrilling!—and nobody's told me. Who with?'

'I thought you were against confessions.'

'*Touché*,' Mona exclaimed. 'But I have an idea that you are trying to drive a hard bargain—I'll tell you if you'll tell me. But how do I know there's really anything to tell,'

'Of course, that dark, handsome reserve of yours has its points. The strong, silent man, an English Gary Cooper. Michael, I believe you are a dark horse and I have never realised it.'

'And what happens now you do?' Michael inquired.

'I can't think,' Mona said mockingly, 'except it's rather more exciting for me to realise that here, next door, is a strange and, shall we say, attractive man about whom I know nothing. I believe I shall have to flirt with you.'

'Your mother would be delighted.'

Mona laughed.

'All right, that's one to you. You have altered, Michael. I have a feeling that you most definitely might be amusing. Let's go down and see what the others are doing, now. I expect they'll only play one rubber. The General never stays out late.'

She rose to her feet and stood shaking out the folds of her dress. Michael had risen, too, and was looking down at her.

'A most interesting little talk, Major Merrill!' she said frivolously.

Then she gave a little gasp for Michael, coming suddenly close to her, put his arms round her.

'Michael!' she exclaimed, but the words died on her lips as his mouth crushed hers.

He kissed her fiercely, almost brutally, holding her so tightly that she could hardly breathe. Then abruptly he let her go.

She stood swaying with the surprise of his action, one hand against her breast, the other against her cheek.

'Michael!' she exclaimed again.

'Isn't that what you've been asking for?' he inquired, and his voice was as insulting as if he had slapped her. 'I thought you were trying to flirt with me.'

For a moment she stared at him as if he had suddenly gone mad, and then the warm colour flooded up her white neck and over her cheeks.

She drew in her breath, and without speaking swept across the polished floor towards the door.

7

They came down the oak stairway in silence, Mona moving in front of Michael, her head held high. As she reached the hall she heard someone knocking on the front door.

'I expect Nanny's gone to bed,' she thought, and crossing the hall raised the heavy iron latch.

A man stood outside, and when the light shone on him Mona could see that he was wearing Air Force uniform.

'Is Dr Howlett here?' he asked.

'Yes,' Mona replied. 'Do you want to speak to him?'

'I want him to come at once,' the man answered. 'My child's hurt himself badly.'

'I'll fetch the Doctor,' Mona said. 'Won't you come in?'

'It's Squadron-Leader Archer, isn't it?' she heard Michael say.

A few seconds later Dr Howlett came hurrying into the hall.

'What's the matter, Archer?' he asked. 'One of the kiddies ill?'

'Gerry's cut himself,' the Squadron-Leader replied. 'He woke up and asked for a drink of milk and my wife gave it him in a glass. She only turned her back for a moment but he managed to break it and he's bleeding pretty badly.'

'I'll come at once,' the Doctor said. 'Thank goodness, my bag's in the car! I have the sense never to leave it at home these days.'

He put on his thick coat.

On an impulse Mona slipped into one of the old tweed coats which her mother habitually kept hanging in a cupboard near the front door.

'I'm coming with you,' she said shortly, when Dr Howlett looked at her inquiringly.

'Tell Dorothy where I've gone, will you?' the Doctor asked Michael.

He nodded.

'I'll tell her and follow you,' he said. 'I might be useful, one never knows.'

It was only a few minutes' run to the lodge.

'This must be the husband of the "writing woman" Nanny spoke about,' Mona thought as they went. 'He looks young to be a Squadron-Leader, and still younger to have three children.'

She wondered what they had made of the lodge.

She remembered the sitting-room as it had been in the days when the gardeners lived there—frowsy, over crowded, with heavy lace curtains veiling the windows so that the room, eerie and connected in her mind as a child with stories of witches and hobgoblins.

They drew up at the door and, not standing on ceremony, Dr Howlett made no attempt to let Mona go first, but hurried into the house.

Mona followed him. The room seemed far larger than she remembered it, and she had a quick impression of primrose yellow walls, of orange chintz curtains, of small, suitable pieces of old oak furniture.

Then all her attention was concentrated on the girl sitting by the fire holding a screaming child in her arms.

She had a piquant prettiness, dark hair cut like a page-boy and almond-shaped eyes wide with fright.

The child was about three and he was screaming with all the might of his lungs. There was blood everywhere. blood on his mother's dress, blood on his own legs, on the floor. . . .

'I tried to put a tourniquet on him,' Mrs Archer was saying in a voice which held a rising note of fear.

'That's all right,' the Doctor said. 'Don't worry now, we'll fix it in a few minutes.'

There was a large, ugly gash which seemed as if it had severed the child's left hand in half.

'Hot water,' he added curtly, 'and a basin if you have one.'

The Squadron-Leader stood helplessly, as if paralysed by his son's appearance. Mona and Michael made a rush for the small kitchen.

Michael found a bowl and Mona put the electric kettle on to boil. She went back into the sitting-room just in time to hear Mrs Archer murmur weakly :

'I'm terribly sorry, but I think I'm going to faint.'

Mona wasn't sure afterwards how it happened, but the child was in her arms, there was the sickly sweet smell of chloroform, and then she was conscious only of a small, warm, and surprisingly hard head nestling against her breast.

The Doctor was sewing up the cut. He took no notice of the mother who was lying back in a chair with an ashen face while her husband fetched her a glass of brandy.

'Move him round a little bit, Mona,' Dr Howlett said. 'That's right. Hold him steady now. That's splendid.'

He finished the job.

Mona could not look at that tiny hand with its ghastly wound, instead she kept her eyes on the curly head, thinking how soft and fair it was and how white the little forehead against the flaming gaiety of her dress.

She glanced up just once and found Michael's eyes fixed on her. She looked away again, remembering almost with an effort that she was angry with Michael.

It somehow seemed unimportant beside the child, so warm, heavy and strangely comforting in her arms.

'I like children,' she thought suddenly. 'I ought to have had dozens of them—Lionel's children and mine. I wonder what they would have been like? Handsome and naughty, I expect.'

For a moment she drifted into a reverie in which the child she held was really hers. She was almost startled to hear Dr Howlett say :

'That's splendid, thank you, Mona. Will you carry him to his cot?'

'Is it upstairs?' she asked the Squadron-Leader.

'I'll show you,' he said. 'No, sit still,' he commanded his wife, 'there's no reason for you to move, Lynn.'

Mona followed the young father up the tiny, twisted stairs. He opened the door of the bedroom. Inside there was darkness and the sound of even breathing.

He switched on the light and Mona saw two small beds and a cot in a row. Gently she lowered the child from her arms to the empty cot and covered him over with blankets.

'Lucky the others have slept through it,' the Squadron-Leader said in a low voice.

She looked in the other beds. A little girl of about five and a boy perhaps a year older were sleeping peacefully, their faces almost angelic in the relaxation which comes with sleep.

The Doctor came up the stairs.

'He's all right now,' he said. 'He won't be round for a little while. And I'll leave your wife something to give him as soon as he wakes, something that will put him to sleep again. I expect you both want a good night after this.'

'It was a bit of a shock,' the Squadron-Leader answered with a grin. 'What about a whisky, Doctor?'

'That's just what I was going to prescribe for you,' Dr Howlett answered. 'And I'll join you.'

They all went downstairs again. Mrs Archer had moved now from the chair and was sitting on the hearthrug.

83

'I'm terribly ashamed of myself,' she said. 'Will you forgive me, Dr Howlett?'

'There's nothing to forgive, my dear,' he replied. 'I thought you behaved very well. At least, you waited until we got here.'

Mrs Archer looked at Mona and cried out:

'Oh, your lovely dress! how awful! I'm so sorry.'

Mona looked down and saw that a long stream of blood had stained the delicate chiffon.

'It doesn't matter,' she answered. 'I don't expect I shall ever have the opportunity of wearing this dress again here in Little Cobble.'

'But I couldn't be sorrier it's happened,' Mrs Archer insisted. 'What can we do about it, Bill?'

Bill Archer looked as troubled as his wife.

'I can't think,' he said. 'Unless Mrs Vale puts a shilling a week on the rent and we take the rest of our lives to pay it off.'

'Oh, of course, you are Mrs Vale's daughter,' Mrs Archer exclaimed to Mona. 'I wondered vaguely who you might be. We heard you were coming home—in fact, everybody's been talking about your return.'

'I'm gratified,' Mona replied.

'I was so looking forward to seeing you, too,' Mrs Archer said, 'and now I have blotted my copybook—or rather Gerry has for me—the very first moment of our acquaintance.'

'Gerry could never blot his own copybook,' Mona answered lightly. 'He's the most adorable baby I've ever seen—even when he's screaming he has a unique charm. In fact, when you are tired of him I'll adopt him.'

'There's not a hope, I'm afraid,' Mrs Archer smiled. 'Both Bill and I are crazy about him, in spite of the fact that at times I'd give the whole three away with a pound of tea. That's when I'm trying to write.'

'But can you—here?' Mona asked. 'It must be almost impossible. I mean the noise, and being so cramped.'

'It is rather difficult,' Mrs Archer confessed, 'except on

fine days when I push them all into the garden and tell them to stay there.'

'You've hit on a rather sore subject, as a matter of fact,' Bill said. 'Lynn is stuck for a new book and unless some sort of inspiration comes to her we shall all find ourselves camping in the park, being unable to pay the rent.'

'I must come and inspire you,' Mona suggested gaily, 'but tonight you must be longing to see the last of us. I'll come and call formally tomorrow.'

She got to her feet and held out her hand. Dr Howlett looked at his watch.

'I think I'll stay another quarter of an hour. Tell Dorothy if your mother's bored with her she can start to walk down the drive.'

'Oh, Mother won't be,' Mona replied. 'Besides, its quite early.'

'If she's ready to leave,' Michael said. 'I'll bring her back in my car. If not, we'll expect you when we see you.'

'Good,' Dr Howlett approved.

Mona and Michael said good night to the Archers and Mona got into the front of Michael's car. He started up the engine and drove slowly up the drive. She was silent and after a moment he spoke first.

'I'm going to apologise,' he said.

She fancied that there was a note of humour in his tone.

'Why?' she inquired.

She suddenly felt terribly tired and sad.

There was something about the Archers, cosy and together in that tiny house with their three babies, which had brought her a new and tender sorrow, a yearning for what might have been, for a quiet domestic peace which had never before entered into her longings for Lionel.

'For losing my temper,' Michael answered.

With an effort Mona dragged her thoughts back to what he was saying.

'Did you lose your temper?' she asked. 'What a funny way of showing it!'

'I've got no excuse—merely that you infuriated me. I

85

thought that many years ago I'd grown immune to your teasing, but apparently I haven't. Still, I had no right to behave as I did, even—if you deserved it,' he added with a flash of humour.

Quite suddenly Mona laughed.

'I'm bewildered,' she confessed. 'I don't quite know where I am. All my ideas of you have undergone a revolution. I suppose I'm angry with you—I ought to be, anyway—at the same time, as you've so rightly pointed out, I deserved it.'

'Why can't we be friends?' Michael asked.

'We can be,' Mona replied. 'I want to be, really, but oh, Michael!—I can't explain—it's some devil within me. I'm so low, so utterly miserable, that I am trying to drag down on top of me all the solid pillars of security and strength that I admire and envy in you.'

Before he answered, Michael drew up the car and stopped the engine. He had made no attempt to get out or to open the door, instead he turned a little in his seat so that he could see Mona's face faintly in the light from the dashboard.

'What's gone wrong?' he asked.

'Everything,' she answered, and there was a throb in her voice. 'I can't talk about it, Michael, to you or to any-one else, but I've come to the end of everything, to the end of the world, to the end of my faith, and I think to the end of my courage.'

'Oh, no, you haven't,' Michael said soothingly.

He reached out and took both her hands in his.

'Listen,' he said. 'When things seem like that it's only be-cause it's the end of a chapter. Tomorrow you start a new one.'

'And if I don't want to?'

'A new chapter will be starting.'

Mona gave a little sob.

'Oh, Michael, if only one could die when one wished to.'

'It would be too easy.'

'Too easy!' she echoed, surprised at his choice of words.

'Yes,' Michael answered. 'We are put into this world for a purpose. If we could deny all our obligations at the first defeat and because we found it hard to fulfil that purpose, wouldn't it be a travesty of all faith and all aspiration?'

'Sometimes we are tried beyond our strength.'

Michael shook his head.

'Never,' he said firmly. 'One's strength will always just stand the strain, believe me.'

Mona had a sudden vision of him crawling towards a deserted machine-gun post, dragging his injured leg, tortured by pain, yet determined, utterly and relentless determined, to get there.

Instinctively and unconsciously her fingers tightened on his, then with a little sigh she relaxed.

'I'm being very foolish,' she said.

She tried to make her tone light. She felt Michael's reaction to her change of mood and somehow she knew instinctively that he was disappointed.

'One day, Mona,' he replied, 'you will learn a little about yourself and then you'll be surprised.'

'I shall have to learn something about you, too, Michael.'

'That wouldn't be very difficult if you were interested enough.'

She felt a sudden weariness descend upon her again.

'To be honest, I don't think I'm interested in anything, and I feel I never shall be again.'

'Wait and see,' Michael advised, 'don't be in a hurry to generalise either about yourself or about other people. There's one thing being a farmer teaches one—patience. Perhaps that is the lesson you have got to learn here, Mona —to be patient, to wait for the seeds that you plant to come up, not to rely on another person's sowing?'

'What do you mean?' she asked, suddenly curious.

But Michael didn't answer; instead he got out of the car, slowly and a little clumsily with his stiff leg, and limped round to open the door for her.

As she stepped out in the cold night air, she put her hand on his.

'I need a friend, Michael.'

'You've always had one. Am I forgiven?'

'I've forgotten about it.'

That was not true. While Mona undressed that evening she found herself thinking of Michael, of his hard, brutal embrace, of his lips which bruised hers.

She knew that her instantaneous reaction had been one of humiliation. Michael's action had merely comfirmed her own uncertainty and insecurity as to what people really thought about her.

'It's my guilty conscience,' she told her own reflection in the glass. 'I've been what the world knows as "a light woman," and so I expect to be treated as one.'

She was glad that she had made it up with Michael; he was a solid stalwart rock on which one might lean and she felt now that she needed such people—would that there were more of them!

How hopeless, how utterly, ridiculously hopeless it was to concentrate on one person to the exclusion of all others! Now that Lionel had gone, what had she left? Nothing.

Nothing at all except the memories of the years they had spent together. And yet she knew that if she could have her time over again, if she had the choice of going with Lionel and doing all she had done in the past years, she would not hesitate.

She could see him now walking into the sitting-room of her flat in London—the flat that she and Ned had furnished so extravagantly, but which was being sold up to meet his debts.

She had been sorting the jade in a cabinet when Lionel was announced; for a moment she could hardly believe that he was not a figment of her imagination and had stood clasping a cool green ornament in her hands staring at him with wide, surprised eyes.

'Mona!—I had to come.'

The words sounded as of they were dragged out of him

and she saw that he looked older than when she had last seen him.

'Lionel!—I can hardly believe it's true.'

Then, in an effort to hide her emotion she had said lightly:

'But it's lovely to see you. Sit down and tell me all the gossip of Paris. I haven't been there for some time.'

He had ignored her idle words and coming slowly across the room had advanced until he stood beside her, nearly touching her.

Then she knew that she was trembling and she could not look up and meet his eyes, but must clutch the great lump of jade, moving her fingers desperately over its smooth surface in a feverish effort to still the tumult within herself.

'Mona!' Lionel's voice was deep and held the note of urgency she knew so well.

'Don't, Lionel!' she whispered. 'I can't bear it! Go away. You can't come here and do this to me. Don't you understand?'

'I can't live without you.'

His voice was raw and broken with emotion.

Just for one wild moment she had believed that he was free to offer her fulfilment of all her dreams—marriage. Then without anything being said, without a gesture or movement, she understood. Lionel wanted her, but on his terms.

She hesitated . . . something exquisite and beautiful within herself which had tentatively raised its head died. And yet the world stood still—awaiting her answer.

Uncertainly she had raised her eyes.

'I don't understand,' she murmured, but her words were lost.

She was in Lionel's arms, his lips were on hers, they were clinging to each other as sailors might cling to a raft in a wild, tempestuous sea.

'Mona! . . . Mona! . . .' he was murmuring her name over and over again.

But the joy of feeling his lips and hands kept her silent. She had no words, her whole being was submerged in one vast throbbing ecstacy—half pleasure, half pain.

'Come back to me—you've got to come back to me.'

Mona knew then that no decision would be required of her—she would go to him because she was his; because life held nothing—no interest, no joy—when he was not there.

After that she remembered packing up the flat as in a dream.

People came and went; they told her how wonderful she was not to mind parting with all the beautiful things that had been hers in her brief married life; they told her, too, how her bravery and courage over poor Ned's tragic death was an inspiration to all who met her.

They couldn't understand that it was difficult for her even to think of Ned, who had killed himself trying to break the record from London to John o' Groats in a mad race when every competitor must wear a grey top-hat and spats.

It had been one of Ned's ridiculous, publicity-seeking jokes which had ended, as usual, in headlines—but this time the last that Ned himself would ever invoke.

What did it matter what people said or what they did, Mona wondered?

That Ned's mother was resentful and reproachful—that Ned's trustees were horrified when it was discovered that his entire fortune had disappeared and that only debts remained?

That Ned's friends who had seemed so true and so affectionate were shrugging their shoulders and looking for someone else from whom to borrow or seek excitement?

What did anything matter but that in ten days' time she would be in Paris?

And so, in the spring, Mona had gone to the Paris she had always dreamt of—to the Paris which had seemed more bewilderingly beautiful than any dream, any fantasy.

The tiny little flat at the top of the Champs-Élysées with a view over the roofs and chimneys of the city, the exquisite things with which Lionel surrounded her, the clothes he bought for her, the jewels with which he decked her, they all mingled in a kaleidoscope of colour, of music, and of passion merging into the throbbing, pulsating happiness of knowing that she loved and was loved.

Now, looking back, it was easy to forget the long hours of loneliness, the days which had passed like centuries, the nights of tortured longing when Lionel could not come to her.

When she had nothing to do but to stare out of the window; when she might make neither friends nor acquaintances but must wait, seeming to herself only an aching want, the incarnation of all yearning, of all desire.

Then Lionel would arrive and everything would be forgotten except that they were together.

It was seldom that they could go out in case he was seen; generally they stayed in that tiny flat, content to be together, wanting nothing in the world save each other and their love which consumed them both like a burning, searing flame.

At the sound of his key turning in the lock, Mona's heart would leap.

She would rush across the room into the tiny hall and without need for words, without explanations, his arms were round her, their lips would be seeking each other's hungrily.

Yes, Paris had been the happiest, the gladdest, the most vivid time in her whole life, but Paris had not lasted. Lionel had been moved to Egypt.

He need not have accepted the position and over his decision he and Mona had their first row.

It was then that she had run away, leaving Paris, the flat and Lionel's presents behind. Without a word she had come speeding home to the Priory, arriving without explanation or any previous announcement of her intentions.

'Here I am,' she had said defiantly.

'Have you lost your job, darling?' Mrs Vale had asked.

Mona remembered then that she had told her mother

that she had a position in Paris as buyer for an English shop.

'Yes, I've lost everything,' she replied briefly.

The words in themselves at least were true.

But after three days the summons came. Lionel on the telephone—Lionel in London demanding to see her. Because she was weak or because she knew it was inevitable, she went up to London to see him.'

'To say good bye,' she told herself, knowing just how feeble and easily shaken her resolution would prove.

She had been shown into the suite he had engaged at Claridge's. He kept her waiting for a moment in the sitting-room and then he came through the door from the bedroom.

His expression was stern, but suddenly at the sight of each other everything was forgotten except an irresistible joy.

She was in his arms again, she was touching his hair, pulling his dear face down to hers . . .

'Oh, my sweet, how could you?' he asked.

Gaily, through the tears and laughter, her answer came :

'I must have been mad! How could I ever live without you?—how could I, my darling?'

And so she went to Egypt. It was Lionel's wish and she went. Lionel always had his own way. She was the one to suffer, and yet wouldn't she have suffered more if she had remained behind? She remembered once Nanny saying . . .

'There are givers and takers in this world, and, mark my words, there are many more takers than givers.'

Lionel was one of the 'takers.' Imperiously he demanded of life its best. He demanded, too, that his desires should always be satisfied—that he should have what he wanted unconditionally.

'He always got it,' Mona thought wearily.

But for the people who were left behind when he had gone, there were debts to be paid—debts different from poor Ned's, but nevertheless debts—of suffering and loneliness, unhappiness and reparation which will have to be paid in full.

8

Mona was waiting for Dorothy in the Howlett's sitting-room.

The Doctor's house was an ugly red brick building with high square rooms, which always appeared out of proportion whatever you did to them; but Dorothy Howlett had done her best to make them fresh and gay.

It was not her fault if the years of hard wear had taken the shine from the furniture, the colour from the yellow chintz curtains and the pile from the brown carpet. The room had a shabby, threadbare appearance, but it also had an atmospher of home.

There were a few photographs dotted about; a pile of mending in a basket stood on the window-seat, and a child's toy car showed underneath the flounce of the sofa-cover, while a blue Persian kitten slept peacefully on the hearthrug.

There was nothing pretentious or ornate about the room. The chairs were big, comfortable, and good of their kind; the rugs were cheap but in good taste and there was a big pile of logs in an old oak cradle by the fireplace waiting to be put on the fire.

The door opened and Dorothy Howlett came in.

'I'm sorry to have kept you waiting, Mona,' she said apologetically. 'It's that awful woman again!'

93

There was no need to ask whom she meant—there was only one 'awful woman' in Little Cobble who was continually upsetting everybody.

'What's she done know?' Mona asked sympathetically. 'And don't look so worried, Dot, it puts years on to your age.'

Dorothy Howlett pulled off her hat and ran her fingers through her greying hair.

'I've given up thinking about my age long ago,' she said, 'but if it registered what I feel I'd be in a bath-chair!'

She picked up a log and put it on the fire.

'Now,' she said, 'we've got nearly an hour in which we can chat. The children won't be back from school until four o'clock.'

'Thank goodness for that!' Mona exclaimed. 'It's easier to see the King of England than to see you alone these days.'

'I know,' Dorothy answered with a grimace, 'but I can't help it. What with my own four and three evacuees I'm pretty busy. I've only got a girl of fifteen to help me and she's almost as bad as having another child, although she tries her best.

'And then there's the W.V.S. Oh, Mona, what am I to do about Mavis Gunther?'

'What's happened?' Mona asked.

'To use a current phrase, she's "sabotaging" everything,' Dorothy answered. 'What's upset me now is that she's taken away two of my very best women; the two on whom I can rely to help, not only with the knitting, but the jam-making and the dozen and one things that we are supposed to do.'

'How?'

'Sheer blackmail. If it wasn't so annoying it would be funny. One of them—you remember Mrs Watson, the fat old body who lives down Elmtree Lane?'

'Yes, I remember.'

'Well, she's got a child who's rather delicate but quite extraordinarily clever. She adores that child and she is frightfully keen for her to win the Sunday School prize.'

'Well, it has been intimated to Mrs Watson, very tactfully, of course, that unless she works for the Knitting Party and gives up the W.V.S. little Vera won't get the prize.'

'But it's unbelievable!' Mona exclaimed. 'Mavis Gunther must be out of her mind.'

'On the contrary, she's very much in it.'

'And the other woman?'

'Mrs Young—I don't think you know her. A very nice woman in every way but she's got a rotten husband who drinks and can't keep a job. They've been on parish relief for some time, the children would starve otherwise.'

'Well, unless she does what is wanted, the Vicar is likely to give her a report which will alter the relief benefit.

'Really,' Mona exclaimed, 'it's medieval. We ought to be able to do something about it.'

'But what?' Dorothy asked. 'You see, the village people look at things sanely. They know that, whatever happens, Arthur will do his best for them, and I would never do my worst, so, "knowing which side their bread is buttered" —or whatever the expression is—they play up to her.'

'And who can blame them?'

'I'm sure I don't,' Dorothy agreed, 'but really, Mona, if I could commit murder and get away with it, I would.'

'The person I feel sorry for is that wretched man.'

'Stanley Gunther. Sorry!—my heart bleeds for him. Just think of being cooped-up with that fiend day in and day out!'

'Is she still awful to him?' Mona asked. 'I remember some of her tricks in the old days.'

'If possible, she's worse,' Dorothy replied. 'She nags him in public, she's spiteful, cruel, and beastly—and like a snake waiting to strike she wounds him when he's not expecting it.

'She hardly bothers to hide her pleasure when she can make him look a fool in front of the village, or humiliate him before his friends.'

'Murder's too good for her!' Mona said. 'It's funny,

Dorothy, but I suppose people are the same all the world over.

'I've known other women like Mavis Gunther in a very different strata of society, but the instinct to be cruel, to torture others, and to grasp power by whatever means they could, was exactly the same.'

'I suppose power is what she does want,' Dorothy said. 'That's why she hates me. You see, Lady Beaumont, the Lord-Lieutenant's wife, asked me to start the W.V.S. here. If I'd had any sense, I suppose I'd have refused, but I felt it was my duty. There's so little I can do here to help the war.'

'Little!' Mona exclaimed. 'I should think you're doing a great deal more than most people—certainly more than anyone in Little Cobble.'

'Well, that isn't saying much,' Dorothy replied. 'They don't know there's a war on here. Do you know what was said at the Knitting Party last week? As a matter of fact, your mother told me. Someone—one of the women—suggested they might knit for the Air Force, and Mavis Gunther replied.

' "Why should we? There are no Little Cobble men in the R.A.F." '

'One would expect such a remark from her,' Mona said. 'But tell me about yourself. I want to forget Little Cobble and all its petty worries, troubles and squabbles. Tell me what you've been doing all these years. I've thought about you being gay and lovely in all the gayest and loveliest places in the world.'

'I suppose that's what it sounds like to those at home,' Mona sighed. 'Actually, like everything else in life, it was rather disappointing when one was there. The gaiety rang a bit hollow at times and the beauty-spots were either scattered with orange-peel or smelt of garlic-chewing natives.'

'Nonsense!' Dorothey said emphatically. 'You can't put me off with stories like that. When it rained here I used to pad through the mud in my old mackintosh thinking to my-self . . .

'I expect Mona's lying on a golden beach waiting to run into an emerald sea—or . . .'

'I expect Mona's watching polo in a thin chiffon dress and a shady hat with a crowd of young men waiting to bring her an iced drink if she should want one.'

'I sounds like a musical comedy,' Mona laughed.

'But haven't you learnt by this time that's how your life appears to us? Perhaps "comedy" is the wrong word. "Background by Hollywood" is better and it's brought glamour and a reflected excitement into our drab lives just to have known you.'

'How ridiculous you are !' Mona exclaimed. 'But even in chiffon dresses and shady hats one's heart can break and one can feel very like tears.'

She had meant to speak lightly but her voice broke on the words. Quietly Dorothy put out her hand and laid it on Mona's.

'I'm sorry, dear. I thought somehow it sounded all too good to be true.'

Mona blinked away the tears which rose in her eyes.

'I don't want to talk about it, Dot, in fact I can't. But it hasn't always been fun—at times it's been damnable. And now I am home.'

Dorothy gave her hand a quick squeeze.

'Our gain,' she said briefly. 'I'm going to be selfish and hope you stay here.'

'I expect to for ever,' Mona answered.

She spoke tragically but Dorothy ignored her tone of voice.

'I'm going to get you a cup of tea—the Doctor's remedy for every ill,' she said. 'You'd like one, wouldn't you?'

'No, really,' Mona replied. 'I've got to be home for tea. I promised Mummy I would.'

There was the sound of the front door slamming, and a second later Arthur Howlett put his head in at the door.

'Visitors!' he exclaimed. 'Oh, it's you, Mona. What are you two girls doing?—gossiping?'

'Of course we are,' Mona replied.

'Well, that's nice for Dorothy,' he said, coming into the room. 'She's not had a chance to unburden her soul since you went away. To tell anyone anything in Little Cobble is the same as shouting it from the house-tops. Well, I can't stay long, I've got a case over at Willington. I only came in to pick up some medicine.'

'You'll have a case here in your own home if you don't look out,' Mona said severely.

'Who's that?' Arthur Howlett asked. 'One of the children?'

'One of the children nothing!' Mona replied scornfully. 'Dorothy's doing too much. She's wearing herself out fussing round with this W.V.S., the evacuees, and heaven knows what else.'

'I know,' Arthur Howlett agreed. 'She ought to have a medal for it.'

'Medal!' Mona retorted. 'She doesn't want a medal—what she wants is orchids.'

The Doctor looked at Mona as if she had taken leave of her senses.

'Yes,' Mona insisted. 'And I'd just like to ask you one thing, Arthur. How long is it since you took Dorothy out for an evening, took her to the pictures, took her out to dinner, or, indeed, made love to her?'

'Oh, Mona, really!' Dorothy interrupted, 'you mustn't say things like that. Arthur will think I've been complaining, and I haven't, have I?'

'Of course you haven't,' Mona answered. 'You wouldn't complain if he asked you stand still while he hammered nails into you. You're too good to that man, Dorothy, and you always have been.

'But he's always been the same—taken up with his beastly profession—treating the house like a hotel, and noticing nothing unless his supper was late or his bed wasn't ready for him when he came in dead tired.'

Arthur Howlett looked uncomfortable.

'I say, Mona, you're being a bit hard on me, aren't you? I dare say there's a lot in what you say, but really, ever since the war, I don't seem to have a second to myself. Two doctors have gone from the neighbourhood and I have taken over their work.'

'I don't care if ninety doctors have gone,' Mona said, 'Dorothy's got to come first. I don't mind telling you that when I saw her last week it gave me quite a shock. Why, she isn't much older than I am, but she looks a hundred!'

'Don't mind me,' Dorothy interposed. 'Don't spare my feelings, will you?'

'I shan't,' Mona said. 'I'm being brutal for your own good. I'm taking you into Bedford tomorrow or the next day to get a permanent wave and what's more you're going to have some nice clothes and use all Arthur's coupons. If anyone goes barefoot this winter it's going to be him.'

'I've used most of them already for the children,' Dorothy said apologetically.

'You've made as much a fetish of the children as Arthur has of his patients,' Mona scolded. 'They're both charming in the right place, but you're losing your grip on life, both of you. It's no use sinking lower and lower into the mud of Bedfordshire until you wouldn't recognise a dance tune if you heard one.'

'I only wish to goodness there was an attractive young man in the village who would make love to Dorothy and give you, Arthur, the fright of your life.'

'Well, I must say, Mona, you don't mince your words,' Dr. Howlett said.

But there was a twinkle in his eye and a smile touching the corners of his mouth. He ran his fingers through his hair and looked for all the world like a school-boy who had been caught out stealing the apples.

'What about it, Dorothy?' he said. 'As this tornado has entered our lives I suppose we must pay some attention to it. Would you like me to take you to the pictures to-night when I get back from Willington?'

'Tonight?' Dorothy exclaimed. 'Oh, I don't think I can.'

'Of course you can,' Mona said fiercely. 'Don't you dare refuse him. You'll go, and you'll enjoy it, if I have to come down here and look after your squalling brats.'

'They're not squalling and they're not brats,' Dorothy said with a flash of spirit. 'They're perfectly charming children.'

'In which case you can leave them with an easy conscience,' Mona retorted. 'In fact, to make quite certain that you come I am going to ring up Michael now and ask him if he will give us all dinner at the Swan.'

'Oh, but you can't do that!' Dorothy protested. 'He will think it so extraordinary.'

'Let him think,' Mona replied. 'Besides, what's he got money for? If I don't spend it for him I expect someone else will.'

She went out of the room to telephone but noted with satisfaction as she left that Arthur Howlett, who was chuckling, bent to kiss his surprised wife.

'They just want waking up,' she thought to herself. 'They're a darling couple but they've got into a groove.'

She rang up Michael and found that he was at one of his farms. She put through another call, then waited for nearly ten minutes while he was fetched to the telephone.

She explained to him what she wanted and heard him laugh at the other end of the line.

'I knew you couldn't manage to be subdued for long, Mona,' he said. 'I thought you'd have to get your fingers into some sort of pie, even if it weren't your own!'

'Don't be rude, Michael,' Mona replied. 'Will you fetch me this evening?'

'I will,' he promised.

Mona ran back to the sitting-room with the good news. She found Dorothy alone with a somewhat flushed face.

'I don't know what you've done to Arthur,' she said. 'He quite embarrassed me with his affection.'

'Arthur's the nicest man in the world,' Mona answered, 'but he's as blind as a bat. Things have to be very obvious for him to see them. Subtlety will never work with Arthur, as you ought to know. If you don't draw attention to yourself, he'll forget that you're not a robot.'

'That's not quite true,' Dorothy said loyally, 'but I admit that sometimes I have felt as if everything exciting that had ever happened to me was in the past and that the future was pretty drab and uninteresting.'

'That's what I feel myself,' Mona thought with a sudden pang.

Then quickly she put her personal feelings on one side, concentrating determinedly and fiercely on her friend.

'What have you got to wear?'

'Not a thing,' Dorothy said cheerfully.

'Then I'm going back now to find you something.'

Dorothy Howlett laughed.

'Sweet of you dear, but nothing of yours would go round my hips by yards.'

'Oh, yes, it would,' Mona said. 'I've got some pleated dresses somewhere and those will easily fit you. Anyway, Dorothy, don't be so difficult. You've got to look your best tonight—you've got to flirt with your own husband.'

'I swear you're making me feel quite shy. Why are you doing this?'

'To make you look young again. Also, to be selfish, it makes me feel so terribly ancient myself to see someone who is not much older than I am looking a million.'

'Do I look as bad as all that?' Dorothy asked.

'Quite,' Mona answered ruthless, 'but you won't when I've finished with you. I shall be sending you down some astringent lotion for your face, some rouge, and a lipstick— and kindly use them.'

'My dear, if Mavis Gunther sees me going out like that what will she say!'

'Nothing worse than she's said already.'

'I think you are right there,' Dorothy laughed. 'Well, now I must get the children's tea. Are you quite sure you won't stay and have some?'

'I've got a lot to do.' Mona told her. 'And if you don't

look your prettiest tonight I shall flirt with Arthur myself, I warn you.'

'He'd love it. He's always admired you.'

'I wish I could believe that, but he first saw me when I had mumps and I have a sneaky feeling that he's never quite forgotten the spectacle I presented. No, I'll confine myself to being pleasant to Michael—your job is to make Arthur feel that he's twenty-two again.'

'I'll do my best,' Dorothy promised.

Suddenly she bent forward and kissed Mona.

'You are a darling! We need you here among us. We've got so self-centred.'

As Mona walked down the road she thought—'I don't deserve that. I'm the one who's been self-centred all these years.'

She looked back and tried to remember someone to whom she had been kind, someone in whom she had taken an interest beside Lionel.

But all her searchings could recall nothing save the moments of supreme happiness with the man she loved and moments of utter despair and misery when she was alone.

'I won't think about it,' she muttered.

Blindly, not looking where she was going, bumped straight into Mrs. Gunther.

'Well, Lady Carsdale, this is a surprise!' Mrs Gunther exclaimed, in her high metallic voice which had been known to send cold shudders down the spine of those whom she reprimanded.

'Is it?' Mona asked. 'The village is a small place, Mrs Gunther, and I have been home nearly a week. We were bound to meet sooner or later.'

Mrs Gunther for a second looked taken aback at having her words siezed upon so literally, then she remarked:

'And how delightful it must be for you to be back. I am sure you are quite a stranger. Your poor mother must have been wondering if she was ever going to see you again.'

There was malice and enmity in the words which she

spoke with a smiling mouth, her beady little eyes watching Mona to see the effect of them.

'She's trying to make me feel uncomfortable,' Mona thought, amused at anyone doing exactly what was expected of them.

'I'm afraid it has been rather lonely for my mother,' she replied, 'but here I am at last and now I shall be able to be with her and make up for lost time.'

'And you are making a long stay, Lady Carsdale?'

'Very long,' Mona replied. 'God willing—of course—I was thinking of remaining here for the rest of my life.'

'Indeed! We should be very flattered at the idea,' Mrs Gunther said, 'but I am afraid you will find it very dull. We haven't many diversions in Little Cobble.'

There was a wealth of meaning in the word 'diversions' as Mrs Gunther said it.

'Oh, don't you think so?' Mona asked innocently. 'I find it very amusing, especially the people. Most of them are so true to type but one or two are surprising—but then there's no need to say that to you. You know all the secrets of the village, of course.'

'Secrets!' Mrs Gunther said. 'Are there any . . .'

She checked the words and substituted.

'I expect, being quite a stranger, you see things from a different aspect from we who have been here all these years.'

Mona laughed.

'I wonder?' she said. 'But perhaps I'm being indiscreet. I mustn't tell tales out of school, must I, Mrs Gunther? Although I'm sure I know nothing that you do not. Well, it's been nice meeting you. Good-bye. Tell your husband that we hope he will drop in to the Priory for a glass of sherry one evening if he's up that way.'

Mona nodded and started off down the street.

She was well aware that she had left Mrs Gunther perturbed and uncertain—wondering if there was something going on that she didn't know—wondering what Mona could have meant by 'secrets.'

'That type always wants to know everything,' Mona thought to herself. 'She's just like Char Strathwyn, always nosing about—always frightened that she's going to miss something.'

She walked past the church and took the right-of-way across the fields, then, as she neared the Priory, she thought she would go in and see Lynn Archer.

She called most days to inquire about Gerry, who was better, although he had been in pain for forty-eight hours and was suffering now from shock and loss of blood.

She tapped at the door of the lodge and heard Lynn's voice call out—'Come in.'

She found her alone, seated at her desk by the window, a pile of papers in front of her.

'Am I disturbing you?' Mona asked.

'No,' Lynn replied. 'Come in, I am trying to write and I can't. Why didn't I choose any other profession? Even scrubbing floors would be preferable to sitting with a pencil in one's hand and a persistently blank piece of paper to look at.'

'Where are the children?' Mona asked.

'Your angelic Nanny has taken them for a walk,' Lynn replied. 'Your mother came in this morning and said she thought I was looking tired, so Nanny came down after lunch, bundled the two babies into the pram and John has taken his tricycle.

'Oh, why haven't I got a Nanny like that! They were all fighting and screaming and in two minutes she had calm and order, had buttoned them into their coats, pulled on their leggings, dared them on pain of death to take off their gloves again, and they were out of sight before they could get their breath.

'I feel a free woman—but still I can't write.'

'What's the matter?' Mona asked.

'It's this country,' Lynn said with a gesture of despair. 'It sounds absurd, I know, but I've always lived in towns, I've always had gaiety, excitement, noise and traffic round me. I can't write when its quiet, flat and uneventful. People have said to me for years.

' "Lynn Archer, if you could go away for six months to the country you'd write a marvellous book."

'I believed it until I came here, and I know that my books are conceived on cocktails and parties and that unless there's some sort of fun going on I can't write so much as a post card.'

'That's a bit unfortunate,' Mona said.

'Unfortunate! It's desperate,' Lynn replied. 'Here, have a cigarette.'

She walked across the room, a vivid figure in her navy blue slacks and cherry-coloured jumper.

'Am I boring you?'

'Of course you're not,' Mona answered. 'I like listening to other people's troubles, it takes my mind off my own. Go ahead   I'm listening.'

'It's a dull story,' Lynn said. 'If I tried to put it in a book people would die of boredom and I'd only sell one copy and that would be to my old mother, and the plot can be explained in one word. A word which is, I suppose, one of the most common words in the English language—a disgusting, mean, crafty little word.'

'Which is?' Mona prompted.

'Debts,' Lynn replied. 'Debts . . . debts . . . debts. Bill and I got married on debts, and we've lived on debts, and we've very nearly died on them, too, when the bomb came through the roof of our house in London.

'We've pledged everything we ever possessed to try and get straight. With any luck, and if Bill's an Air-Marshal before the end of the war, we may get clear by the time the grave is waiting for both of us—but in the meantime we have got to eat.'

'And to do that you must write?'

'Exactly. And I can't—I tell you, I can't. It's impossible. I got a letter from my publisher this morning asking for the blurb of my spring novel. Blurb!—I haven't begun to think out a plot.

'And where can I find one in this deadly place? Do you think people want to read about cabbages mating in the fields or potatoes committing adultery with turnips in the barn? I tell you—I'm sunk!'

'Nonsense!' Mona said. 'I don't believe that books can be entirely dependent on outside influences. It must be something inside you and that's still there. What we have got to do is to conjure up the atmosphere.'

'So easy, isn't it?' Lynn said sarcastically. 'Do you know, I haven't seen a soul in months except your mother—who's an angel—yourself, and Dr Howlett. Bill gets home three, perhaps four nights a week from the aerodrome, the rest of the time he's on duty.

'They're so madly busy that he can't even bring the other officers along with him, and if he does we can't really afford the drinks.

'Not that that would matter if they gave me something to write about, but most of them have nice, straightforward, charming characters and when you have used the adjectives "eager," "enthusiastic," "clean-limbed," et cetera, et cetera, there's nothing left to say.'

Mona laughed.

'Poor Mrs Archer!'

'And for heaven's sake call me Lynn!' her hostess said sharply. 'That's another thing—this awful formality. I suppose if I live here another six years someone will call on me.'

'My dear, I'm sorry for you,' Mona said. 'I've felt like this myself. I used to think of all the nice things that were happening in the world while I looked like being marooned here for ever.

'That was when I was seventeen and nothing dramatic ever happened except a choir-boy fainting in church or a cow getting loose in somebody's back garden and destroying the flowers they were cosseting for the local flower show.'

'Well, you understand then,' Lynn said. 'What can I

do? I can't go back to London with the children. You see, mad though I sound, I rather love my babies.'

'I'm not surprised. They are adorable—in fact they all three look as though they've stepped out of a story book.'

'You understand, then! The last time we were bombed was bad enough. Thank God, I had all three of them down in the cellar—but the next time we might not be so lucky. Besides, Bill's here and I wouldn't leave him for anything in the world.'

Lynn's face lit up when she spoke about her husband.

'She loves him!' Mona thought.

'Well, then, we've got to do something about it,' she said aloud. 'The question is—what? Have you thought of getting to know some of the people here? There are stories enough in everyone's life if you begin to look for them—even in a village like this.'

'What sort of stories?' Lynn asked half scornfully.

'I'll tell you one, about the Vicar's wife.'

She told Lynn briefly but vividly the story of Mavis and Stanley Gunther.

It was at least three parts the exact truth, for although neither of the parties concerned had ever confided in anyone in some strange way people's lives became known.

A half sentence here, an indiscreet word there, and the chatter of those who have known them since childhood do, in the sum total, complete a story which is generally not far from the actual facts.

Lynn listened, her feet curled under her on the sofa, her dark eyes fixed on Mona's face.

'I like that,' she said. 'Is she really diabolical to him?'

'She couldn't be worse,' Mona answered. 'One of her favourite tricks when he's annoyed her is to play the organ in church slower and slower. She knows that it upsets him. And when she's really angry she alters the hymns, pretending she hasn't brought the right music.'

'Poor Stanley Gunther gives out the one that's been chosen, then there's a pause, no music starts and his wife leans forward and whispers to one of the men at the back of the choir who slowly marches down the aisle and informs the Vicar that another number will be sung instead.

'All the choir-boys smirk—they know, as do the whole of the congregation, what's happened—and Stanley Gunther has to put the best face on it that he can and make another announcement.'

'I shall go to church on Sunday,' Lynn said. 'I'd no idea there were such excitements going on.'

'It's rather tragic, really. He was once a fine man. When he first came here I can remember how enthusiastic he was about everything.

'We had a village cricket team and he was the captain, we played the other villages—and the children's sports were really good, famous for miles around.

'People used to come and watch them and give really lovely prizes. But gradually he lost interest and so did everyone else.'

'I'm not surprised. Tell me more. I can't tell you how interesting this is to me.'

'I'll tell you about Nanny,' Mona went on. 'You'd think on the surface that she was a fairly dull, staid person who had never had any interest beyond bringing up other people's children. But Nanny has had her moments. She started her existence by being born in a lifeboat.'

'Really?'

'Yes, really,' Mona replied. 'The lifeboat of a ship which had been sunk—not in war-time, of course—it hit a rock or something. Anyway, her mother got away safely although her father was drowned, and Nanny was born some hours before the rescue ship found them.

'She was brought back to England and spent her childhood in a little village not far from here. As soon as she was old enough, it was decided that she should go into domestic service and she chose the nursery.

'The people she was with were going out to India—they took Nanny with them. They were in the north of India and there were riots.

'I can't remember her exact story, Nanny will tell you all

about it if you ask her, but for over a week they were besieged in Government House, and when they were down to their last crust of bread relief came.

'Some years later she came home, and Mother engaged her, as I was on the way. When I was about two, Nanny fell in love. He was only a labourer and it was considered that she was marrying beneath her.

'Her relatives made a great fuss and she promised to wait until he could better himself before getting married. He went off to Austraila to make money and from that day to this she's never heard of him again.

'What happened to him none of us have any idea, but I think Nanny, even now in her old age, still believes that he might come back?'

'Oh, I do wish he would!' Lynn exclaimed.

'I don't think there's a chance,' Mona answered. 'He must have been killed or something; but Nanny goes systematically to every fortune-teller she hears of and if there's any gipsy woman in the neighbourhood you'll find her in our kitchen telling Nanny's fortune.'

'I believe you're right,' Lynn said reflectively. 'There must be stories everywhere only I don't go and look for them.'

'Of course there are.'

'And what about yours?'

Mona got to her feet hastily.

'I've talked quite enough for one afternoon. Besides, my life is too complicated, too mixed, to make a good novel.'

'I still want to hear about you,' Lynn insisted.

'Well, you'll have to wait,' Mona answered. 'One day when I'm feeling really garrulous perhaps, not now. Go back to your writing. Nanny will be home soon and then pandemonium will break out.'

'It certainly will,' Lynn laughed. 'But thank you. Come again soon. I feel a different person for seeing you.'

Mona said good-bye and walked on up the drive.

'I wonder what she'd make of my story,' she thought.

'One day, perhaps, I shall be able to talk about Lionel to someone,' Mona thought. 'Perhaps to Lynn.'

It would be easier to a stranger than to someone she knew well. But at the moment she knew that any expression of her own unhappiness would be choked by tears.

The numbness with which she had come home to England was passing and now her emotions were dangerously near the surface.

'I must try not to think,' she told herself. 'I must learn to live in the present, to forget the past and not to worry about the future.'

She would try to rouse her interest in the people round her. She liked Dorothy and Lynn Archer and there might be others, too. She mustn't forget her advice to Lynn to look for stories in the people near at hand.

How easy it was to give advice, she thought, and so desperately hard to follow it oneself!

Just for a moment the drive with its avenue of trees appeared to be only a vista in a dream and the Priory at the end just a mirage. In a moment she might awake—awake to find Lionel alive, not dead. . . .

Then coldly and logically her brain told her the truth. Lionel was dead—dead and buried—and her life, like the road beneath her feet, stretched out into a grey, lonely future without him.

9

'This is England at it's best,' Mona thought.

She stood still for a moment looking at the scene before her. The sun was setting and there was a reddish glow in the western sky.

Vision was limited by a fine mist from which the barren branches of the trees rose sharp and distinct like some exquisite etching, but the lake in front of Cobble Park was unveiled.

It lay like molten silver, with the swans moving gravely and majestically on its rippling surface while the ducks splashed and fluttered round its green edges.

Beyond the lake stood the house itself, its Elizabethan red brick rising to beautiful and balanced heights of architecture, its chimneys like miniature towers, its surrounding yew hedges, perfected after years of care, giving the whole picture a quaint geometrical appearance.

It was lovely, and peculiarly English, and as Mona watched, a flight of pigeons wheeled above the roof-tops, encircling the flag which fluttered languidly in the dying breeze.

It was hard indeed to realise that war with all the ruthless brutality of modern weapons was being waged all over the world and was expected at any moment to devastate this 'green and peaceful land.'

'The whole thing's like a nightmare from which one cannot wake up,' Mona thought.

She recalled her own passage across the Atlantic only a few weeks ago; how, despite everyone's outward air of cheerfulness and confidence, the least unusual sound would make the passengers start nervously.

It had been difficult to sleep at night, wondering if the dawn would find them hurrying to the lifeboats with only a few minutes' grace before the ship might sink under them.

But here in England, although both town and country bore deep scars, there were perfect and untouched pictures such as that which now lay before her.

Even as she contemplated the peace and beauty of Michael's home, she heard the hoot of a motor-horn behind her and an Army lorry, camouflaged and full of grinning soldiers, passed her and, approaching the house, turned through an ancient gateway and disappeared from sight.

Then Mona remembered that half the Park had been given over to the military and she noticed strange new features—a gun emplacement near the lake, several ammunition dumps hidden among the trees surrounding the drive, the broken and scarred surface of the drive itself caused by frequent and heavy traffic.

One couldn't really avoid the realities of war, she decided—not even for a moment.

She walked on; and now the beauty of the Park seemed even more poignant, as if she must fix it indelibly in her mind in case one day it was no longer there for her to see.

The door was opened by the family butler, who had been in service with the Merrill's since he was a little boy. He was getting deaf now, and his movements were slow from arthritis.

'Where's the Major, Bates?' Mona asked him.

'He's in the library, m'lady—at least, he was when I last saw him.'

'I'll go through,' Mona said. 'Don't bother to announce me—the Major's expecting me.'

She walked along the wide passages hung with valuable paintings, through the big high-ceilinged sitting-room which had once been the baronial hall but which Michael preferred to use as an ordinary living-room of the house, and beyond it to the library—a small book-lined room where he did all his work and which was his own particular sanctum.

Mona opened the door and as she did so heard voices and was surprised to learn that Michael was not alone.

He was usually on the doorstep to welcome her if he knew she was coming, but this afternoon he seemed to be engaged with someone else.

Mona had an impression of large, rather lovely eyes turned towards her, of fair, almost flaxen hair, braided round a well-shaped head, and then Michael had risen from his desk and was walking towards her.

'Hello, Mona,' he said. 'I'm afraid we've been rather busy or I'd have come to meet you. I don't think you've met Stella Fairlace. Miss Fairlace—Lady Carsdale. Stella's in charge of the home farm since Gallup was called up.'

'A land girl!' Mona thought, and recognised the armlet worn against the emerald green jumper.

'How do you do?' she said, holding out her hand. 'I do hope you aren't finding Major Merrill too hard a task-master.'

'Indeed I'm not,' Stella Fairlace replied.

Mona noticed that her voice was low, rather hesitating and shy.

'She's pretty,' she thought swiftly, 'very pretty—a Juno in uniform.'

'There's no question of driving my land girls,' Michael said with a smile. 'They're too efficient to need any inter-ference from me—in fact, I don't mind telling you that I'm beginning to suspect Gallup and many of my other male employees have been very lazy these past years.'

'There's certainly a lot to be done and perhaps I'd better be getting back to it,' Stella Fairlace said. 'Thank you, Major Merrill.'

'I'll see you in the morning, Stella,' Michael said, and walked with her as far as the door. 'Can you find your own way out?'

'I ought to be able to by now,' Stella replied, 'even if it is the largest house I've ever been in.'

She gave him a small, shy smile, then looked at Mona.

'Good-bye, Lady Carsdale.'

'Good-by,' Mona replied.

She walked across to the fire, seated herself on the high brass and leather seat which surrounded the hearth. As Michael closed the door she pointed an accusing finger at him.

'Michael,' she said, 'you've been very secretive. How have you managed to keep anything as pretty as that hidden for so long?'

Michael laughed.

'Is this the first time you've seen Stella? She is pretty isn't she? She's living here.'

'My goodness! And do you mean to say there's no scandal about it?'

'It would be difficult to make one. She's in the housekeeper's quarters and you know what Mrs Meakers is like. I've always thought she was one of the original Grundy family.'

'Is the fair Stella your only lodger? Or have you a whole harem of them?'

'There are four others here, and six billeted in the village.'

'Well, I'm most intrigued. Tell me about your lovely Stella. Who is she and where does she come from?'

'I really know very little about her. She's a very quiet girl and "keeps herself to herself" as the saying is. I gather that her father was a lawyer in Devonshire so she's led a very quiet life up till now, but when the war came she volunteered to be a land girl.

She had the sense to set about it in the right way—go through an agricultural college and pass the examinations —and the result is that she's really well-qualified and what's more—intelligent.'

'A paragon, in fact,' Mona said.

She wondered to herself if her voice sounded sour. She half resented the fact that Michael was so enthusiastic about anyone.

She herself was used to holding the limelight where he was concerned, at least she thought she had managed to do it very effectively these last weeks.

But he was a continual surprise to her.

He had altered, there was no doubt about that, and she found herself watching him for new characteristics, new twists of personality which she would not have thought for one moment that he was likely to possess.

He had a subtlety, too, which she would never have suspected in him.

The night she had asked him to give her and the Howletts dinner in Bedford, for instance, he had grasped exactly what was expected of him and without being ostentatious he had managed to enthuse the right atmosphere into the party from the very moment they had all met.

He had ordered a very good dinner and plenty of drink; he said all the right things to Dorothy Howlett, who was feeling a little nervous in her borrowed plumes—a dress of Mona's and a fur cape which she swore made her feel too opulent to be comfortable.

Nevertheless, she seemed to have lost ten years in the process of dressing-up for the evening and going out for a few hours' enjoyment. The children were forgotten; the cares and troubles of the W.V.S. and the village billeting were left behind.

It was a young, excited Dorothy who sat beside her husband and squeezed his hand tightly, who wept at the sentimental parts of the picture, and who agreed without prevarication to going back to the hotel when the film ended for yet another drink and chat before they all went home to bed.

Mona had been grateful to Michael that evening.

She would have hated it if he had devoted himself entirely to her and ignored or behaved with ordinary casual politeness to Dorothy—whom he saw practically every day of his life.

But he had understood what was required of him, had played up magnificently, and the result was an evening which exceeded everybody's anticipations.

Even the Doctor, driving his glowing, if sleepy, wife home in his car had been taken out of himself.

Half-way to Little Cobble he had stopped the engine and putting his arms round Dorothy had kissed her affectionately.

'I'm not good enough for you, Dot,' he had whispered, 'but you know I'm fond of you, don't you?'

She had looked up at his face in the dim light.

'Need you ask that?' she replied.

'I don't ask it often enough, that's my trouble,' Arthur Howlett said. 'When our daughter grows up I'm going to make her promise me that the one thing she'll never do is to marry a medical man. They're so busy looking after other people's families they forget their own.'

'That's not true, Arthur,' Dorothy protested loyally. 'You are wonderful to us, but you do work too hard.'

'And in consequence, at times I'm like a bear with a sore head. I know it, Dot, but continue to put up with me, old girl, won't you?'

'If course I will, you old stupid.'

She put her arms round his neck and gave him a quick, affectionate hug.

Awkwardly he stroked the soft fur of Mona's cape.

'I wish to God I could give you something like that. Oh, damn! How I hate poverty and everything that goes with it!'

'Arthur!' Dot had exclaimed, between laughter and tears.

It was so strange to hear him complain. He never did, and yet she knew that in his awkward way he was trying to tell her that he wanted to give her such things and was never likely to be able to afford them. But Arthur had started up the engine.

'Ready for bed?' she asked.

'Yes,' his wife replied, 'but it's been a lovely evening, hasn't it? I hope the children are all right.'

They had gone home in silence, only as they reached the front door did Dorothy, as she tumbled out of the car, say sleepily:

'I do wish Mona would marry Michael—they'd be a perfect couple, wouldn't they?'

And so intent was she on her own thoughts that she hardly heard her husband's reply:

'My heavens!—that's women all over, match-making at every opportunity!'

Yes, Michael was marvellous that evening, Mona thought.

Looking at him she wondered what she had really thought about her desire to bring a new happiness, or what she called sunshine, into the Howletts' lives.

Did he think she was interfering, she wondered? He had seemed amused and yet she knew instinctively that Michael queried many of the things she said and did.

He never attempted to argue with her, or, indeed, to cross her wishes in any way; but whenever they were together she had a notion that he was standing a little aloof from her, not entirely a part of her schemes but outside them, watching them, and—she felt uncomfortably—criticising them.

'What are you thinking about?' she asked.

She noticed that he was frowning as he lit a cigarette.

'I was wondering,' he replied, 'if it was true that there was a case of foot-and-mouth disease at Blunham. It isn't a nice thing to have in the neighbourhood.'

Mona said nothing and he smiled at her.

'I'm sorry. I'm boring you with these farming problems.'

'You aren't boring me,' Mona replied, 'and don't be so irritating, Michael. You've got into the habit of talking like that lately and it couldn't annoy me more.'

'Why?' Michael asked.

'Well, can't you see it's so insulting,' Mona said. 'Take a girl like Stella Fairlace, who's very pretty but because she isn't painted and isn't well-dressed—or over dressed if you like —men like you will sit down and confide in her all their troubles from cows to carrots and feel sure that she will be interested.

'I'm just as interested, but because I look sophisticated everyone feels that they must talk to me about night-clubs and caviare. I can't tell you how boring it is, especially from people who know little about either!'

Michael laughed.

'It's all very well to laugh,' Mona said hotly, 'but it's infuriating for me. Anyone is interesting on their own subject, the subject on which they have specialised, and everyone—whoever they may be—is boring when they talk about things of which they know nothing.'

'You shall hear every detail of the foot-and-mouth disease if we get it,' Michael promised, 'which God forbid!'

He was teasing her and Mona knew it.

'If you aren't going to be nice to me I'm going home,' she said.

'Aren't I always nice to you?'

He got up and stood beside her in front of the fire. He surprised her by reaching for one of her hands, but there was no sign of affection in his gesture.

He looked at her long pink-tipped fingers in an absent-minded manner, then he turned the hand over casually and stared at the network of lines on the palm.

'What do they all, mean, I wonder?' he said. 'Have you ever been to a palmist?'

'Heaps of them,' Mona replied, 'and they all contradicted each other and nothing they told me had any relation to the truth—except, perhaps, one.'

'And what did she say?'

'It was a he—an Egyptian. He sat on the steps of the Winter Palace Hotel at Luxor and he said:

"You are in the sunshine but everything is dark. When everything is dark, very dark, under a cloud bigger than the world, you will find sunshine."'

There was a pause.

'Most fortune-tellers are thought or mind readers,' Michael said lightly.

He released her hand. Mona had a feeling that before he had spoken he hesitated as to whether to ask her more.

Perhaps he had wanted to know if while living in the sunshine she had been in the dark of unhappiness. She could have told him that part of the prediction was true, at any rate.

She had been unhappy.

How she hated Egypt! Yet it remained in her mind a vision of colour, of golden sun-kissed desert, of the blue and glittering Nile, of a sky hazy with heat and the distant shimmering of a mirage on the hot sand.

She conjured up the shrill cries of the natives driving their camels, of the Arab boys fighting in the rising dust, of the call to prayer from the tall slender minarets, and mixed with it all was a feeling of blank misery, a yearning for escape and a sense on interminable frustration.

Mona shook herself and turned towards the window.

'Don't let's talk about the past,' she said, 'it makes me depressed, and to anticipate the future is even worse. Shall we go for a walk?'

'It's too late,' Michael replied. 'Besides, there's tea waiting for you in the hall and someone I want you to meet.'

'Who?' Mona asked curiously.

'My aunt,' Michael replied. 'She's come to stay with me for a little while. She's closed her house in London and is making a tour of her nephews and nieces.'

'It sounds formidable. What's she like?'

'What are aunts usually like?'

'Well, in that case I'd better go home and put on my lavender and lace.'

'You'll do very well as you are,' Michael answered.

He looked at her checked skirt and short beaver-fur coat.

'Well, I shall be interested to meet her,' Mona said. 'Somehow, I never think of you as a man with many relations.'

'Which, of course, infers something rude,' Michael retorted.

'How touchy you are! I think it's a compliment, really I've usually hated all my relations.'

'Except one,' her heart whispered—'except one.'

Michael opened the door and they walked into the great sitting-room. Tea was laid before the big open fireplace, with its huge logs supported on steel dogs.

Seated in front of the tea-table was a woman. She was small, with grey hair beautifully arranged, and her hands, moving among the tea things, glittered with rings.

The first impression was that she was old; and then one was not so certain. She might have been any age.

She was distinguished but from the moment she held out her hand in greeting Mona was conscious of a twinkle in the bright eyes that looked her over and seemed to see more than was on the surface.

'Aunt Ada,' Michael said, 'this is Lady Carsdale, about whom I've talked so much. Mona—my aunt, Mrs Windlesham.'

'How do you do?' Michael's aunt said. 'I have heard a great deal about you, and don't look so startled—all nice things. How I loathe people who don't say that at once! One always wonders what they have heard and if one should take steps at once to contradict everything that is likely to be untrue.'

Mona laughed.

'In this neighbourhood everything is certain to be untrue,' she said. 'Except about me, and then it isn't bad enough. Has Michael told you I am the black sheep of Little Cobble?'

'On the contrary,' Mrs Windlesham said, 'he told me that you were a great beauty, and I must say for once I agree with every word he said.'

'Thank you,' Mona replied. 'How nice you are to me. Michael, can I have a crumpet?'

'Yes, but I don't think you need one after that tribute,' he said.

Then handing them to his aunt, added:

'Mona wondered if she ought to go home and put on her lavender and lace when she heard she was to meet you, Aunt Ada.'

Mrs Windlesham chuckled.

'People always expect Michael's aunt to be a staid old body with lace-up corsets and a bustle,' she said. 'I'm beginning to think there must be something wrong with Michael.'

Mona laughed and Michael said grumpily:

'This is really the end—if both of you are going to set on me. It's not fair! I thought at least I should have one person to be kind to me when you arrived, Aunt Ada.'

'Kind! Nobody's ever asked me to be that,' Aunt Ada said. 'Most people nowadays seem to want one to be amusing or daring—don't you think so, Lady Carsdale?'

Mona had come to the quick conclusion that she liked Michael's aunt. She had a sharp, amusing way of talking, but, although she appeared to know the world, there was also something wise and rather restful about her.

'A really nice relation to have,' she thought.

'Tell me all the excitements,' Mrs Windlesham went on. 'You know what men are like when you ask them to tell you about people in the neighbourhood. I've got as far as their names and addresses, their ages and the number of children they have, but as for knowing their peculiarities Michael's about as informative as *Who's Who*, which I always thought was very dull reading.'

'My aunt likes inside information about people,' Michael explained. 'She makes a hobby of collecting specimens of mankind as other people collect stamps or odd bits of china. When I go to her house in London. I find all sorts of oddities there. One man I'm certain was a murderer.'

'Now who was that?' his aunt said with a puzzled face. 'Oh, I know who you mean. No dear, he was never had up for anything worse than arson.'

She turned to Mona.

'I'm afraid it is rather a failing of mine to study people. I like knowing about them—watching for characteristic traits—it's far more interesting than reading a book.'

'But often far more expensive,' Michael interrupted.

His aunt smiled at him.

'You are thinking of that young man who persuaded me to put money into a non-existent gold mine,' she said. 'Oh well, we must all pay for our pleasures, and I don't suppose that the gold mines in which I have speculated over my whole life would add up to more than you have expended giving young women orchids and taking them to the theatre.'

'Oh, but those are not Michael's extravagances,' Mona laughed. 'When he's feeling reckless he indulges in a cow or a new tractor! But I'm on your side, Mrs Windlesham, I think that one's pleasures are worth paying for, but I can't say I enjoy people as a whole. Some of them are too queer, to peculiar, to be anything but nauseating.'

'I rather like being nauseated,' Mrs Windlesham said with relish.

They all had to laugh at the tone in which she spoke.

'It's no use, Mona,' Michael said, 'you could no more talk Aunt Ada out of a collecting people than you could stop a dipsomaniac when you caught him beside a bar.'

'Not a very elegant simile,' Mrs Windlesham interposed, 'but I understand what you mean. Now, Lady Carsdale can you tell me about the people in Little Cobble. You are useless Michael—so run away and add up the farm accounts or do something to keep your mind occupied. We shall be at least an hour.'

'All right, I'll leave you then,' Michael said. 'Don't encourage her too much, Mona, otherwise she will find out all about everyone too quickly and leave me. I rather like having her here.'

'Don't flatter me too fulsomely,' his aunt said.

Then as he left the room, she turned to Mona.

'A nice boy, but he never had many party graces. His father was just like him. I can't think what you've been doing to let him grow up like that.'

'Like what?' Mona asked.

'Gruff and abrupt,' Mrs Windlesham said. 'It's a form of shyness, of course, all the Merrills are shy although they'll never admit it.'

Mona smiled.

'I can't believe that,' she said. 'I always think of Michael as above such things.'

'And that's where you are quite wrong,' his aunt replied. 'Michael is both shy and sensitive. As a little boy he was particularly so and then he adopted that rather hard veneer to protect himself, just as a tree grows bark. I'm not certain that you haven't a good deal to do with his bark being so tough.'

'I!' Mona exclaimed. 'Why should you think I have made Michael shy and nervous?'

'Well, haven't you?' Mrs Windlesham asked.

She looked at Mona with such knowing eyes that she had to laugh.

'Kamerade!' Mona cried. 'I see I'm up against an expert in psychology. All right, I have teased Michael, but I never thought he minded. In fact, that's why I went on, hoping that one day he'd squeal.'

'Of course you did—and then they say we aren't barbarians,' Mrs Windlesham sighed. 'My dear, very few of us are civilised, the instinct to be cruel is strong in the best of us.

'So you were cruel to Michael with your teasing and taunting and you sharpened your quick wit at his expense and he got more and more hoary and prickly to the touch?

'Oh dear, don't I know it! Men and women are the same the world over.'

'You're making me feel guilty,' Mona exclaimed.

'Not I,' Mrs Windlesham replied. 'You are feeling rather pleased with yourself to think that you had such an effect on Michael. I only hope one day he gives you the spanking you deserve.'

'I'm not certain he hasn't,' Mona said.

She was remembering that kiss in the Long Gallery—that hard, brutal, insulting kiss for which Michael had apologised afterwards.

'I'm very glad to hear it,' Mrs Windlesham said, 'but I'm not certain that you've been punished enough. There's a glint in your eye when you tease Michael that bodes ill for the poor lad. But never mind, I shall know more after I have been here a few days.

'Tell me about the other people in this flat and rather desolate-looking country.'

As Mona walked home she smiled at the remembrance of Mrs Windlesham's interest. She had a quick perceptive mind and the way she managed to pierce through what was unimportant to the kernel or root of the matter was entrancing to watch.

'I shall go up and see her tomorrow,' Mona thought. 'It's so like Michael to have an aunt like that and never talk about her. I wonder what the story of her life is? That would be worth hearing.'

At the same time, Mona had made up her mind that she herself must be careful. It would be difficult to hide anything from Mrs Windlesham, she thought, if she were really determined to hunt one down, though instinctively she knew that Michael's aunt was trustworthy.

Thinking over the afternoon she realised that she had told Mrs Windlesham a lot to hear nothing in return. That was the secret of learning—to be a good listener and to be able to impart wisdom without making it boring.

'Perhaps old age to such people,' Mona thought, 'has its compensations, and yet who wants to be old?'

For the first time since Lionel had died she wanted not death but life. A life that was vivid and vital again, holding interest and hope—having a future instead of only a past.

'Am I getting sensible or merely older?' she asked herself. 'Perhaps both.'

She was singing as she opened the door of the Priory. The hall was in darkness, Nanny and Mrs Vale had already put up the black-out. Mona switched on the light and saw a letter waiting for her on the hall table.

'Who can have written to me?' she wondered, and hoped it was from Ned's lawyers to say there was some money waiting for her in the bank.

She picked up the envelope, and then, as she stared at it, was suddenly very still. That slanting, flowing writing —where had she seen it before?

Wildly she thought it was impossible, that she was mistaken, but her fingers trembled and even as she slit open the envelope she knew she was not deceived—there was only one person in the world with handwriting just like that.

IO

Mona could remember very clearly the first time she had met Char Strathwyn.

It had been at the races in Cairo; she was waiting to draw her winnings on a previous race, and noticed a woman standing not far away from her looking disconsolately at the fortunate queue of those who had gambled successfully.

She was an ugly woman, exaggeratedly thin and dressed with almost masculine severity in a tussore coat and skirt and a hard panama hat.

She might have been any age, for she had that dried-up, weather-beaten look which women get after spending years in the East and indulging in too much whisky after sun-down.

Without thinking Moan stared at her. Suddenly the woman smiled and, ashamed of her rudeness, Mona smiled back. The woman sauntered across to her.

'You have been lucky then?' she said in a deep, slightly husky voice which somehow was in keeping with her appearance. 'I wish to goodness I had. You don't know anything good for the big race do you?'

Mona looked at her card. It had been marked for her by Lionel the day before, and when she followed his advice she nearly always made money.

125

'I don't know much about it myself,' she confessed, 'but I have been told "Mizpah" is a good choice. He's an outsider, of course.'

'Thanks very much,' the woman said. 'Perhaps you will bring me luck. I need it.'

She hurried away to place her bet, and Mona forgot about her until an hour later, when, as she walked towards the paddock, a voice at her elbow said :

'I couldn't be more grateful—you've done me a good turn.'

She turned to see the woman in the tussore coat and skirt.

'Oh, you backed "Mizpah" then,' she exclaimed. 'I am so glad. It was a good price too, wasn't it ?'

'Thank you a thousand times—I'm so grateful,' the woman insisted. 'Do you know anything else ?'

There was a greedy look about her eyes and the way she spoke, and Mona's instinctive reaction was to say 'No' and to leave her, but she was too good-natured.

It struck her that perhaps the woman was really in want, and so, looking through her card, she said :

'I've got nothing for the next two, but "Le Prince" in the last race is, I am told, a certainty. He's the favourite, so I'm afraid you'll only get a very short price.'

'Thank you,' the woman said fervently, then added : 'Are you going to the paddock now ?'

'I thought of it.'

'Let's so together,' the other suggested.

Mona accepted because it would have been difficult to refuse.

'My name's Strathwyn,' the stranger went on, 'Char Strathwyn.'

'Mine's Mona Vale.'

She was reserved, for suddenly, without reason, she disliked this encounter. She was used to meeting people casually, and yet something about this woman repelled her.

'I'll get rid of her,' she thought. 'I'm certain to see someone I know and that will be an excuse.'

But she was soon to learn that having once met Char Strathwyn it was impossible to shake her off. She was persistently at one's heels like a raffish and rather disreputable dog.

She followed one about—at least so it seemed to Mona in the next few weeks. For she grew used to seeing that tussore coat and skirt loom in the distance and know with a sinking of the heart that it was Char again.

They soon got to Christian names; they soon assumed a friendliness that Mona was far from feeling—somehow it was difficult to analyse her feelings about Char Strathwyn.

She was sorry for her; sometimes she almost hated her; but she could not bring herself to be really rude, to tell her that she did not want to know her and ignore her eagerness to be friends.

Occasionally it was a relief to have another woman to talk to. When the hours of loneliness were too frightful Mona even welcomed that thin face with its bright restless eyes like those of an inquisitive monkey.

She learnt little about Char's personal life for, in her desire to avoid confidences, Mona made no effort to inquire closely either into Char's past or present.

Gaunt and unattractive, Char had a distinctive personality, although one could find many such middle-aged women, usually widowed, wandering about the East alone because they had no homes and no belongings, having given the best years of their lives to upholding some outpost of the Empire.

They journeyed from port to port, from capital to capital, as if in search of something which they never found —perhaps the will-o'-the-wisp was only their own youth and enthusiasm which had been lost during their first years of Suez.

Char knew a lot of people; and if she did not know them she would manage, sooner or later, to scrape an acquaintance.

Sometimes Mona would shudder as she watched her, asking herself if one day she might become like Char in her desire for companionship—in her search to find an antidote to an inner loneliness.

Char also knew a lot about people. She made it her business. There were few secrets or intrigues of which she did not manage to get an inkling. She was like a dog with a hidden bone—she scented it and dug on indefatigably until it was discovered.

Whether of diplomacy, international politics, or scandal, sooner or later Char knew all there was to know, and Mona guessed that at times she made a good thing out of her knowledge.

She soon realised that Char was a dangerous person with whom to be acquainted in her position. It was so essential that her association with Lionel should never be disclosed.

In a place like Cairo, where everything about everybody was common property, they had to be more careful than they had ever imagined would be necessary when they were in Paris.

There it had been easy for Mona to have a flat and for Lionel to visit her. In Egypt such a position was impossible and all her anticipations of the unhappiness and sufering which awaited her with Lionel's new appointment were justified.

She must live in a second-rate hotel, and when she had the chance to see him they met in a villa on the outskirts of the town, which he had borrowed from a friend.

The latter was away big-game shooting and the only people left in charge were two well-trusted servants. Lionel and Mona would motor there in separate cars to enjoy a few hours together—hours ecstatic with passion and the release of repressed longing, but shadowed by fear and the consciousness of danger.

Yet for Mona, at least, such meetings were worth all the hours and weeks of lonely misery that she must spend waiting for them.

The garden of the villa sloped down to the Nile, and sometimes they would sit under the palms on a patch of lawn that was kept green by hours of watering.

They would talk, they would laugh, and they would be happy, but they were always feverishly aware that the minutes were speeding past and that soon they must separate again.

Lionel must return to his wife and Mona to the sordid, dismal discomfort of her hotel.

Her position was sometimes almost insupportable.

Due to Lionel's insistence on her being dressed expensively, Mona caused a great deal of gossip whenever she appeared in public.

In a place as small as Cairo everyone knew everyone else's business and 'the mysterious Miss Vale' soon began to be pointed out. It was inevitable that she should make a few acquaintances.

Lionel warned her it was playing with fire, but she found it impossible to live a life of complete seclusion unless she shut herself in her hotel bedroom and never went out. People spoke to her, and unless she were offensively rude she must respond pleasantly.

Few were as persistent as Char Strathwyn, but nevertheless her circle of acquaintances increased.

Lionel talked of making a trip to Luxor and Aswan and he suggested to Mona that while he was going by train, she might go by river in a steamer.

She agreed at once, not only because Lionel suggested it but because she was glad of the chance to get out of Cairo, away from the heat, dust, noise and the everlasting round of racing and restaurants.

Lionel gave her the money for her ticket and told her that he expected to be staying at the Winter Palace Hotel, but anyway she would find a letter with all his plans when she arrived.

She clung to him desperately at their last meeting. She felt as if this everlasting see-saw of 'Hail' and 'Farewell' was getting on her nerves.

'If only just for once we could go somewhere alone together,' she cried. 'One day, darling, I shall run away. I don't think I can stand this much longer.'

He had laughed at her, but she felt that he did sympathise; and she knew that, although her words were threatening, it would be impossible for her ever to leave him or to sever their personal relationship.

It was a blazingly hot day when Mona stepped on board the Nile steamer, native boys carrying her luggage.

There was a faint breeze on the river and the covered decks of the boat, cool, dark and shady, were inviting after contact with the heat rising from the tarmac streets and the smell and stench of motor-cars and camels—a mingling of East and West which was only attractive in books.

Mona unpacked a few things in her cabin, then went on deck to watch them cast off and start their slow and leisurely movements up the blue waters of the Nile.

The last gangway was being removed when suddenly she saw an Arab gesticulating and shouting at the officers to hold the ship.

She leant over the rail curiously and saw to her horror who the late arrival was—Char Strathwyn!

She was wearing her usual tussore coat and skirt, but it was crumpled and dishevelled as if she had dressed in a hurry; and her panama hat was pushed a little to the back of her head, giving her a rakish air so that for the moment Mona thought she had been drinking.

She very likely had, but Char Strathwyn was the type of woman to whose appearance it made little difference however much she drank.

Only her mind became vague and somewhat disconnected, but her looks remained the same, ugly, dried-up, colourless, and as ageless as the Sphinx itself.

'Why is she here?' Mona wondered. 'Did she know I was to be aboard?'

She had had the idea for some time that Char Strathwyn was deliberately following her around, finding out by some methods of her own what were Mona's engagements.

The woman seemed to have a kind of affection for her, although it was difficult to imagine Char having sentimental or affectionate feelings for anyone but herself.

Perhaps there was a simpler explanation. Mona knew that Char thought she was lucky. Ever since that day at the races she had bombarded her with requests for tips—for information of any sort which might lead to her being successful at her eternal gambling.

Char was an inveterate gambler. She could not resist a bet even on the most ridiculous things; and she was also very unlucky.

It seemed to Mona absurd that anyone who was so unfortunate at cards and racing, should continue with a persistence which was almost fanatical, day after day, week after week, in an endeavour to turn the scales of fortune in their favour.

But Char plagued the Fates and was equally importunate in her anxiety to hang on to Mona.

With the best grace that she could muster, Mona smiled as she saw Char coming down the deck towards her.

'This is a surprise!' she said.

'I only heard half an hour ago that you were going,' Char panted. 'I just had time to throw a few things into a case. Why didn't you tell me?'

'I didn't think you'd be interested,' Mona answered.

She longed to ask 'Why should I?' but remembered that they had some weeks together ahead of them. There was nothing to be gained by quarrelling.

'Of course you knew I'd be interested,' Char said impatiently. 'You weren't trying to push me off, were you? Have you come with some other friends?'

She looked suspiciously at Mona, who suddenly felt exceedingly bored with the whole situation. What a nuisance the woman was!

Why couldn't she go away and leave her alone? She had rather looked forward to the trip—to the long, lazy days ahead. There might have been some quite amusing people on board, new people she had not met before, and in all probability would never see again.

It would have been a rest, an interlude, to associate with them and get away from her Cairo acquaintances;

but now it was as if she had brought all Cairo with her in the person of Char Strathwyn.

She leant over the rail, feeling annoyed and yet wise enough not to show it.

'I wonder who's on board?' Char chattered. 'Sometimes there are some very decent people on these trips—rich ones, too. We might get up a game of poker.'

'I can't afford to play.'

'Nor can I, but that's all the more reason to find someone rich and stupid. If we could win their money it would be a good holiday.'

They were moving now; the green palm trees bordering the banks of the river and the white roofs and minarets of the city looked fairy-like in the haze which was rising above them towards the golden sky.

Mona suddenly felt irritated at the idea of spending the time in which they might be enjoying the scenery in playing cards.

'I'm not going to gamble while I'm on board,' she answered shortly. 'I'm not even going to play bridge.'

She walked towards her cabin, but Char was irrepressible.

'Nonsense!' she said. 'I'll have a five fixed up for after dinner this evening, you see if I don't.'

Mona was quite certain that she would achieve her aims —Char always did.

Angry and resentful, she took off her hat and dress and lay down on her bed. It was too hot even to unpack. She rang the bell and ordered a gin-and-tonic—and when it was brought to her in the long glass filled with ice she sipped it reflectively.

Char Strathwyn was becoming a nuisance, she thought, but what could she do about it. She wondered if Char thought she was rich. It would be quite easy for her to be under such a misapprehension.

She had seen her clothes and Char would know to a penny exactly what they had cost from Molyneux, Chanel, and Scaparelli. She had seen her jewels—the fabulous gems which Lionel had wisely insisted on her putting into the bank in Cairo before she left on this trip.

Yes, Char might easily be mistaken, but she knew where she was staying; she was not fool enough to think that anyone would choose the blowsy garishness of that second-rate hotel if they could afford Shepheard's or Mena House.

'I don't care what she thinks,' Mona muttered angrily, but she knew that it was no use ignoring Char, she had got to face up to her.

She was there waiting—as inevitable as the bill at the end of an evening's enjoyment—one could not escape her. Those curious, self-seeking eyes missed nothing, they knew everything.

'Except one thing,' Mona told herself. 'Whatever happens she shall never find out about Lionel and me—it would be ghastly.'

She knew that Char being on the steamer was going to complicate things considerably when they got to Luxor.

'Lionel will find a way out of it,' she thought confidently.

But she felt uncomfortable, for she had not told Lionel about Char. He was impatient if anything complicated their already complex life still further.

'It's all very well for him—he doesn't know or understand how hard it is for me.'

She had begun to learn that Lionel had a lot of blind spots where other people's happiness or interests were concerned.

Once or twice she had accused him of it, but somehow her words lost their sting, her accusations their point when she had to say them within his encircling arms or with his mouth near to hers.

No, it was no use relying on Lionel, she would have to run her life as best she could. But why worry? Perhaps Char would find someone else on board to whom she could attach herself.

Mona's hopes were not fulfilled. Char certainly collected a small number of people who were willing to gamble, but it was to Mona she clung, going along to her cabin in search of her if she were a few minutes late for meals or if she tried to have a longer siesta than usual.

It was also quite impossible to avoid gambling with her. Char insisted on it.

'I'm nothing more or less than a mascot,' Mona told herself.

Yet she knew it was deeper than that. She represented all that Char had missed in her life—beauty, glamour, a charm which gained popularity without effort, and the superficial trappings of wealth and extravagance.

Char certainly had none of the latter. Mona never saw her in anything save her plain tussore suits and one black evening dress which she wore with a coat that was somewhat similiar in design to a man's dinner jacket.

Yet she always managed to get to places. She had travelled all over the world, the trip on the Nile steamer to Luxor was not a cheap one, but she had found the money.

She had money, too, to spend on drinks and—even if whisky was cheap and she was treated by many people—Char's drink bill at the end of the week must have amounted to a considerable sum.

Sometimes Mona longed to ask her for an explanation of these things and yet she dared not for fear that Char might in return question her.

'Thank goodness, she doesn't know England well!' Mona thought. 'I'd hate her to find out that I've been married and that I have a title. I feel that somehow or other she would turn it to her advantage.'

She certainly used Mona's looks to attract odd men to play poker with them in the evenings and often in the afternoons as well.

'She's a lovely girl—you'll like her,' Mona heard her say once to a bluff, dour old man who was reputed wealthy but had withstood all Char's advances and efforts to make him join their game.

She knew quite well of whom Char was speaking and was disappointed when the old man capitulated and was one of their number that evening. Yet she was too lazy to make a protest.

'What does it matter?' she told herself, and knew that the only thing that counted was the passing of time until she should see Lionel again at Luxor.

There was one other woman in their party. She was an American widow, travelling ostensibly on a sight-seeing tour, actually in search of another and, if possible, a European husband.

She was apparently very rich and she was equally apparently a drunkard. Despite everyone's advice, she insisted on starting to drink early in the morning and kept it up all day.

She was pretty in a rather ordinary manner and she would have been far prettier if the lines of dissipation had not already begun to destroy the freshness of her looks.

Sadie, as they called her, began to be rather a nuisance after the first few days, when she had been on her best behaviour.

Half-way through the evening it seemed to be either Char's or Mona's job to help her along to her cabin and ring for the stewardess to undress her and put her to bed.

'That woman's an absolute sponge,' Char said. 'I can't think how she goes on doing it day after day. At this rate she'll hardly be alive at the end of the trip.'

'Perhaps she'll pull herself together when we get to Luxor,' Mona said. 'She's bored, that's half her trouble.'

'She's lucky, too,' Char said furiously.

She had been annoyed that Sadie, having won quite a considerable sum had collapsed over the table before anyone had a chance of taking their revenge.

But that night Sadie won again, and Char came to Mona almost despairingly in the morning.

'To think that pig of a woman should get away with it!' she said. 'It makes me furious—but still there's plenty of time. She isn't getting off here and I've arranged that we'll all start to play at four o'clock. If we can keep her sober enough to hold the cards until dinner-time we ought to get our money back.'

'I don't know that I shall be here,' Mona said.

She was doing her hair as she spoke and in the glass she saw Char's face move convulsively.

'You're getting off?' Char stammered.

'I may be, I don't know yet.'

'But you can't do that—you can't go,' Char said frantically.

'I tell you I'm not certain. I'm expecting a letter waiting for me at the Winter Palace Hotel.'

Char swallowed quickly.

'Don't you understand? You're lucky to me. If you go now I'll never get my money back—never!'

'Oh, yes, you will,' Mona said soothingly. 'It's nothing to do with me, you know. You've just got this fancy into your head, Char. One person isn't more lucky than another.'

'You're wrong,' Char said, and there was a note of hysteria in her voice. 'Ever since I first saw you at the races my luck changed. I've got to hang on to you, Mona, otherwise I'm lost.'

'Nonsense!' Mona said impatiently. 'You mustn't let yourself think like that. The heat's getting you down. Have a drink.'

She pressed the bell as she spoke and Char sat there on her bed saying nothing until the boy came and the order was given.

'She looks like a sick monkey,' Mona thought. 'How idiotic women are!—even the ones who seem most self-possessed and likely to be able to look after themselves.'

To cheer Char up she lied.

'I think there's every possibility of my staying, so don't look so depressed.'

Char brightened.

'You really think so?'

'Yes, I do.'

'You don't understand what it means to me. One day I

will tell you about bad luck—my bad luck—and it will open your eyes. I don't suppose you've even dreamt of such things.'

'I'd like to hear about it—one day,' Mona said, warding off the confession, 'but at the moment I shouldn't upset yourself.'

She noticed that Char's fingers as she lit a cigarette were trembling.

'Perhaps she's ill,' she thought, unsympathetically hoping it was true.

She had a feeling she was being held by the inescapable tentacles of an octopus. Char twined herself round people —one couldn't get away from her.

'Funny,' Mona thought. 'You'd never think she was the ivy type. She looks so independent, so completely self-sufficient, but she's a leech and she's trying to batten herself on me.'

She finished dressing and went ashore.

'Miss Vale?' the clerk at the Winter Palace Hotel said. 'Oh, yes we have a letter for you.'

He handed it to her and she saw Lionel's writing.

She went into the garden fragrant with flowers where soft-eyed deer and other small animals were caged for the amusement of the hotel guests.

Under a great shady tree were long mattress-covered chairs. Mona sat down in one.

She opened Lionel's letter, of which, as usual, the first words brought a throb to her heart and a flush to her face. Lionel was always original in his choice of endearments. Then she read on.

'*A most wonderful thing has happened, my darling. It will be possible for us to have a week together alone in Alexandria. The reasons why make too long a story to tell you now, sufficient to say that I shall be there the day after you get this letter. You will have to fly back of course. Catch this morning's plane and remember as you come that I shall be waiting impatiently for you at the other end. Oh, Mona. . . .'*

There was a lot more, then a postscript.

'Be careful no one guesses about us or where you are going.'

Had he been clairvoyant, Mona wondered, when he wrote that? Did he sense there was someone like Char haunting her like a shadow?

She bought her air ticket and went back to the boat. It was nearly dinner-time and she was planning how she could pack and get away without Char knowing. She walked down below to go to her cabin. As she passed the door of Sadie's it was half open.

Hardly realising she did so, Mona glanced inside. Sadie was sprawled on the floor drunk. But Char was with her. Mona was just going to slip by, hoping she had not been seen, when something happened.

Sadie's bag was lying on the floor. It was open as if it had fallen from her arm when she collapsed. The lipstick and vanity case had spilled on the floor, but a great wad of notes was still caught in the bag. As Mona watched, a hand —Char's—had come out and taken the notes!

It was all over in a flash. Then Mona had run into her cabin, shut the door and locked it.

She sat down at the dressing-table feeling physically sick. She didn't know why the sight of Char stealing from the drunken Sadie upset her so much, she only knew that she personally felt humiliated and degraded beyond words. This is what she had sunk to, these were the depths to which her life of sin had brought her.

She thought of her mother, of her home, and knew she could bear no more. This was evil, filthy, unclean. She felt as if she was sinking into a pit of stinky mud from which she could not escape and would finally be submerged.

She could hear Nanny all down the ages warning her.

'You can't touch pitch and not be defiled.'

'Birds of a feather flock together.'

'Like goes to like !'

She wasn't like those women, yet could she become like them? For in the years ahead what other companionship would she be offered, what alternative was there to Char and her associates?

There was a knock on the door.

'Who is it?'

'It's me, Char.'

'I'm resting.'

'Let me in.'

'No, I'm tired. I've got a headache and I'm going to bed.'

'But you must come down for dinner—you must.'

'No, Char, leave me alone !'

Mona felt as if her voice rose, then with an effort she spoke firmly.

'I'm going to bed. I'm not going to argue.'

There was silence as if Char debated whether to try and force her way into the cabin. Then to Mona's relief she said surlily :

'Very well then, if that's what you want.'

She moved away. Mona sat tense, listening until she could no longer hear footsteps and there was only silence. Then feverishly, frantically she started to stuff her clothes into their cases.

She felt such a desperate desire to escape it was almost hysterical.

'I never, never want to see those ghastly women again,' she told herself.

11

Mona and Lionel had a perfect week together in Alexandria.

It was made even more perfect for Mona by the knowledge that she was not returning to Cairo, Lionel had been moved to Vienna, and that was the reason their holiday had been possible.

Mona's clothes and jewels were sent down to meet her on the ship which took her from Alexandria to Naples. As she stood on the deck and watched the great harbour at Alexandria, with its ships of all nations lying side by side, recede slowly into the distance, she thanked heaven that she had shaken the dust of Egypt from her feet.

'I loathe the country, the heat, the smell, the people,' she thought.

But she knew it was Char she loathed because she still felt unclean from the contact with her.

And yet she told herself defiantly, that it had been worth anything to be with Lionel, to charm the lines of care and worry from his face, to know that he was as gay as a child, as irresponsible in his laughter and his loving as any young boy.

For she was not the only one who was beginning to suffer by this unnatural existence. Lionel loved her with all the force of his dynamic personality and his conventional domestic existence was a continual strain.

Ann got on his nerves. She could never have been the right type of wife for him for he needed someone intelligent and sensitive who could respond to his moods. Ann had a solid, sensible character and no imagination.

When she accepted Lionel as her husband she believed their happiness to be complete, with no doubts or misgivings as to the future. She expected, and she found, neither light nor shade in her married life.

To her is was a straightforward, charming existence,

with few ups and downs, and those only of a material character. The spiritual issues of life were no problem to Ann —her world was made up of black and white with no half-shades, and in her sheltered existence she had known only the white.

She filled her life with small things, with entertaining, with amusements and with seeing to her household. She had no interest in diplomacy—the intrigues of either dictators or statesmen were completely beyond her and she made no effort to understand them.

Her horizon was bounded by her home, and she meant to bring up her children sensibly, neither spoiling them with too much affection nor fashionably ignoring them.

In other words, Ann was the perfect wife for someone who could have been the perfect husband in a moderate sort of way. But Lionel had never understood moderation.

He was a clever man, acknowledged as brilliant in his profession, and he suffered, as most brilliant men do, from moods of high elation and deep depression.

He had learnt, however, to control himself so that to the outside world he appeared invariably suave, courteous and distinguished.

Only Mona knew at times he was tortured by his own emotions, and overwrought until it seemed as if the fine strings of her nerves were stretched almost to breaking-point.

He brought to her sympathetic understanding all his troubles and problems, for she alone could save him from himself and charm away his moods of black depression.

It amused her sometimes to think how much she knew and how dangerous she might be as a traitor to her own country. There was no doubt that many of Lionel's successful negotiations which earned him praise in high places were due to Mona's inspiration.

Lionel had no secrets from her, and she hated hiding facts from him.

But she could not bring herself to tell him about those

awful women and the degradation she had felt at having been so-called friends with them.

She had felt that it was almost too fortunate when Lionel had told her that there was no need to return to Cairo and that they were leaving for Austria.

Vienna had indeed seemed a paradise after Cairo. Mona had loved its grey shabbiness, which even in its direst poverty had never become tawdry.

Vienna had for her a charm beyond words; she felt as if she perpetually moved to the soft strains of a Strauss waltz. And the people with their smiling faces, their hands outstretched in friendship even while they were in a desperate plight financially, moved her to tears.

The poverty in Vienna was horrifying and yet the courage and bravery of its citizens gave a glamour and beauty even to starvation and penury.

Mona stayed at a small hotel, which had remained unchanged through the centuries. There were big blue-tiled stoves in the corners of the rooms, religious paintings on the walls, and great gilt beds reminiscent of the days when Vienna really was a city of music and love and laughter.

But the time there had passed all too quickly. Clouds were sweeping over Europe; there were the ominous rumblings and thunderings of the German War Machine. Mona left Vienna on Lionel's insistence two days before Hitler marched in and captured Austria without a shot being fired in her defence.

She went to Paris, and Lionel arrived a week later in the diplomatic train.

'What's going to happen to you now?' Mona asked, and he shrugged his shoulders.

'I don't know,' he replied, 'and for the moment, my darling, I don't care.'

They soon found out. Lionel was posted to Buenos Aires.

Once again Mona realised that she would be cut off from social contacts and condemned to continue the only life she had led in Cairo. Almost her nerve failed her and she felt that she could not go, but it was useless to tell Lionel that when he turned to her for reassurance—so certain of her love—so sure that she would not fail him.

She agreed; but the night before she left Paris to travel across the Atlantic in a slow Highland boat while Lionel crossed with Ann in one of the big Royal Mail liners, something happened which might have proved a warning.

They were alone in Paris, for Ann had flown back to England to say good-bye to her parents. They had decided to dine together at one of the little restaurants in the Madeleine.

It was so seldom that they had the opportunity of going out together in public that it was something of a gala occasion.

Lionel had bought her a huge bunch of orchids to pin on her shoulder against the cool green of her dress and the table at which they dined was decorated with the same flowers.

'How extravagant you are!' Mona had teased him, but he had laughed.

'Nothing is extravagance where you are concerned, darling—only the best is good enough.'

A trite enough saying, but not when Lionel said it.

The band had played while they ate a dinner chosen with the taste of a connoisseur and drank wines which had lain for years covered in cobwebs in the cellar waiting for just such an occasion.

There was a cabaret, but they had been too happy to watch it. Lionel's hand had held Mona's beneath the table, and she had felt as young and as gay as if she were only eighteen and they had just become engaged again.

'I wonder,' she asked herself, 'if our love would have lasted had we been married all these years? Would we still have felt this passionate need for each other—this yearning of heart, mind and soul for the other when we are apart?'

She turned to tell Lionel something of what she was thinking when the words froze on her lips and she sat staring at the doorway, for there, peering in at the crowded room, was Char Strathwyn!

She was with a party, and a moment later they were being shown into another part of the room.

Quickly Mona picked up a menu card and held it in front of her face, but she was certain in her mind that Char had seen her, and noticed Lionel also.

'Why should it matter?' Mona asked herself. 'I'm leaving Paris tomorrow.'

But despite common sense and her own endeavours at reassurance, she knew that it did matter. Char was dangerous.

If she did not know who Lionel was she would find out in some way and she would make use of the information; Mona was certain of that.

Lionel had noticed nothing, but instinctively he realised a few moments later that some magic had gone from the evening.

'You are tired,' he said. 'Let us go.'

She accepted gratefully, and pulling her sable cloak round her, they went, leaving the restaurant by a different door, so that Char did not see them depart.

And yet Mona was uneasy. She felt there was something relentless, something inevitable about Char as far as she was concerned. Would she ever be able to shake her off?

The next morning she had sailed for Buenos Aires—a year there and then New York. Her fears were forgotten. It was a long time since she had thought of Char until this moment when, like a bombshell, she had found her letter waiting in the hall.

Mona had a longing to throw it straight into the fire unopened, and yet she knew how useless such an action would be. If Char wanted to see her she couldn't escape as easily as that.

Slowly she drew the letter from its envelope. She looked first at the signature in the wild hope that she had been mistaken, but there it was—'Yours always affectionately, Char.' With a sigh she began to read.

It was only as she read the words 'My dear Mona' that she turned back and looked at the envelope. Yes, it was addressed to Lady Carsdale. So Char knew her right name! Again Mona started the letter.

'*My dear Mona,*

I hear you are back in England. Welcome home—and you are lucky in that you have one to go to.

I am here in London and feeling rather blue. I suppose you wouldn't be an angel and put me up for a few days? I know what an imposition this is in war-time, so of course I will be only too willing to "pay my way", as they say. If you can't manage the extra bed what about the local pub?

Let me know soon, as it would be lovely to see you again, and anyway I shall be in that part of the world, as I have a friend who is running one of the Aeroplane factories near Bedford.

Yours always affectionately,
CHAR.'

To anyone reading the letter casually, it would have seemed pleasant enough, but to Mona, Char made her intentions very obvious. Reading between the lines she knew that Char said:

'I am coming either to the Priory or the local pub, and it's no use trying to put me off because I shall come into the neighbourhood and then fasten myself upon you.'

'What am I to do?' she wondered desperately, and knew there was no hope of reprieve—Char would attain her object.

'How Mummy will hate her!' was her next reaction as she went in search of Mrs Vale.

Her mother was writing letters and looked up smiling as Mona came into the room.

'Did you have a nice time with Michael?' she asked.

'Yes,' Mona replied briefly, her thoughts concentrated on the letter she held in her hand.

'Mummy,' she said tentatively, 'there's a woman who wants to come here and stay. I knew her when I was in Cairo.'

'Well, I think we can manage it,' Mrs Vale said. 'It would be nice for you to see one of your old friends again.'

'She isn't really a friend. I don't like her, but it is rather difficult to refuse. Look, you can read the letter.'

She handed it to her mother, who read it through and passed it back.

'Of course you must have her, dear. Drop her a line and ask her to come on Thursday or Friday—not Wednesday, if you can help it, it's always such a commotion when the Knitting Party is here.'

'I'll tell her,' Mona said hopelessly.

She could not explain her horror at the idea of seeing Char again; it all sounded too ridiculous, and there was nothing she could really say against Char except that she was a gambler and the sort of person that one did not usually find staying in people's homes.

'Oh, Heavens!' Mona thought to herself. 'What a mess I make of things! Why can't I live a normal life like anyone else?'

It seemed as if nothing was ever simple. Here she had come home hoping to lose herself and her memories in the quietness of the country, but now Char, with her inquisitive restless eyes looking about for trouble—and usually finding it—was intruding on her seclusion.

For one wild moment Mona thought of telling Michael everything. Supposing she took him at his word and confided in him, told him what her life had been with Lionel, told him, too, about Char and how without reason she was afraid of her?

Then she laughed bitterly at the idea.

'I think Michael would die of the shock!' she thought. 'What would he say? How could he ever begin to understand people could live like that. No I got myself into this trouble, now I shall have to get out of it again. After all, what can she do?'

But despite every effort to reassure herself, the fear persisted; and when Saturday came and she drove down to the station in the governess car to meet Char, she knew that she was as nervous as if the train contained a policeman coming to arrest her.

But to the people who saw her passing through the village she looked merely her usual attractive self in a green check tweed suit and velvet peaked hat pulled over her curls. Opposite the post-office, Lynn Archer hailed her.

'Where are you off to?'

'I'm going to the station,' Mona replied, pulling up the pony. 'Do you want a lift?'

She noted that Lynn had the two elder children with her and she felt it might be a relief to meet Char with a party.

'Can't spare the time, I'm afraid,' Lynn answered. 'Bill's coming home today and we have been buying crumpets for the occasion.'

'My loss, then,' Mona smiled, 'but I will come and see you tomorrow and bring you somebody who will be a real type for your book.'

'Don't speak to me about the book!' Lynn cried disgustedly. 'I've written two chapters and I'm stuck again.'

'You're hopeless. Unless someone commits a murder right on your doorstep you can't find a plot.'

'I wish somebody would! What's your friend like?'

'Straight from the Mysterious East.'

'It sounds exciting. Ask her if she'll entrust her memoirs to me.'

'I will, but I'd better get on now or she'll find no one to meet her.'

'Good-bye, and don't forget to come in tomorrow.'

'I won't,' Mona promised, and drove on down the hill.

She liked Lynn Archer and she was amused to find that Lynn shocked the village, which was not used to Lady novelists in trousers or women who said 'Damn' when she couldn't get the groceries they required at the local shop.

Mrs Gunther had already declaimed her as being a scandal to the neighbourhood, but Dorothy Howlett agreed with Mona that she was an asset and they had discovered too, that underneath her superficial sophistication she was an adoring mother and a very domesticated wife.

The train was pulling into the station just as Mona arrived. She jumped out and, telling the stationmaster's small boy, who was playing in the yard, to hold the pony, hurried on to the platform.

Though she was expecting her, it was quite a shock to see Char's weather-beaten narrow face smiling at her from the window of a first-class carriage. She got out on to the platform and held out her hands.

'Here I am, safe and sound,' she said. 'How are you, Mona? But there's no need to ask.'

Char spoke in her dry, abrupt manner, which made any compliment she paid sound as if she was being critical. Her voice, too, was deep and dry. Mona had forgotten that particular dryness of Char's voice—as if, like her skin, it needed oiling.

'I've got a suitcase in the van,' Char said.

When the porter got it out for them they carried it between them to the governess-cart.

Char was looking just the same, Mona thought. She had merely changed her tussore coat and skirt for one of brown tweed of an indefinite speckled pattern which made her look rather like a shaggy, unattractive bird. Now that she was actually here, some of Mona's apprehension vanished.

'Why did I worry?' she asked herself. 'After all, she's only a woman, middle-aged, lonely and unwanted,'

They started off in silence, and then as they reached the hill approaching the village and the pony started his slow climb, Char leant forward and put her gloved hand on Mona's knee.

'I am glad to see you,' she said. 'It's a long time since we met, isn't it?'

'Years.'

'But I did see you once after you left Egypt—in Paris.'

Mona felt the blood surge up in her face. She had not expected Char to be so blunt and while she knew that she ought to be expressing surprise, asking where, and pretending that she had not seen her, somehow she could do none of these things.

Instead she flicked the pony lightly with the whip and said :

'I don't suppose we shall see Paris again for a long time.'

'Doesn't look like it,' Char agreed.

Mona knew that her eyes were on her face, taking in every detail of her expression.

They were nearing the top of the hill and Mona pointed ahead.

'Here's the village. You will see it's very rural, in fact, I'm afraid, Char, you will find it very dull.'

'I don't mind that. Nothing could be duller than London when one has been away for years and all one's friends are dead or lost.'

'I haven't been to London except for the day since I came home.'

'Did you see anyone you knew?'

Mona shook her head.

'No, I went up on business to see my solicitors.'

'Why did you come home?'

'I couldn't get any money out to America,' Mona replied.

Even as she said the words, she knew that Char was playing with her as a cat plays with a mouse. Char knew why she had come home—Char knew a great many things about her !

She waited, and Char's voice, dry and arid as the desert sands, confirmed her suspicions.

'I saw that your cousin Lionel died very suddenly in Washington,' she said. 'It must have been an awful shock for you.'

12

Char pulled off her hat and threw it down on the bed with a sigh; but the sound she made did not express weariness but rather triumph—as if she had reached her journey's end and achieved some task to which she had set herself.

She looked round the big bedroom with appraising eyes; she noted the heavy oak four-poster with its tapestry hangings, the walnut chest-of-drawers, the Chippendale mirrors and ancient oil paintings on the walls.

She guessed their value and noted, too, the shabby, threadbare carpet, the curtains that were faded, patched and darned, the old-fashioned Victorian washhand-stand with its badly cleaned brass hot-water can.

Char's scrutiny missed nothing—then she crouched down for a moment in front of the fire, holding out her thin fingers to the blaze.

She was delighted to be at the Priory. She had half-expected that Mona would prevaricate, or make excuses when she replied to her letter, and she had been prepared to fight her way in. But her resolution had not been tested, instead she had received by return of post an invitation to stay.

Char wondered if Mona had any idea how pleased she was to see her again. She had sensed that her own feelings were not reciprocated, but that was to be expected.

Char was used to being unwanted, to knowing that people preferred her absence to her company. Meeting dislike and distrust wherever she went, she had grown immune to their power to hurt, except very rarely.

This was, perhaps, one of the rare occasions.

Mona meant something to her which no one else had ever meant. She could not explain it even to herself. It was not affection, that would have been too alien an emotion for Char's make-up.

No, it was a kind of instinct—almost a superstition—to cling to Mona because she believed her lucky.

'A golden girl,' was how she thought of her.

From the moment Mona had come into her life at the races it seemed to Char that her luck had changed. The tips Mona had given her had brought money—afterwards everything she did seemed literally to turn to gold in her hands.

She had been on her beam ends; she had no idea how she could carry on, until Mona had turned the tide which had threatened to submerge her.

Even when Mona had disappeared out of her life, she had left an aura of luck behind her, for that trip up the Nile had been lucky for Char. She had made a contact on the boat which was to have far-reaching effects.

One of the men who made up their party at poker was to prove immeasurably useful to Char for some years afterwards. She attributed all her good fortune to Mona—she made the girl a talisman and the mere thought of her seemed to invite success.

It gave Char confidence, just as Mona's presence had given her confidence when they went anywhere together. Mona was so vital, so alive, she seemed to leap forward on the upward wave of life and that was what Char had never been able to do.

Feeling the warmth now on her hands, she felt as if it had penetrated her heart—a heart so withered, so shrivelled-up by the experiences of years, that it had ceased to have any existence save as an anatomical organ.

All her life Char had believed in Luck.

She had followed the Luck unremittingly; and although it had taken her into strange places and guided her at times down to the nethermost hell, she still trusted it, still had an undivided faith in that will-o'-the-wisp which deceived so many and finally disappointed all who depended upon it.

But Luck was Char's god, and Luck to her had become identified with Mona.

When she discovered that Mona had escaped her at Luxor she had made herself ill with rage.

Only the knowledge that she was penniless and must somehow get her money back from Sadie had prevented her from drinking herself into a coma and taking no further interest in what went on around her.

When her mind cleared a little, she looked back over her life and over the past, an account of which Mona had so successfully avoided receiving in confidence, and realised vaguely—for Char was not skilled in introspection—that Mona's attraction lay partly in the fact that she was the complete opposite to herself, and was, therefore, all she had always longed to be.

Char, most inappropriately christened Charmain, had been born of Anglo-Indian parents.

Her father had a small government post at Cawnpore and, as soon as Char was a few years old, she was sent back to England to live with her cousins. They were a large family, rough, improvident, and always on the verge of bankruptcy.

They found Char—an unprepossessing child—both a nuisance and an expense. She had an unhappy childhood and the trouble lay partly in a sensitive reaction to being teased incessantly about her looks.

She was unaccountably ugly with no redeeming feature. She was also ungainly, awkward, and delicate in health. Her female cousins being attractive and boisterously healthy, the contrast between them was always there to taunt Char, and she was made bitterly conscious of her own deficiencies.

When she was seventeen she went back to her parents in India. Her mother, by this time, had turned into a shrew who nagged incessantly and complained both at the country in which she lived and at the prospect of a retirement which would enforce their return home.

Char had looked forward to India as an escape from the miseries of her life in England. She soon found that life for her was much the same wherever she went. She had none of that commodity which was to be labelled in later years 'sex appeal'.

Men shunned her, even in India, where it was conventionally assumed that any girl, however unattractive, could find a husband.

She found herself partnerless at dances and excluded or forgotten from the numerous parties with which the Anglo-Indians filled their days. She grew bitter.

She found it some solace to be able to jeer and sneer at people, to repeat and even invent unkind things about them.

Consequently, people avoided her more than ever, but this only spurred her on to greater indiscretions.

Finally, when she was twenty-four, she got married. She married an acquaintance of her father, a man nearly three times her own age, who was a tea-planter in Ceylon.

He lived on the estate, which was twenty-five miles from the nearest white neighbour. He drank, he was a rotter, and he had a brutal streak in him—but still he was a man.

Char married him gratefully. In later years, she used to look back and wonder if, had she known what she was going to, she would have refused her one and only proposal of marriage.

Even then, with the marks of where he had bruised her still sore on her thin body, she was doubtful whether she would have had the courage to say no.

It had meant so much to have the status of a married woman, to salve her pride with the knowledge that one man had wanted her—even if he were a man like her husband.

He had got what he had set out to get—a housekeeper—but he made no bones about the fact that he found her physically unattractive and preferred to seek his amusement with native girls.

When he died, Char found herself with a few hundred pounds, a large experience of vice and debauchery, and not a friend in the world. Two places she disliked—one was England, the other Cawnpore, otherwise the world was open to her.

She decided that somehow she would manage to enjoy herself. If men were not going to seek her out because she was a woman, there were yet other ways in which she might arouse their interest.

The bars and cheap hotels of the East cater for just such dregs of humanity as Char Strathwyn became. Sometimes when she was fortunate she moved amongst a higher strata of dregs, but always she lived by the same methods, the same ideas.

She had one ambition—money. She wanted money not only to live, but because it gave her power.

Every penny she could wrench unwillingly out of a man or woman gave her the satisfaction of feeling that she was getting a little of her own back on a humanity which had treated her badly.

She knew quite well that people pointed her out as being undesirable, that young men and women were warned against her, and that the authorities had on more than one occasion debated the desirability of deporting her from British possessions.

But even in her wickedness, Char was not really effective. She was that strange mixture of rogue and fool which displays sometimes the astuteness of the rogue, at others the weakness of the fool.

She was human, after all—human because the vulnerability of her youth had never quite forsaken her : it was there, a tender spot, and it would catch up on her unexpectedly so that she lost her grip and many of her victims drifted away from her, thankful to escape and not realising quite why or how they had been so fortunate.

Deep down inside, Char had a longing for the peace and comfort which financial security could have given her.

Her fevered search for money was unsatisfying because in reality, although she did not know it, she was still seeking for the affection she had lost in her childhood.

She was pathetic ; but only to those who could see through the hard veneer of vice and self-seeking which had accumulated over her character through the years.

It had been only by chance that Char had learnt of Mona's return to England. She had been having a drink in one of the small bars in the West End of London and she had heard a man standing next to her say to his companion :

'Do you know anything about Hughes?'

'I met him once when he was training for Ned Carsdale,' the other had replied. 'Not a bad fellow, although he never got a winner for poor old Ned.'

The first man had laughed.

'Ned never could back a winner in anything. He was born to lose money. They tell me that he left his wife with a packet of debts and not a penny to meet them with.'

'I shouldn't think that worried her with a face like hers.'

'Yes, she was a good-looker all right,' the first man agreed. 'Funnily enough, I saw her a month ago getting out of an aeroplane at Croydon. She didn't recognise me, so I didn't speak to her. I think she'd come over from Lisbon.'

'I'd like to see her again,' his friend said. 'By Jove, she was worth looking at ! Remember how mad old Ned was about her—it was "Mona this" and "Mona that," but I will say there was every excuse for it.'

'All the Vales are good looking,' the first man asserted. 'I was at school with one of them—best-looking chap you've ever seen, but he was killed at Passchaendale.'

Char had started by listening to the conversation idly, then she had become alert and made an excuse to join in.

When she left the bar she had learnt all she wanted to know and she went straight back to her lodgings and wrote to Mona.

Not only was she wildly anxious to see Mona again—as usual she was in need of luck—but she also knew that she could fit her into a scheme which she had on hand at the moment.

It seemed to her providential that Mona should come back into her life at this particular moment. For, of course, she was intriguing. She wouldn't have been Char if she had been able to sit quiet and not work on something or some-body.

Her whole life for the last twenty years had consisted in spinning webs round people and forcing them to fit like bits of a jig-saw puzzle into a pattern which would be to her advantage.

Since her return to England she had attached herself to a man called Jarvis Lecker.

Char had met him on the ship in which she returned from abroad when war started. She had realised immediately that here was one of her own sort, someone as calculating as she was herself, someone to whom she could be useful and who would prove inconceivably useful to her in return.

Jarvis Lecker was a self-made man, clever and shrewd, with the faculty of being in the right spot at the right time. He had started by working in a bicycle fitting shop in Coventry; his grandfather had been a German Jew; his father a somewhat ne'er-do-well engineer.

When Jarvis Lecker was thirty-five he owned a motor company which was experimenting with a new type of engine. Fifteen years later this engine proved itself to be excellent in the air, and just before the war started Jarvis Lecker had gone into the aeroplane business in a big way.

He was middle-aged and, although very rich had not yet begun to make for himself a place in the social world. But like many men of his type, he was socially ambitious.

Money, once he had got it, seemed unimportant in that it could only buy him things from shops and none of the things which he now felt were important.

He wanted a position; he wanted power not only in finan-cial circles but in that section of the community which has always counted in England, the section labelled 'Society'.

Char, with her usual uncanny instinct, sensed Jarvis Lecker's need long before he brought himself to tell her about it. She had managed with some cleverness to make an impression upon him.

He was a fool where women were concerned, and Char, with her abrupt manner, her bitter tongue and her disdain of all her fellow passengers, both amused and intrigued him.

To a certain extent he was impressed, too, that Char had travelled, had seen a great many things in the world for which he had never had time.

When she talked to him he appreciated the shrewd sharpness of her brain which found some parallel to his own. He, too, had lived by his wits as he soon realised Char lived by hers.

It was Char who told him frankly what he wanted.

'A wife,' she said. 'Someone who will spend your money well and introduce you to the right people.'

'She's got to be the right sort of woman, then,' Jarvis Lecker growled, and Char had agreed with him. The chance conversation in the bar had given her an idea.

She had been very anxious not to lose Jarvis Lecker, and she knew that, sooner or later, it was inevitable he would see through her bluff of making herself his social cicerone. She was desperately anxious to make him think she was essential in his life.

She knew there were a lot of pickings round Jarvis Lecker, but she knew, too, that he was ruthless. The moment he found she was of no further use to him he would throw her out as he would discard an inefficient employee.

The thought of Mona was like a glowing torch in the darkness of fear and desperation. There was, of course, Mona herself to be considered, but Char knew why she had come home, or at least she had a very good idea.

That night in Paris when she had seen her across the crowded restaurant and realised that she had not wanted to be seen, had told Char all she wanted to know. That, then, was the man.

She had always known that there must be a man hidden away somewhere. Char's deductions about people worked on simple lines and usually her conclusions proved the right ones.

She had gone to endless trouble in Cairo to discover what was the mystery concerning Mona and had drawn a blank, the seclusion of the little villa on the banks of the Nile had eluded her even as it had eluded other curious people.

She had bribed the servants in Mona's hotel to no avail —they could tell her nothing, and when Mona had disappeared from the boat at Luxor, Char knew as little about her personal affairs as she had known when she first came into her life. It was one of her few failures.

But those fleeting seconds in a Paris restaurant had given her the clue she sought. She had found out who Lionel was. That wasn't difficult; the head waiter knew all the distinguished people who visited his restaurant. Lionel's career was in books of reference for all to read—Paris, Egypt, Vienna. Char had noted the dates.

There was no need to tell her then why Mona had disappeared from Egypt just about the same time as Lionel's appointment to the Embassy at Vienna was listed.

Char made inquiries in London after she had learned of Mona's return. She found out that Lionel had died in America. That was what she wanted to know. Mona was at a loose end, living in the country, perhaps bored, maybe anxious to see her old friends.

Char had almost hoped that she might have been welcome, but the look of fear on Mona's face when she mentioned Lionel had told her quite plainly why she had been invited. Mona was afraid.

That, Char thought now, was all to the good. She was used to dealing with people who were frightened of her, used to getting her own way when she could use fear as a weapon, and yet in some ways she was still bewildered. Of what was Mona afraid?

The man in question was dead, what harm could she, Char, do him now? When she met Mrs Vale she understood. Mona's devotion to her mother was obvious, her mother's adoration of Mona was palpable.

Within three minutes of entering the Priory, Char knew that she held a trump card in her hand.

She was so excited that it was with difficulty she restrained herself from rushing to the telephone and telling Jarvis Lecker to come over at once. She had already described Mona to him in glowing terms.

It was satisfactory to find that she had not exaggerated. The house, a description of which she had conjured up out of her imagination, was just as old and solid with tradition, respectability and heredity as she had made it out to be.

This, indeed, was the background for which Jarvis Lecker was looking. And to get a wife who was not only 'county' but also beautiful, well-known, and titled, was almost more than even the most grasping millionaire could expect from fortune.

'We are all in clover!' Char told herself gleefully, for she thought astutely that the Priory could do with money being spent on it and that Mona would not be averse to spending it.

When she had changed her shoes and combed her hair, she went downstairs. Mona was waiting for her in the sitting-room.

'Mother's getting the tea,' she said. 'I hope you found everything you wanted upstairs?'

'Everything, thank you,' Char replied. 'It is nice to see you again, Mona. You haven't altered.'

'A few added years. I expect if you look for them you will find my grey hairs beginning to sprout.'

She spoke lightly but she was ill at ease, moving restlessly as she talked, not looking directly at Char but into the fire. Finally, with an effort, she brought out the words as if they would choke her.

'Char, I'd be grateful if you'd not talk about my cousin Lionel in front of mother. She feels his death and there is no need to refer to it.'

Char chuckled to herself. Outwardly she said suavely :

'No, of course I won't, and anyway I always think condolences are unnecessary and rather grim. I only mentioned it to you knowing how upset you would be.'

Mona accepted this in silence, then she jumped to her feet.

'I can hear Mother with the tea-tray,' she said. She moved forward to open the door of the room.

It was after tea that Char began talking about Jarvis Lecker.

'You don't mind if I ask him over?' she asked Mrs Vale. 'He's a brilliant man and in charge of this factory the other side of Bedford. He's very anxious to come out and meet you. Now when would it suit you for him to come?'

'What about lunch tomorrow?' Mrs Vale suggested. 'If you are quite certain he won't mind the very simple way we live.'

'That will be delightful,' Char said. 'You'll like him, Mona, he's clever.' She got to her feet. 'You don't mind if I telephone him now?—I might catch him before he leaves the office.'

'Yes, of course, please do,' Mrs Vale replied, and Mona showed Char where the telephone was in the little study off the hall.

She came back into the room and said to her mother in a low voice :

'Why did you ask him to lunch? Tea would have done quite as well and we'd have got rid of him quicker.'

'But, darling, he sounds a very interesting man. It would be nice for you to meet someone new and amusing. It's been rather dull for you here this past month.'

'It hasn't,' Mona protested. 'I've loved it. I don't want new people, strange people, coming here.'

'Now you mustn't let yourself get into a groove,' Mrs Vale said, reaching over and patting her daughter's hand.

'She's doing it for me,' Mona thought, and found it difficult to put her dislike and distrust into words. She was uneasily aware that Char was up to something but wasn't quite certain what. Yet what could she say?

It was impossible to argue with Char once she had determined to get her own way; one could only accept it and let her go ahead, and yet Mona had a curious reluctance to let Char insinuate her friends into the house.

It was bad enough to wonder how much she knew, how

dangerous she was—but to have her friends forced upon them, to allow her to hoodwink her mother with grandiloquent phrases about cleverness and brains was too much!

Mona had the feeling that she was being rapidly caught into a web, which was spinning round her so finely that it was quite impossible to see it or feel it, but which, when it was complete, would be strong enough to imprison, if not to destroy, her.

She was afraid and her fear lay chiefly in the fact that there was nothing tangible of which to be afraid.

Char came back. She was looking pleased; Mona knew that expression well, it was the one she wore when she had made money on a lucky coup.

'He's delighted,' she said purringly. 'He'll be over tomorrow at one o'clock.'

'He can't be working very hard,' Mona remarked, feeling inwardly resentful, 'or he wouldn't be able to get away for luncheon.'

'This is an exceptional occasion,' Char replied. 'You'll like him—I know you will.'

Mona found herself without words, but something within her shivered, and she turned away from what she feared to see in Char's glittering, triumphant eyes.

13

There was the sound of laughter and of many voices as Bates threw open the door and announced :

'Lady Carsdale, Mrs Strathwyn, and Mr Lecker.'

The great sitting-room at the Park was a festive sight;

festooned with streamers, holly and mistletoe, and filled with a company of laughing, dancing and chattering people.

The land girls out of uniform were gay in brightly coloured dancing-frocks, their hair waved and set for the occasion, their feet—usually hidden in thick, cumbersome boots—now wearing the neatest and trimmest of dancing sandals.

Michael was doing his party on a grand scale, Mona thought, as she noted through the open door at the end of the room a cocktail bar and a buffet.

She and her small party were late, as they had been forced to wait for Jarvis Lecker, and all Little Cobble seemed to have arrived before them.

There was Dorothy Howlett, looking flushed and exhilarated by the unexpected excitement of the occasion, dancing with a burly major in the Pioneers. There was Lynn Archer, surrounded, as might have been expected, by young officers from her husband's aerodrome, and standing alone, scrutinising the throng as if in search of some misdemeanour, was Mrs Gunther.

Michael came limping across the room.

'I thought you had forsaken me,' he said reproachfully. 'You promised to be here early.'

'I'm sorry, but it couldn't be helped,' Mona replied. 'You know Char, I think, and Mr Jarvis Lecker—Major Merrill.'

The two men shook hands and Mona was aware of the contrast between them. In other surroundings Jarvis Lecker might have appeared fairly good looking, but beside Michael any attractions he might have claimed were lost.

He was too short and there was something slightly coarse about his thick neck and heavily set body. Whatever Michael's faults, Mona realised that even his worst enemy could not call him undistinguished, and, despite a tentative effort at loyalty she felt slightly ashamed of her companions.

She caught Mrs Windlesham's eye across the room and moved towards her. Michael's aunt held out both hands in welcome.

'You are quite a stranger, dear child,' she exclaimed. 'Why have you deserted us like this?'

'I don't seem to have had a moment to myself,' Mona explained; but Mrs Windlesham was not listening.

'Is that the Mrs Strathwyn of whom I have heard so much?' she asked, peering at Char. 'Introduce her to me.'

'A new addition to your collection?' Mona asked with a mischievous smile. Mrs Windlesham glanced up at her, but did not smile in response.

'Perhaps—go and fetch her, my dear.'

Mona did as she was told, and instantly Jarvis Lecker was at her side again. He had an irritating way of walking so close that his arm touched hers. He had, too, an almost possessive attitude towards her whenever they met other people.

She realised that it was not entirely personal but a characteristic gesture of awkwardness. Because he was not used to the company of women he over-emphasised his attentions to them.

For the last week, Jarvis Lecker had been continually at the Priory. He had come to lunch and had stayed to tea; the following day he had invited himself to dinner, and every day after that he had made some excuse or another to call.

He took Mona and Char for drives in his car, he escorted them into Bedford for shopping. He also loaded the household with presents.

He brought them a turkey—a luxury which was almost unprocurable in the neighbourhood; he produced a ham which he said had been sent from Ireland, caviare from Fortnum and Mason, and several cases of wine.

There were flowers, too, bunches of orchids, carnations and violets which must have cost exorbitant sums. Mona and Mrs Vale were embarrassed by such ostentatious generosity, but Char was delighted. She made no secret of her admiration for Jarvis and grew annoyed with Mona when she would not enthuse about him.

'Millionaires don't grow on gooseberry bushes—not in these days, at any rate.'

'But I don't want them to,' Mona retorted.

'Don't be absurd,' Char said. 'Everyone likes to have a rich man about the house and you could do with one, too. Don't let's pretend between ourselves. It can't be much fun for your mother to manage this big house on her tiny income.'

Mona shrugged her shoulders. She resented fiercely that Char should discuss her mother's private affairs, yet she hesitated to say so.

But Jarvis Lecker did not need Char to champion him, he was quite prepared to speak for himself.

He had the dominating assurance of a self-made man; he was used to riding roughshod over people's feelings, to overwhelming them with his personality, to getting what he wanted by sheer force of determination.

Mona would have been blind indeed if she had not realised very quickly indeed exactly what Jarvis Lecker wanted now, and she felt, almost hysterically, that she could not cope with the situation.

Char had been at the Priory a week and showed no signs of terminating her visit. Mona had been trying to summon up the courage to ask her point-blank when she thought of leaving.

She had decided she would do so tonight or tomorrow morning, however difficult it might be to approach the subject.

Perhaps after Michael's party would be a good time, she thought, for during the week everyone they met had talked of little else and it would have seemed unreasonable to have suggested Char's leaving before it took place.

Having introduced Char to Mrs Windlesham, Mona turned away from Jarvis Lecker who was trying to monopolise her attention and, finding Stanley Gunther at her side, plunged into a conversation with him.

'Isn't this fun,' she asked. 'Aren't you proud of your idea,

Mr Gunther? I had no idea that we might expect anything so gay in Little Cobble.'

'Nor had I,' the Vicar replied smilingly. 'The Major's been most extraordinarily kind about it. I never meant to ask him for anything on such a grand scale.'

'It's very good for him,' Mona said. 'This place is far too large for a bachelor.'

She was talking without really thinking of what she said, then Jarvis Lecker's voice broke in on the conversation.

'So our host's a bachelor? Well, it doesn't look as if he will be for long. That's a very attractive young creature he's talking to now.'

Mona glanced across the room and saw Stella Fairlace gazing up at Michael. She was looking particularly attractive tonight in a simple black dress, poor in quality and cut, but which showed up the colour of her hair and the creamy quality of her skin.

'She is pretty,' Mona admitted, and realised what a handsome couple Stella and Michael made.

They might have been the models for 'The Perfect English Man and Woman, A.D. 1942'. Strong and healthy, lovers of the country, such people would maintain a high standard of civilisation, would serve their country to the last drop of blood, and give to a world torn and damaged by war a new generation capable of reconstructing a finer and better type of democracy.

Yes, doubtless Jarvis Lecker was right, Mona thought. Michael would marry Stella Fairlace, or someone like her, and absorbed in farming would find a steady, uneventful happiness.

Suddenly she felt alien to the whole party. Here were a collection of simple people enjoying an evening's entertainment which for them was the height of gaiety and amusement. How could she and the people she had brought with her be anything but a foreign element in their midst?

She looked at Char and thought of the sort of parties at which she had seen her in Cairo; parties in some low night-club, where the atmosphere was thick with smoke and more than half the guests would have had too much to drink.

Parties when large sums of money would change hands —when perhaps the dawn would bring misery and maybe even thoughts of suicide to some who had lost, not only more than they could afford but everything they possessed in the world.

Yes, that was Char's milieu—surrounded by people to whom 'adultery, fornication, and all other deadly sins' were not merely words but familiar acquaintances to be treated casually and indifferently.

And Jarvis Lecker. Mona knew his type so well; the businessman who had got himself to the top by methods not too clean or too open to close inspection, and having got to the top wanted to buy the best.

Nothing would convince him, she knew, that some things could not be bought, that there were things beyond price, beyond the purchase of any man, be he as rich as Croesus.

To the Jarvis Leckers of this world everything had its cash value—even herself.

With an effort, she dragged her thoughts back to what was going on around her. She realised that Stanley Gunther was staring at her and thought he must have asked a question to which he had received no answer.

'I am sorry,' she said. 'What were you saying to me?'

'It was Mr Lecker who asked you if you'd care to dance,' the Vicar replied, 'but you were far away from us in the land of dreams.'

'Actually I was thinking about you all.'

The Vicar smiled.

'Nice thoughts, I hope.'

'But naturally.'

She saw Mrs Windlesham beckoning to her and crossed to her side.

'Mrs Strathwyn has never seen the Long Gallery, Mona,' Mrs Windlesham said. 'I must get Michael to take her round.'

'May I be allowed to be your escort?' the Vicar asked Char. 'I have studied the pictures here for many years and flatter myself I know them almost as well as their owner.'

'Yes, that's a good idea, Vicar,' Mrs Windlesham said. 'Take Mrs Strathwyn along and don't forget that the large Van Dyck has been moved to the library.'

'I won't,' Stanley Gunther promised and they moved away.

'Well?' Mona asked.

Mrs Windlesham knew what she meant.

'How long is she staying, my dear?'

'I haven't any idea.'

'I shouldn't keep her too long,' Mrs Windlesham said.

Mona understood the significance of her words. Michael's aunt was as shrewd at summing up a person as was Char Strathwyn herself. She was just going to say something more when she realised that once again Jarvis Lecker was at her elbow.

'Will you show me the pictures? I'd like to see them.'

'In a moment,' Mona replied shortly. 'I must speak to Lynn Archer first.'

'Here is my guardian angel,' Lynn said, introducing Mona to two of the officers she hadn't met before. 'She's saved the Archer family from starvation.'

'How did she do that?' a young pilot-officer asked.

'She convinced me that a novelist can be a reporter. Before Mona talked to me my plots were personal experiences —now I watch other people commit the crimes!'

'Sounds dull!' a wing-commander commiserated.

'It is,' Lynn answered dolefully. 'I shall get fat and uninteresting, I'm afraid! But, Mona, your friend, Mrs Strathwyn, thrilled me. She told me some quite extraordinary stories about people she had met, and I'm mixing them all up into a lurid cocktail and making a sensational romance out of them.'

'Char will want a commission on the book when it's published,' Jarvis Lecker interposed.

'You're much more likely to be had up for libel,' Mona suggested.

'If all Mrs Strathwyn told me is true,' Lynn retorted, 'no one would dare to identify themselves with any of the characters—they'd be much too ashamed.'

Lynn, Mona thought drily, was about the only person in the neighbourhood who was pleased to see Char Strathwyn or who had any use for her. She was well aware how much her mother disliked their guest and Michael did not trouble to hide his feelings.

After meeting her on two or three occasions, he had been so openly hostile that it was wiser to refuse other invitations to the Park, except for this particular party.

One amusing feature was that Mavis Gunther and Char had hated one another on sight. They had eyed each other like two bantam fighting-cocks and then, as if each realised the invincibility of the other, had subsided into a bristling and menacing silence.

It was strange how out-of-place Char could seem even at a party like this. She was not smart, she was by no means spectacular, and yet she looked like a person from another world among these fresh young girls and the incontrovertible respectability of their elders.

'What about those pictures?' she heard Jarvis Lecker say again, and unwillingly she rose to her feet.

'I'm going to take Mr Lecker to see the pictures in the Long Gallery,' she told Lynn. 'Why don't you come?'

'Too lazy,' Lynn smiled back at her.

'She means she prefers looking at us,' one of the Air Force officers teased, and they all laughed.

Mona moved away with Jarvis Lecker. She felt annoyed at his insistence, knowing quite well that his interest in the pictures was inspired by a desire to get her away from her friends.

Like other clever men, he hated not being the centre of interest; he wanted to talk—to have the undivided attention of his audience and he had no chance of showing off among this gathering of happy, irresponsible young people.

'If only he would get bored and go,' Mona thought savagely, but she knew there was no likelihood of this while she remained.

As they turned into the Long Gallery, they met Char and the Vicar coming out.

'Have you finished your tour already?' Mona asked in dismay. 'You'll have to come round again, Vicar; I know so little about the pictures and you can explain them much better to Mr Lecker than I can.'

Char, however, would not allow this.

'The Vicar's going to get me a drink first,' she said. 'I feel quite thirsty after imbibing so much information. You two go on and we'll join you later.'

Mona knew just what that meant, and she led the way in silence towards the finest portraits in the Merrill collection, which were kept at the end of the Gallery. Here they were alone and the sounds of merrymaking came only faintly to their ears.

'Well, tell me about them,' Jarvis Lecker said as they stood before generations of Merrills painted by famous artists, but he looked at her.

'I'm not a very good guide,' Mona admitted nervously. 'You ought to have got Michael to tell you about them himself, or the Vicar.'

'I'd much rather listen to you,' Jarvis Lecker replied.

As he spoke he laid his hands on her bare arm. Swiftly Mona moved away from him.

'Don't be unkind to me,' he said.

'I'm not,' Mona replied, 'but I dislike being touched.' She spoke coldly.

Jarvis Lecker was quite unaffected by her tone.

'I imagine it depends on who touches you.'

'Perhaps you're right.'

'You're a funny girl. Char warned me you might be difficult, and I'm beginning to think she spoke the truth.'

'So Char warned you. What did she say?'

Mona sat down on one of the wide window-seats covered with tapestry cushions.

'She's told me not "to rush my fences",' Jarvis Lecker replied. 'She said you'd lost someone of whom you were very fond.'

'She told you that, did she.' Mona spoke very quietly.

'Yes. And I replied that hearts could be mended.' Jarvis Lecker sat down beside Mona and put a heavy hand on her knee. 'What about letting me mend yours?'

Mona looked at him with distaste.

'No one could do that,' she said distinctly, 'no one in the world.'

She jumped to her feet before he could say another word and moved across the Gallery.

'Come and see the miniatures,' she said over her shoulder. 'They are here in the Tower.'

It was only when she had switched on the light in the small octagonal room which held only the glass-covered cases of valuable miniatures that she realised she had made a mistake, for, as Jarvis Lecker entered the room behind her, he bore on his face the inscrutable smile of the conquering male. He shut the door.

'Listen, my dear,' he said softly as he came across to her. 'You've been elusive long enough. I'm a downright sort of chap; I'm used to coming straight to the point when I want a thing in business and I don't see why I should use different methods because I am in love. I want you—you know that, don't you?'

He put out his hands and would have grasped her shoulders but Mona backed away from him.

'I'm sorry,' she answered quietly, 'but you're making a mistake about me. Whatever Char's told you, whatever encouragement she's given you—is wrong.'

'I'm not relying on Char or anyone else,' Jarvis Lecker said roughly. 'I don't need a go-between to get me what I want. Now, you listen to me, Mona my dear.'

She had backed until she was against one of the cases and could go no further. He had followed her until his body was almost touching hers, and Mona had a feeling of being overpowered, of being beaten down, relentlessly pursued.

The man was dynamic; there was no denying that, and she felt small, weary, and ineffectively armed to do battle with him.

'Please, Jarvis,' she pleaded; but she got no further, for at that moment, the door was opened and two people stood in the doorway.

There was no disguising the fact that Mona and Jarvis Lecker were in the middle of an intimate conversation, and although Jarvis moved quickly, if resentfully, to one side, Mona had time to see the astonishment on Stella Fairlace's face and know that Michael was not only surprised but angry.

Nobody said anything until Mona, in an attempt to carry off the difficult situation, broke the silence nervously.

'I was just showing Mr Lecker the miniatures.'

'I hope he was interested,' Michael replied, and his voice was icy.

Jarvis Lecker's eyes narrowed. He looked across the tiny room at his host, and the atmosphere was tense with antagonistic vibrations which passed between the two men.

'You've got quite a nice little collection of antiques here, Merrill,' Jarvis Lecker said. 'Any time you want to dispose of the better ones let me know.'

He could have said nothing more calculated to infuriate Michael, who looked him up and down with an arrogance which would have withered any man less self-possessed and sure of himself.

'The majority of my possessions are heirlooms, the rest are not for sale.'

'One never knows in these hard times,' Lecker replied. 'Well, Mona, what about a dance?'

'I think I ought to find Char,' Mona prevaricated. 'After all, she doesn't know many people here.'

'You will find her in the dining-room,' Michael said.

He held open the door with a gesture which not even Jarvis Lecker could fail to interpret.

Mona walked down the Long Gallery in silence but her cheeks were flaming. What must Michael think? she wondered, and felt humiliated and ashamed that he should have come in at just that moment.

She minded that he should think she was allowing this unprepossessing and common man to make love to her. For that, she knew, was the only interpretation he was likely to put on the scene he had interrupted.

In all fairness to Michael, Mona admitted that she would have suspected the same thing herself had the circumstances been reversed. As it was, she wondered why Michael was taking Stella Fairlace to that particular room.

The Tower was a joke. When they were young and there were parties at the Park, if a couple were missing someone was always sent to look for them in the Tower. She had forgotten this when, to avoid Jarvis Lecker's embarrassing conversation, she had taken him there from the Long Gallery.

Never had she regretted an action more. She realised with a kind of horror that he was quite unperturbed by what had taken place, in fact, she sensed that he was rather pleased with himself.

He thought that Michael was jealous of him and it gave him a feeling of superiority. As he said, he always got what he wanted, and he was quite prepared to fight for it—if need be to fight Michael.

Suddenly Mona felt she could bear no more. The net which was being wound round her was tightening and life was becoming too complicated. She might have known it would be like this; Char's presence was always disruptive.

Here, through her instigations, friends of a lifetime were being antagonised, misunderstandings were rising.

'She must go,' Mona thought, 'she must!'

The party was still in full swing. Char, a whisk-and-soda in her hand, had joined Lynn's party and was making some of the young officers laugh, but in rather a shamefaced way, as if what she said was slightly embarrassing.

Mona guessed that she was either telling dirty stories or making unkind and cruel remarks about other people in the room.

Char could be amusing, there was no doubt about that, but her kind of wit was not usually heard in Little Cobble, and certainly would never be appreciated.

It was too early to go home, but Mona moved across the floor to where Mrs Windlesham was sitting and sat down firmly beside her.

'Come and dance,' Jarvis Lecker begged, but she shook her head.

'You can get me a drink if you like,' she suggested, and when he had gone turned to Michael's aunt. 'I want to stay here.'

'Then you shall,' Mrs Windlesham replied. 'I'm enjoying myself. I like seeing young people have a good time. It's a sign of old age when one can get one's pleasure second-hand, but I find it quite consoling.'

Jarvis Lecker came back with Mona's drink.

'Can I get you anything?' he asked Mrs Windlesham.

She shook her head.

'Nothing, thank you,' she answered, 'but now, Mr Lecker, you must go and dance with some of these young girls. They'll be pleased to have you for a partner. Mona and I are going to sit here like a couple of dowagers and criticise those who are dancing.'

'I'd rather stay and listen to your criticisms.'

'Run along,' Mrs Windlesham insisted. 'You must do your duty.'

Surprisingly, he obeyed her and Mona gave an audible sigh of relief. Mrs Windlesham chuckled.

'You aren't so sophisticated as I thought you were, my dear. If you haven't learnt to manage that type of man by this time you ought to have.'

Mona smiled wanly.

'There are such a lot of things I've got to learn. I've come to the conclusion I don't know half as much as I thought I did.'

'We all come to that conclusion some time in our lives,' Mrs Windlesham replied, 'but don't worry—it's a sign of grace. It's often a sign, too, that one's reached the bottom of the hill and now one must start to climb again.'

Mona understood the meaning of the parable.

'I suppose I'm being stupid.'

'On the contrary,' Mrs Windlesham remarked, 'you are being human, and I like you that way. So would Michael, if you allowed him to see you like that.'

'Like what?'

'Helpless,' Mrs Windlesham replied, and there was a twinkle in her eye.

'I wouldn't give him the satisfaction,' Mona retorted, and she heard Mrs Windlesham sigh.

'The young are so knobbly.'

'Now what do you mean by that?'

'Well, aren't you?' Michael's aunt inquired.

'Perhaps,' Mona answered. 'But you don't know how difficult things are.'

'Things always seem to be far worse when we insist on fighting our own battles without any assistance. What you need, my dear, are a few reinforcements.'

'Not the ones you suggest,' Mona said, and suddenly she felt that she could bear it no longer.

She couldn't stay here and wait for Michael to come back from the Long Gallery—wait to see his look of disapproval, a look, perhaps, also of contempt and disgust. She got to her feet.

'I feel ill,' she said quickly, 'but I don't want to spoil the party. Could you explain to the others that I've gone home? I'll walk; it won't do me any harm, in fact, it may clear my head.'

Mrs Windlesham accepted her explanation and made no protest. She was unique in that she never tried to interfere with another person's actions.

'I'll tell Mrs Strathwyn and Mr Lecker later in the evening,' she promised.

Mona knew that it would give her pleasure to keep them guessing as to what had happened to her. Swiftly she bent down and kissed the older woman's cheek.

'You're a darling !' she whispered.

'And you aren't half as lost as you think you are,' Mrs Windlesham replied, and Mona, as she slipped unnoticed from the room, wondered what she meant.

14

The moon had risen and shone with almost unearthly beauty over the countryside.

There was a faint mist over the lake and it reminded Mona of the lakes of Austria, whose soft white mists had often seemed to her to take the forms of wraiths or nymphs in the light of the rising moon.

She pulled her fur coat closely round her and started to walk down the drive. She and Char had come to the Park in Jarvis Lecker's car, which was now parked with dozens of others in the wide sweep before the front door.

It was freezing hard and bitterly cold, and yet Mona welcomed the icy fingers of the wind as they touched her face and lifted her hair from her forehead.

There was something invigorating, bracing, and almost cruel in the severity of the frosty air, yet she felt that it cleansed her a little from her sense of humiliation.

Once, it seemed to Mona she had been proud—proud of herself, of the life she lived, of what she thought and did; but that had been a very long time ago, so long that it was hard now to recollect the feeling.

Instead, during these last years, she had known always this sense of being ashamed, of holding her head high in defiance and not through any inner conviction of nobility.

She had paid the price of a fleeting and evanescent happiness with the loss of her self-respect.

'Why have I been such a fool?' Mona asked the night, but the cold barren beauty of it had no answer for her.

She skirted the lake and could look back now at the house she had left. Its dignity had a touch of arrogance, which accorded well with that of its owner.

What must he think of her? Again the question came to her mind and she was afraid to formulate the answer.

All through her life, she reflected, she had sought Michael's good opinion and it had escaped her.

Perhaps because she had been born under the shadow of the Merrill tradition, she had always instinctively looked up to him.

The Merrills had counted for something in Little Cobble and for her personally; her mother had fostered the illusion that Michael was of importance.

As she had grown older she had laughed, she had teased him, and even jeered at him; this, had he but understood, was a compliment.

Mona's good nature never permitted her to be unkind to anyone she thought vulnerable; only at someone who was as impregnable as Michael appeared would she jeer, conscious of her own inferiority.

She felt as if it were impossible for her even to try to be friends with Michael—she had sunk too low in her estimation now even to recapture even an illusion of glamour and attraction.

For that had been her only advantage—that the sordid realities of her life had been covered by a thin veneer of glamour. It had glittered for those who did not understand that tinsel can be dazzling.

To Lynn Archer, to Dorothy, to so many people in Little Cobble, Mona appeared the personification of all that was gay, irresponsible, and lovely. Their admiration had soothed her into a false sense of security.

Even her mother enjoyed her stories of excitement, endless amusement, and having what was called 'a good time' in all the most spectacular and expensive playgrounds of the world.

It was only she herself who knew how pretentious and garish was the truth.

But now, to Michael, if not all the others, Char and Jarvis Lecker had burst the gaudy bubble in which she had concealed herself.

If Michael did not know the whole truth he could guess at a good deal of it. Mona was sure of that; she had seen it in the expression on his face as he came into the Tower Room; she had known it as she had met his eyes—cold, inquiring, disdainful.

'I'm a fraud,' Mona thought wearily, 'and my deception has been discovered.'

She heard a car coming behind her and drew to the side of the drive, standing still to let it pass, but as it approached her it slowed down and then stopped. The door nearest her was opened.

'Get in,' a voice said, and she knew who spoke.

'I'm all right,' she replied. 'I'd rather walk.'

'Get in.'

It was Michael's most authoritative tone and, without further argument, Mona obeyed. She stepped into the car and he leant across her to pull the door to and to tuck a warm fur rug round her legs.

She said nothing, accepting his attentions thankfully, for she suddenly realised that her feet and ankles were freezing. The wind, too, had blown her hair into a halo of untidy curls. Mona opened her bag and pulled out a looking-glass.

'I must look a freak,' she said, trying to speak naturally.

Michael said nothing and made no effort to drive on. After a moment he bent forward and switched off the engine of the car. Mona stared at him.

'Why are we stopping?' she asked. 'Aren't you taking me home?'

'If that's where you want to go?'

'Of course. That's why I left.'

'Any reason?'

'I've got a headache, and I feel tired and ill. Neither of which is particularly an asset in a party.'

Her head was aching—and although perhaps the pain she suffered was more mental than physical, it had given her a sense of utter weariness and exhaustion.

'I'm sorry.' Michael spoke after a pause as if he had been pondering on her words.

'It's nothing,' Mona said, 'but somehow I wanted to get home and, being selfish, I thought only of myself.'

'All right, I'll take you home then, if that's what you want.'

Michael started up the car. Through the windscreen Mona looked across the lake and saw the house floating, as it were, in a bowl of silvery water.

Breathtakingly beautiful, it still seemed to her that its high walls and roofs looked down haughtily on the weakness of human nature.

They drove on in silence. After a while Mona closed her eyes, to open them as Michael drew up at the door of the Priory.

'Are we there?' she asked unnecessarily.

Michael turned to look at her.

'You're all right?' he questioned.

'I'm not likely to die during the night, if that's what you mean,' Mona replied, trying to speak lightly.

There was a sudden tension between them—a tension of unspoken words, of accusations and demands. Suddenly Mona capitulated.

'I'm sorry, Michael,' she said, and her voice was soft and yielding, 'to have taken you away from your party.'

Michael stretched out his arm, and to her surprise put it round her shoulders.

'They'll get along quite well without me. It's you I'm worried about.'

'You shouldn't worry about me—I'm not worth it.'

Her tone was bitter and Michael's arm tightened around her shoulders.

'You're tired,' he said sympathetically.

Mona let her head rest for a moment against his shoulder.

'Yes, I'm tired, Michael, but it isn't the sort of tiredness that can be cured by sleep. It's an utter weariness of body and soul.'

'That's unlike you.'

'Is it?' she asked. 'Or is it unlike the idea that most people have of me? I feel as if for years now I have been acting a part and suddenly I am too tired to go on with it—and yet without the mask I am afraid of what I will find.'

He made no answer, and they sat for some minutes in silence. There was something comforting in being able to lay her head against him and feel the strength of his arm supporting her.

'How I wish I could remain like this,' she told herself, 'to drift into a kind of coma and not have to cope any longer with my difficulties and troubles. I suppose the point is that I have always had a man to look after me.

'There was always Lionel in the background to whom I could turn if I were desperate, but now there's no one.'

She felt like crying so she galvanised herself into action.

'I mustn't keep you here all night,' she said quickly. 'Good night, Michael, and thank you. I'm sorry I've been a nuisance.'

'You haven't,' he replied, but the words were lost as she slammed the car door.

'Don't get out,' she called, and was gone before, with his bad leg, he could stumble from the driving seat. He saw the door of the Priory close, and then turned the car for home.

Inside the house she switched on the lights quietly. Mrs Vale was not only a light sleeper but she was also suffering from a heavy cold.

Michael had been particularly anxious for her to come to his party, but instead she had gone to bed after tea, knowing that to go out in her condition would be no pleasure for herself or anyone else.

Mona crept upstairs. She did not want her mother to

wake because she had no reasonable explanation for having come home alone, for leaving Char at the party.

The fire was burning in her room, piled up by the attentive Nanny before she went to bed. Mona undressed and wrapped herself in her dressing-gown. She was crouching on the hearthrug, staring at the flames, when the door opened.

She looked up, expecting to see her mother, but it was Char who came in.

'I didn't hear the car,' Mona ejaculated.

She had meant to lock her door before she went to bed so that there could be no chance of Char coming to her room when she returned.

'Jarvis dropped me at the end of the drive,' Char replied drily. 'He's in a bad temper.'

'I'm sorry.' Mona felt the words were inadequate even as she said them.

'So you should be.'

Char moved across the room, seated herself in a chair by the fireplace and fitted a fresh cigarette into her long black holder. Mona watched her in silence, then, throwing the smoked-out stub into the fire, Char said:

'He's coming over tomorrow for lunch.'

Mona took a deep breath.

'That won't be convenient.'

Without removing the cigarette-holder from her mouth Char asked: 'Do you mean that?'

'I do.'

'Why?' Char shot the question at her as if it were a bullet from a revolver.

Mona looked into the fire.

'I don't care for Mr Lecker—in fact I see no reason to continue the acquaintance.'

'You're a fool!'

'Maybe, but that's my business, isn't it?'

'On the contrary,' Char said, 'it concerns us all.'

Her tone was angry and Mona decided that she must be firm, once and for all.

'I'm sorry, Char, if you are disappointed, but after all, we can't all like the same people. I dare say there are lots of women in London who would be only too pleased to play around with Jarvis Lecker, and I'm sure he would find them far more amusing than I am at the moment. When were you thinking of going back there?'

It was an effort to say the words, but Mona had got them out. Char gave her an inscrutable look which she did not understand and, getting up, walked restlessly about the room, her cigarette-ash falling on the carpet as she moved.

She looked like some kind of animal—gaunt, cadaverous, but with no grandeur or feline grace. It was rather as if she were some ungainly bird—a vulture, Mona decided, and remembered how once she had seen those monstrous creatures wheeling above a carcass in the desert.

Suddenly Char came back to the chair and sat down abruptly.

'Shall we put our cards on the table?' she asked, and her voice was hoarse and harsh.

'I have no cards to show, but let me see yours, Char.'

'This isn't really a game,' Char replied. 'It's damnably serious to me.'

There was a ring of sincerity in her voice.

'Why?' Mona asked. 'Explain—I don't understand.'

'Then you're more dense than you used to be. Jarvis Lecker's a millionaire. When I met him I was on to a good thing. I soon knew that he wanted a wife—the right sort of wife, one who'd give him the background and position that he needs. When I introduced him to you I had hopes that things might work out smoothly.

'I knew that Jarvis would admire you—a few men have been able to help themselves doing that where you were concerned; but now he's in love with you—madly and crazily in love with you.

'If you turn him down there's no hope of my finding him anyone else.'

'I'm sorry, Char,' Mona said with a smile, 'but really you don't seem to have consulted me in all this.'

'Don't be such a little fool,' Char said savagely. 'You don't want to spend the rest of your life here in this dump! Oh, I know it's the old family homestead and all that sort of thing, but, my dear girl, you'll be bored stiff in a few months if you're not already. Look at the life you've led and look at what you're getting now!'

Mona didn't answer and Char went on:

'You've only got to think of what Jarvis can do for you. He's rich—perhaps one of the richest men in the country— and he will be richer still. All he wants is a little polish and you could make him very presentable.'

Mona got to her feet, stretching herself.

'I don't care how presentable he could be,' she said coldly. 'I never want to see him again.'

'Have you told him so?'

'No, but I dare say you can do that for me.'

Mona spoke rudely. She was suddenly tired of Char and of her machinations. It was one thing to watch her intriguing over other people and quite another thing to be the one intrigued over.

'It's no use, Char,' she said. 'There's nothing to argue about one way or another. I've made up my mind, and that's that. Now I suggest that you ring up Jarvis Lecker in the morning and ask him to give you dinner in London. You can then explain the whole situation to him.'

There was no misunderstanding Mona's meaning, and Char turned towards her with a snarl.

'So you are turning me out, too?'

'Hardly that, but you see that it's very difficult for me to have my friends to stay for long. Nanny's getting old and another person in the house makes a lot of extra work.'

'You can't do this to me—you can't!' Char cried.

Mona saw that she was gripping the sides of the chair with her hands.

'Now do be sensible, Char,' she begged. 'I've come home for a rest and to be with my mother. It's sweet of you to worry about me at all, but, honestly, I don't want either young men or husbands at the moment. I just want to be left alone to vegetate here in my own home.'

Char suddenly jumped up and Mona saw that her eyes were full of tears.

'I've had such a hell of a time,' she said, 'and now, just as things looked like being lucky again, you've gone and smashed them all up! I believed in you, Mona—I believed that you'd bring me good fortune.'

'I've always told you that idea was a fallacy,' Mona replied. 'Cheer up, Char. Perhaps something really good will happen to you though not through me at the moment I'm unlucky to myself and to everyone else.

'With your looks' Char said bitterly 'you'll always be lucky. You don't know what it is to have to grasp at things, to fight for everything you want; to have to clutch and grab, deceive and lie, to get one single thing you want in this bloody life!

For you it's different—you smile and every man within miles would go and fetch you the moon if he thought you'd say "thank you" prettily when he brought it to you. But for me—what chance have I got or have I ever had with a face like this?

'I've been kicked and sworn at all my life, I've had knock after knock, rotten deal after rotten deal—and why? Because God made me a caricature. I've never been able to ride roughshod over other people like you can I've had to go down on my knees and be thankful to lick the blacking of their shoes or pick up the crumbs that were left under the table.

'You're one of the lucky ones, born with a pretty face, and a figure that drives men crazy the moment they set eyes on you. Oh, it's a fair world all right! Don't speak to me about justice—there isn't any, at least where I'm concerned.'

The older woman was shaking. Mona moved to her side and putting an arm round her shoulders forced her back into the chair.

'Don't, Char,' she said with quick compunction. 'Don't

upset yourself, it doesn't do any good. Wait, I'll go and get you a drink.'

She opened the door quietly and went downstairs to the dining-room. She found the whisky and siphon of soda, and putting one under each arm hurried upstairs again.

She had seen Char in this sort of mood before—a mood of self-pity usually brought on by too many whiskies or too many gins, and yet the only cure was another drink to drag her out of the despair in which she would wallow as long as anyone would listen to her.

But her tears were genuine enough and Mona was half exasperated, half sympathetic with her. If only she would be thorough about something, she thought wearily—thoroughly bad or thoroughly pitiable.

But one's feelings were invariably flexible where Char was concerned, one hated her and yet in that hatred was compassion and a certain measure of understanding.

'Here you are,' Mona exclaimed cheerily as she returned to the bedroom. 'Now drink this and you'll feel better.'

Char was sitting on the edge of the chair, her elbows on her knees, her chin in her hands.

'She looks like a sick monkey,' Mona told herself, and remembered how once before she had thought the same thing.

That time on the boat came flooding back to her; the misery and the degradation for which Char was to blame. Life would be insupportable if she had to put up with her any longer. She diffused an atmosphere which was both disturbing and repellent.

She gave Char the glass and said lightly :

'You know you hate the country, old girl, you'll be much better in London. You go back tomorrow and I'll try to come up at the end of the week and have luncheon with you.'

It was a sop to Cerberus and Mona hoped that she would swallow it and agree to go. Char took the glass and raised it to her lips.

'If I go,' she said, 'you will have to help me. You've lost

Jarvis Lecker for me—the least you can do is to make up for that.'

'What do you mean?'

There were no tears in Char's eyes now and her voice had a new shrewish quality. She sat back in the chair and looked up at Mona.

'You can't be so simple as not to understand my position.'

'I'm sorry,' Mona said. 'I may be very stupid but I honestly don't know what you are trying to say.'

Char laughed unpleasantly.

'The "little innocent" always was your line,' she sneered. 'I remember how evasive you were in Cairo when we tried to find out why you were there and how long you were staying. You did it very cleverly.'

Mona had a sudden sense of impending disaster. She wondered what Char was getting at—the unpleasantness of her tone was obvious.

'I still don't understand.'

'Then I'll explain,' Char retorted. 'To put it frankly it would have paid me well for you to have married Jarvis. He would have been both grateful and generous. He's all right if you handle him the right way—I know his type.

'Get him what he wants and he'll make it worth your while, but fail and if you were dying on his doorstep he wouldn't raise a finger to save you. Thanks to you, Mona I've failed.'

'It was asking rather a lot of me,' Mona murmured, half amused despite a growing sense of apprehension.

'But the point is this,' Char went on. 'I've got to live. From now on Jarvis Lecker is a wash-out. Well, he's served his purpose—I've at least lived in comfort for the last three months.'

'And you want me to help you?'

'Exactly. You aren't always so dumb as you look.'

'But, Char,' Mona said in dismay, 'I can't give you very much. Quite frankly I haven't got a penny in the bank myself. I'm living on my mother until I find some sort of work to do.'

'You're lucky to have a mother to live on.'

'I know that.'

'It's marvellous to see how fond she is of you. She adores you, doesn't she?—thinks everything you do is wonderful.'

Mona looked up swiftly. Vaguely she was beginning to understand, to see where this conversation was leading her.

'It would be a pity,' Char went on, and her voice was as smooth and treacherous as the silky movements of a snake on a branch, 'if her trust and affection should be turned into horror and . . . disgust.'

'What exactly do you mean?'

Char took her cigarette holder out of her mouth and flicked the ash into the grate.

'I need at least a thousand pounds.'

Mona sat very still.

'It's impossible,' she said after a few moments.

Char raised her eyebrows.

'Jewellery has never fetched better prices. It's lucky that your cousin Lionel had such excellent taste in emeralds and diamonds!'

Mona clenched her hands together to prevent herself from hitting Char across the face.

There was something in the sneering mouth which besmirched the memory of those moments when Lionel had given her his presents—jewels which now took on the form of payment rather than what they had been at the time—gifts precious, not for their intrinsic value, but because they crystallised moments of happiness.

There was something degrading in thinking of Lionel's gifts being sold to pay Char for her silence—something horrible in the idea of the love which she had given Lionel so willingly, so generously, being translated into terms of cash.

'Blackmail is a nasty word, Char.'

'I quite agree with you,' Char said affably. 'It's a word

I never use, although it merely boils down to being a matter of business.'

There was a long silence.

'And supposing . . .' Mona said at length, 'supposing . . . I give you this money? What guarantee have I got that you won't ask for more and yet more in the future?'

'I can always give you my word of honour,' Char said—and grinned.

The grin was that of a gargoyle—something evil and something inexpressibly frightening.

'I'm caught!' Mona thought desperately. 'Char has got me and she knows it.'

Wildly, desperately, she tried to think of a way out, an escape; but there was only a future made hideous by Char, sitting there doubled up like a sick monkey, her mouth wide in a grinning smile and in her eyes the greedy light of easy victory.

15

The door opened suddenly and both women started. Mrs Vale came into the room in her dressing-gown.

'Is anything the matter, darling?' she asked. 'I heard someone going downstairs.'

Mona answered quickly.

'No, nothing, Mummy. Char wanted a drink, that was all.'

Mrs Vale looked from her daughter to Char and back again to Mona.

'How silly of me to be anxious!'

'I'm sorry if we woke you.'

'Oh, I wasn't asleep,' her mother replied. 'My cough's been rather troublesome. Was the party amusing? I wasn't expecting you back so soon.'

'Yes, it was a splendid effort on Michael's part,' Mona replied, 'but I'll tell you about it in the morning, Mummy. Do go back to bed now. It's so cold and I don't want you laid up.'

She put her arm round her mother's shoulders and almost pushed her from the room. Char had said nothing, she had merely sat in her chair by the fireplace and stared into the fire.

Mona wondered how much her mother had overheard, their raised voices must have reached her across the passage. She took Mrs Vale back to bed and tucked her in.

'Would you like some hot milk?' she asked. 'I can easily run downstairs and get you some.'

'I don't want anything, thank you, darling,' her mother replied.

But Mona felt that she looked at her with a puzzled expression in her eyes.

'Now go to sleep,' she commanded and bent down to kiss her mother's cheek.

She looked very frail, lying there in the big double bed, her hair nearly as white as the pillow behind it.

'Anything is better,' Mona thought desperately, 'anything —than letting her be unhappy.'

She realised suddenly that her mother was the only person left in the whole world of whom she was really fond and the only person, too, who really loved her. It was strange to think that all the men who had meant so much in her life had gone.

So many had loved her and yet now at this moment the only love on which she could rely—the only love which was given her wholeheartedly and selflessly—came from her mother.

'Good night, darling,' she said from the door, 'and God bless you.'

As she spoke she wondered why the conventional phrase came to her lips and yet she meant it. She did indeed believe that God would bless this mother of hers who had been unswervingly loyal and true through all the years of separation and neglect.

She went back to her own room to find Char still sitting before the fire, a fresh whisky-and-soda in her hand. Brusquely, Mona picked up the decanter and the siphon and put them outside the door.

'There's nothing to be gained by talking all night,' she said, 'besides, we shall disturb Mother. I'll tell you my decision in the morning.'

'All right,' Char said and got to her feet. She turned towards the door, then stopped. 'I don't want to lose your friendship, Mona.'

Mona laughed—a bitter, humourless sound.

'Really, Char, if this is your idea of friendship it isn't mine.'

Char stuck out her lower lip in a sulky expression which Mona knew well.

'I've got to live, you seem to forget that. I'm sorry it's come to this—I'd rather have taken the money from Jarvis Lecker.'

Angry and disgusted though she was, Mona understood. The whole thing was a matter of business with Char and, as such, quite apart from her affections and personal interest. If it hadn't been so serious it would have been funny.

As it was, Mona could only look at the gaunt, ungainly figure of the woman who must threaten those she would have called her friends and feel a vague impulse of pity towards her. But such tenderness could not be sustained.

'Good night,' Mona said abruptly.

With a gesture almost of helplessness, as if fate were too strong for her, Char went from the room.

When she had gone Mona locked the door, then throwing herself face downwards on the bed, lay still for a long time.

After a while the fire died down, the room grew colder

and she roused herself to take off her dressing-gown and get between the sheets. She lay in the darkness, but sleep was impossible.

Her brain was in a turmoil—all the events of the past hours recreating themselves in vivid pictures before her eyes. She went over her conversation with Jarvis Lecker; her drive home with Michael; and then, lastly, the scene with Char.

It seemed to her that the whole week had been leading up to this climax—this moment when she would find herself in Char's toils, trapped and unable to escape.

'I'm not quite a fool,' Mona murmured to herself. 'This is only the beginning.'

She knew how quickly a thousand pounds would trickle through Char's fingers. She was certain to gamble with it, there were places in London which would be only too ready to open their doors to her and where high stakes would soon deprive Char of any practical benefit she might gain from the money. Then she would come back for more.

The jewels would last for a time. Lionel's gifts—which he had chosen with such care and such love—each and every one perfect of its kind because it commemorated a perfect moment, a perfect episode in their joint lives. But even those would come to an end.

When the emeralds had gone, and the diamonds too, she would only have a few small pieces of less value to dispose of . . . the zircon bracelet he had bought her in Vienna because he said the deep blue-green of the stones matched her eyes . . . the ruby ear-rings with the little ring to match which he had given her after that perfect week they had spent together in Alexandria . . . the pearl necklace she wore every day which had been his last present, received only a fortnight before he died.

These would all have to go, and when they had gone she could pawn or sell her furs, but after that . . . what then?

When the supply failed would Char spitefully fulfil her threat to go to Mrs Vale? Or would she be content to realise that her victim could, in all honesty, do no more?

Somehow Mona could never imagine Char being content. She would have some scheme, some way of forcing her to be accommodating—another Jarvis Lecker, perhaps!

Mona shuddered.

It was like a nightmare—Char's greedy fingers reaching down the years, never satisfied, never satiated.

'What am I to do?' she wondered. 'What am I to do?'

She sat up in bed and rested her head in her hands. In the distance she heard the church clock strike four and, after what seemed to her only a very little while, she heard it strike again. Yet still her brain found no solution.

The hours might pass, but always her imagination subjected her to fresh tortures rather than to the discovery of any relief from those which were already agonising her.

'If I were brave,' Mona thought, 'I'd tell Char to go to hell and do her worst!'

But she knew that she would never have the courage to risk the destruction of her mother's faith.

She thought of Mrs Vale's happiness when she returned and the pride she had always evinced in her ever since she had been a child. Her mother had suffered so much in her life.

Her husband—Mona's father—had died of cancer, a slow, lingering, painful death. The doctors had been unable to do anything for him, for when the growth was discovered it was already beyond hope of operating.

And before that, when Mona had been six years old, the brother she should have had was stillborn. Mrs Vale had lain then between life and death and when she recovered she was told that she could have no more children.

All her joy, all her interest, was therefore centred in Mona, and after her husband's death she had clung even more closely to her only child.

Mona would never forget her mother's gallant courage during those last months of her father's life.

Then when he had been laid to rest in the family vault Mrs Vale, dry-eyed but with a look of suffering on her face which no one could misunderstand, had walked with her arm through Mona's to the car waiting at the church gates.

As they had driven home alone she had taken Mona's hand in hers.

'We still have each other, darling, we must never forget that,' she had said, her composure giving way at last into slow and painful tears.

'How hopelessly I've failed her in the past!' Mona thought. 'But, please God, I will keep this from her. She must never know.'

Her mother's life had always seemed to her one of crystal clarity. She had set herself a high standard and never swerved from it; she had carried out her duty as she saw it with an unfailing kindness and with an unselfish affection for mankind which had made every task, however arduous, a pleasure and a joy.

She consecrated herself to a life of devotion as completely as if she had taken the vows of a nun. Nothing was too much trouble.

If a village woman was ill, Mrs Vale would always gladly sit up all night with her; if there were difficulties over poverty, children, or pensions, any of the hundred and one little troubles which crop up in parochial life, Mrs Vale worked indefatigably for those who were in need.

Mona knew that, quietly and in her own way, she brought as much help and comfort to the people with whom she came in contact as any priest; yet there was nothing ostentatious in her charity.

She lived the quiet, uneventful life of a gentlewoman; she tended her garden; she looked after her house; she exchanged courtesies with her neighbours; and she never interfered in other people's concerns unless they sought her help

She had a thousand friends yet she was a lonely woman at heart.

Mona knew that her mother missed the perfect companionship enjoyed during her married life more than could ever be expressed in words, for she and her husband in their quiet, conventional way had known happiness in the fullest and most complete sense.

But he had died and then she must have felt the need of someone of her own flesh and blood—the support of her one remaining family tie—their child.

'How I've failed her!' Mona thought again. 'How terribly!—how inexcusably!'

How empty and desolate her mother's life must have been all those years when she had been abroad, too engrossed in her own affairs to come home even for a few weeks!

Her letters had been scanty; and she had forgotten, too, how hard it must have been for her mother to keep explaining away her absence.

'Her pride would not have allowed her to suspect me,' Mona reasoned.

But she knew it was something deeper than pride—it was love, a perfect trust, a confidence which now must never—whatever the cost—be destroyed.

And yet what could she do?

Over and over again Mona faced the issues confronting her, but could find no outlet; she was trapped—completely and absolutely trapped by her own actions.

'It's only what I deserve,' she told herself, 'and yet why should Mummy suffer because I have transgressed against the code of life to which I was brought up.'

She heard the clock strike seven and got out of bed. She dressed, choosing a thick tweed skirt and a warm cardigan; then putting on her beaver coat and tying a handkerchief gipsy-wise round her hair, she cautiously unlocked the door and crept downstairs.

In the kitchen she could hear Nanny moving about—the rest of the house was in silence. She unbarred the front door and went out.

It was dawn; the world was white with the heavy frost of the night, and the rooks' nests of the previous year were dark patches in the delicate tracery of bare branches against a faintly yellow sky.

Mona turned away from the house and climbing over the sunk fence at the bottom of the garden walked across the fields. She felt that she must get away for a little while—must be by herself far from the proximity of Char and her threats.

The ground was crisp underfoot, every blade of grass was stiff with frost and like a tiny pointed knife. It was cold, but the wind had fallen and there was a stillness over the world as if it awaited breathlessly for the coming day.

Mona reached her favourite spot at the edge of the lake where the Priory boundary met that of the Park. She leant over the wall and then as she stood there quite suddenly the first morning song of birds came trillingly to her ears.

As if it awakened some corresponding joy within herself, she felt the lassitude and weariness of the night fade away and some inner spirit respond, something alive which leapt upwards with those first high notes.

'It's like coming to life,' Mona thought.

She knew that was what it was—the life of a new day pouring through her, so that she was united with a revivified and rested universe, impregnated with fresh energy and strength.

That moment of wonder and palpitating beauty gave Mona a momentary vision of the vast, infinite power of creation—of the Life Force flowing through the whole world, through people and things, animate and inanimate.

Then she could see no more, it was too tremendous for her to grasp—she could only feel the loveliness and glory of it permeate her whole being. It gave her a new courage.

'I will fight,' she said to herself. 'I won't let myself be overwhelmed by the past! Somehow there must be a way of atonement, and if there is I will find it.'

She found then that her thoughts had merged into prayer—prayer for help and for the protection of her mother.

She found herself speaking with the simple confidence that she had known as a child, certain and sure that God would understand and that sooner or later He would answer her supplication.

How long she stood with closed eyes and folded hands she did not know, but when she moved it was to see a soldier approaching her across the fields, his khaki overcoat a dull smudge against the whitened brussels sprouts which were glittering in the pale ray of the rising sun.

Idly she wondered who it could be; then, as he came nearer, she recognised him—it was Michael, wearing the uniform of the Home Guard.

She waited until he was almost upon her before she spoke, but as he saluted her she smiled.

'I wasn't expecting to see you, Michael.'

'Just come off my "dawn patrol". This is my quickest way home from the Mound.'

He pointed to where the land behind them peaked up to overlook the valley.

'You didn't have much sleep, then.'

'I might say the same of you.'

Mona looked away.

'No I didn't sleep well last night.'

'Why?' Michael's question was serious, but Mona made an effort to answer lightly.

'Guilty conscience, I suppose.'

Michael did not reply. He put his rifle down against the wall and, taking out his cigarette-case, offered it to Mona. She shook her head.

'It's too early.'

He did not take one himself but put the case back in his pocket, and as if he made up his mind, spoke with sudden resolution.

'Is that man worrying you?'

For a moment Mona looked bewildered.

'What man?'

Her thoughts had been so deeply involved with Char she had forgotten Jarvis Lecker. Then she remembered.

'Oh, no,' she said quickly, 'it's all right. I want never to see him again that's all.'

'I'm glad,' Michael said, and she heard the relief in his tone.

'It's nice of you not to think . . .' Mona hesitated, 'well
. . . what you might have thought last night.'

'I was angry at the time,' Michael admitted, 'but I knew
that you—of all people—would never tolerate a bounder of
that sort.'

He spoke so violently that Mona looked at him in surprise.

'Thank you, Michael. I think that's one of the few com-
pliments you've ever paid me.'

He leant against the wall.

'I suppose you know why I was angry?'

Mona hesitated, and then, as she did not answer, he said
very quietly :

'You see, I'm in love with you. I always have been.'

'Michael !'

There was no misunderstanding Mona's tone of genuine
surprise.

'All my life I've loved you,' Michael went on. 'I've waited
a long time, and I meant to go on waiting until I believed it
was the right moment to tell you—to ask you to marry me
—but last night when I saw that man trying to make love
to you, it drove me wild. I thought then that I was being a
fool—being too cautious and letting other people get ahead
of me.'

'But, Michael !' Mona gasped . . . and then helplessly—
'I don't know what to say.'

'Why should you say anything? I just wanted you to
know that I love you, and that if you want me I am here.'

There was something in the utter simplicity of what he
said and in his quiet, restrained voice which caught Mona
in the throat. She felt the tears were perilously near her
eyes and her lips were trembling.

She tried to laugh and it was a strange sound that came
forth. 'Dear Michael ! We've known each other for twenty-
five years and now you choose dawn in a field of brussels
sprouts to propose to me !'

'Does the place matter so very much?' he asked.

Once again she had no words, but could only stare across

the lake struggling to control her tears. There was a silence between them, but she knew that Michael was waiting and that she must answer him.

'I'd never be the right sort of wife for you, Michael,' she said at length, and her voice quivered.

'That is for me to judge. What you have to decide is whether I could make you happy.'

'I don't know. I think I've lost the capacity for happiness —I think it's left me for ever.'

Michael took her by the shoulders and turned her round to face him. He stood looking down at her, his face strong and determined in the morning light and yet inexpressibly tender.

'Is something the matter?' he asked. 'Is something troubling you? Because if it is, you must tell me.'

He had touched a vulnerable spot and Mona started and tried to draw away from him.

'No, it's nothing,' she said quickly. 'You cannot help me.'

'Why not?' And when she did not respond, he asked : 'Are you afraid of me, Mona?'

'A little.'

'Why?'

'I feel you are almost inhuman. We've all of us got so many weaknesses, so many failings, but you—well, you seem immune to them all, Michael. I could never live up to your standard.'

'You little fool! Don't you realise how wonderful you are?'

Michael's hands released her shoulders, but she was not free—instead she was swept into his arms. He held her close for a moment, then tipped back her head and pressed his lips to hers.

He kissed her very gently—a kiss as tender and as light as one might have given to a child. There was nothing demanding or compelling as his lips met hers, and yet she felt stirred again to the weakness of tears which must prick her eyes and trickle down her cheeks.

'I must be very tired,' she thought.

Yet she knew it was not fatigue that was making her cry but Michael. She closed her eyes because he was looking at her and she could not meet his eyes.

'I'm here to look after you—to take care of you,' he said softly. 'Will you promise to remember that?'

'I will . . . promise.'

Mona's lips formed the words as once again Michael kissed her, pressing his lips gently on her mouth and against each of her wet eyes.

Then, taking up his rifle, he slung it across his shoulder, slipped his arm through hers and turned their steps towards the gate at the end of the field.

'Where are we going?' Mona asked.

'You're coming to breakfast,' Michael said. 'You're hungry and so am I.'

There was joy and a new gladness in his voice.

They walked slowly arm-in-arm through the fields, talking of the party, of the village, of trivial interests, and every now and then lapsing into an easy, contented silence so that there was only the sound of their footsteps on the crisp earth and the song of the birds welcoming the sun.

'Are you hungry?' Michael asked as they reached the front door.

Mona, laughing up at him, forgetting for a moment all her troubles, all the sinister miseries which were waiting for her at home, replied :

'Ravenous—I could eat a week's rations at one sitting.'

They went in together, Michael calling for Bates.

'Isn't your aunt coming down to breakfast?' Mona asked as they reached the dining-room and Bates was sent hurrying for more toast and coffee.

'Aunt Ada's lived in London far too long for me to teach her country ways,' Michael replied. 'She has her breakfast taken to her upstairs with all the morning papers —the result being I have no idea what the news is until she condescends to tell me at lunch-time.'

'How good for you, Michael !' Mona teased. 'After years

of having everything your own way, without feminine interference.'

'As you say, it's very good for me,' he replied, 'but I'd stand it with greater equanimity from my wife.'

Mona felt her face flush as he smiled at her across the table. She did not know why, but she felt very young when she was with Michael.

All her sophistication and all traces of her experiences seemed to vanish, she felt as if she was a girl again, but Michael was wooing her with a charm he had never possessed twelve years ago. Surprisingly, too, she felt at ease with him, more at ease than she had ever been.

It was so comfortable to be able to sit like this, laughing and talking naturally, instead of feeling torn and destroyed by excitement or fear.

Love could be a very happy thing with Michael, Mona thought. She knew then that one of the reasons why she had jeered at him was his capacity for diffusing contentment.

One felt contentment with Michael, with the contentment which comes from security, safety, and a lack of worry of what the morrow may bring, and yet, she thought, it was impossible for her even to dream of marrying Michael.

'Why don't I tell him the truth right away?—tell him that I can never marry him, that there's no such possibility now or ever? I shall love Lionel for ever,' she told herself fiercely in sudden revolt, 'no-one could ever take his place.'

Yet, as she poured herself a second cup of coffee, the question surprisingly presented itself—was Michael attempting to take Lionel's place? Had Lionel ever stood in her life for anything but a lover?

Never had she been able to think of him as a husband—as part of a life of quiet, mellow happiness; a life shared not only in the enjoyment of physical delights but in creating a home and a family; taking up a certain position in the world, and fulfilling it to the best of one's ability.

That's what it would mean to be Michael's wife. Mrs Merrill, of Cobble Park, would have responsibilities; people would look to her for guidance, for an example, for dignity.

And here, in this perfect setting, in this house full of tradition, customs and ceremonies handed down through the centuries there would be the need of a new generation to carry them on.

Children! Mona felt then her heart yearn for the children she had never possessed. That moment when the curly head of Gerry Archer had lain against her breast, she had known how much she had missed. A child like Gerry—her son and Michael's!

She looked across at him and knew that she would be proud of such a father for her children; then impatiently she shook herself. How could she think such things were for her?

She had made her choice inadvertently that evening many years ago when she had gone to the Café de Paris with Judy Cohenn instead of going to bed.

That had been the moment when she had turned aside from all that someone like Michael could offer her and walked blithely down the road which, in true prophetical fashion, got more stony and more difficult every mile it progressed.

Michael's voice interrupted her thoughts.

'Why are you looking so serious?' he asked. 'Tell me what you are thinking.'

Once again she knew that his instinct was a true one. He knew she was in trouble and worried; but, with a decency and understanding which was characteristic, hesitated to intrude even though he wished to help her.

'Shall I tell him?' Mona thought.

For one wild second the truth trembled on her lips. The relief of being able to pour out her fear of Char, of putting her troubles on someone else's shoulders!

She could almost feel the satisfaction of being able to lie back and let events be handled by someone as strong and capable as Michael. But before she could speak the door opened and Stella Fairlace came into the room.

'Oh, Major Merrill!' she said breathlessly. 'I've come with a message from Doctor Howlett.'

'What is it?' Michael asked, realising from Stella's manner that something serious had happened.

'Last night after they left here,' Stella said, 'the Vicar and Mrs Gunther drove into the back of a lorry on the Bedford Road. The Vicar is comparatively unhurt but they are afraid there is no hope for Mrs Gunther.'

16

Michael looked across the table at Mona.

'We'd better go and see if we can help.'

Mona nodded and got to her feet.

'They aren't at the Vicarage,' Stella said. 'They are at the Towers. It was the nearest house, and they were taken there by the lorry driver and an A.A. man who happened to be passing.'

'I'll go and get the car,' Michael said.

He disappeared, and Mona putting on her fur coat, said to Stella :

'One can't pretend to be very sorry about Mrs Gunther, but I'm thankful he's all right.'

'So am I,' Stella answered. 'He's been so awfully nice to us land girls—we should have felt it terribly if anything had happened to him.'

Mona walked through the house to the front door, but she hadn't been waiting on the steps more than a moment before Michael drove up. They said very little to each other as he speeded towards the Towers, which was only a mile and a half from the Park.

When they arrived, they saw the Doctor's car outside and before they could ring the bell, he opened the door.

'I thought I heard you, Merrill,' Arthur Howlett said. 'I hoped you would come—in fact I rang up the Park and they told me you'd just left.'

'Stella brought me your message,' Michael replied. 'I'm terribly sorry about it.'

'It was a bad smash. I saw the car soon after it happened —there's nothing much left of it. Mrs Gunther must have been going at quite a considerable speed when she hit the lorry.'

'She was driving, was she?' Mona asked.

The Doctor turned to her.

'Yes, she was driving.'

'Stella Fairlace said there was little hope of saving her life. Is that true?'

'She died half an hour ago,' Arthur Howlett said briefly. He turned to Michael again. 'There's a lot to be done, Merrill, I want you to help me.'

They walked into the house in silence, feeling, as people always do in the presence of death, the futility of words.

'Come in here,' the Doctor said, opening the door of the big drawing-room. Furnished in imitation Louis XIV style, it was a pretentious room, redolent of its owner.

'Where's Mrs Skeffington-Browne?' Mona asked, lowering her voice.

Arthur Howlett grinned.

'I've sent her to bed,' he said, 'and given her a sedative.'

His twinkling eyes told them just how difficult and excitable the lady in question had been.

'She's not a good person to be with Stanley at the moment.'

'Is he hurt?' Michael asked.

'Not physically,' the Doctor replied, 'but mentally the shock's been a knock-out blow—in fact, I'm glad you've come, Mona. I think you're just the person to deal with him.'

'I?' Mona questioned.

'Yes, you. I want you to talk to him. Let him confide in you. He seems sort of "keyed-up"—I may be wrong, but it seems to me that at the moment you could help him more than I can.'

'I'll go and talk to him,' Mona said, somewhat apprehensively. 'But don't blame me if I can do no good.'

'He's in the study. Do you know your way?'

'Yes, of course.'

'Well, go and see what you can do.'

Mona left the room and the Doctor turned to Michael. 'If anyone can help poor old Stanley now it's Mona.'

'What makes you think that?' Michael asked curiously.

'Haven't you noticed Mona's extraordinary capacity for revitalising people—for making them come alive?

'I'm not expressing myself well because there isn't a word in the English language which describes what I mean, but she's not only vivid in herself—many people are that—but she gets some response, a reaction I suppose one should call it, from those with whom she comes in contact.

'In my profession we often meet healers and people who definitely have a calming effect on others. Nurses are excellent when they have that quality. Mona has the opposite complement.

'She—well, how shall I put it?—makes people give out to their full capacity, or at least inspires them with the idea that they might do so. It's an inestimable gift and, at this moment, I'm glad to be able to use it.'

'Yes, I agree with you,' Michael said slowly as if he were considering the Doctor's theory. 'I'd never thought of it quite like that before, but now I am sure you're right.'

'It's very obvious when Mona joins a party,' Dr Howlett went on. 'The tempo rises—people become more easily excited, their voices are raised, laughter is easier. She's a tonic, and a better one than I can prescribe!'

He laughed at his joke. Michael said nothing, but Arthur

Howlett knew that he was pleased. The expression on his face was almost one of pride.

'By Jove!' the Doctor thought. 'I believe Dorothy's right! And if those two do get married it will be a fine thing for us all. We need a family at the Park.'

With a tact which was unusual, he did not labour the point, but started to talk of the arrangements for Mrs Gunther's funeral, saying to Michael:

'We'd better arrange them in detail as the Vicar's in no state to see to them himself.'

In the meantime, Mona had opened the study door and found Stanley Gunther sitting in front of the fire, pale and dejected. Although a large fire was blazing, and he was wearing his overcoat, he looked cold; and was hunched uncomfortably in the chair, his long legs stuck out in front of him.

'Don't get up,' she said hurriedly, and sat down on a low stool before the fire. 'I'm sorry. There's nothing else one can say, is there? But you know how sorry I am that this should have happened.'

Stanley Gunther stared at her as if he could not take in what she was saying. His lips were blue, and suddenly he moved his hands convulsively only to link his fingers together again, the knuckles white and strained.

'They've told you,' he said hoarsely. 'They've told you.'

'Yes, I'm desperately sorry for you.'

The ensuing silence was embarrassing and yet Mona could find no adequate expressions of comfort or consolation. She stared into the fire, wondering why the Doctor should have given her such a difficult task.

'She'd have hated to be crippled,' Stanley Gunther said suddenly 'hated it—and that is what it would have meant if she had not.'

His voice faltered, but Mona understood without words what he could not bring himself to say.

'It is much better the way it is,' she said gently. 'After all, a long illness, perhaps years of being in pain or on crutches would have been terrible for her. She was so active.'

Stanley Gunther drew up his legs and leant forward in his chair, his head buried in his hands.

'I shall never forgive myself—never.'

'But why? You couldn't help it.'

'It was my fault she was going so fast. You see—we had been having an argument.'

'I wouldn't blame yourself for that.'

'But I do,' he insisted. 'I ought to have agreed with Mavis, let her have her own way, instead—well, I was obstinate and she was angry with me.'

Mona got up and moved across the room.

'I can see why Arthur's worried,' she thought. 'He's working himself up into a passion of remorse—the worst thing possible after years of repression. He certainly looks like a man who might have a nervous breakdown.'

She picked up a box of cigarettes.

'Let's both have a cigarette,' she suggested, 'you'll find it soothing.'

Stanley Gunther shook his head.

'Please,' Mona pleaded. 'It's easier to talk if we're both smoking.'

The Vicar hesitated, then took one.

'I oughtn't to be sitting here talking,' he said weakly. 'There are a lot of things to see to, things to be arranged.'

For a moment his lower lip trembled and Mona was afraid he might burst into tears. He regained control of himself, although it was an unsteady hand that lit a match and held it out to her.

'You can leave everything to Arthur and Michael,' Mona said. 'Don't worry about anything. As soon as you feel strong enough, we will take you home.'

'I'm afraid I'm rather shaken by what happened.'

'Of course you are. You were telling me what you and your wife were arguing about last night. . . .'

Deliberately she reverted to the cause of his self-reproach, knowing it would be better for him to unburden his soul now rather than continue to suppress his feelings.

The expression on his face was tense, but, as he answered,

she felt some of the unnatural reserve and inhibitions of years slipping away.

'It was about my brother,' he said slowly. 'We heard yesterday that he had been taken prisoner in Libya.'

'How awful! I am sorry.'

'I haven't seen him for some time, as it happens. Mavis and he didn't "see eye to eye", but I felt it was my duty to go and visit his wife. She lives at Plymouth—they are very poor—my brother was in the regular Army but he didn't seem to get on very well.'

His low, hesitating voice lapsed into silence.

'And Mrs Gunther didn't want you to go?' Mona prompted.

'She never did care for John or for his wife. She thought the journey would be a needless expense. I expect she was right but, for the moment, I thought differently and that was what killed her.'

His face contorted again in an expression of pain.

Mona flicked out her ash, then quietly and deliberately said:

'Does it matter what killed her? Perhaps her time had come. I don't know whether you are a fatalist—I think I am —anyway, whatever the reason that made Mrs Gunther drive too fast, the fact remains that it is too late now to regret it.'

'But you don't understand,' Stanley Gunther said wildly, 'It haunts me—I shall never be able to forget it—never be able to erase the memory of those last moments when we both spoke unkindly to one another. Poor Mavis—she was hurt—she told me—she—'

Mona had a mental picture of Mavis Gunther reaching out from beyond the grave to hold her husband, to enslave him after death as she had done when she was alive.

She shuddered at the thought—it held something evil— something which was echoed in her own life by Char, who was making her mortgage the Future to the Past.

And then, like a healing hand on a fevered brow—like the strains of immortal music creeping slowly into the senses

—came the memory of that moment of wonder and joy at dawn.

That moment when she had understood the wonder of the Universe, seen the unfolding pattern of progression—life flowing onwards, forwards, outwards. . . .

Mona felt life powerful and transcendent within the shell of her own body, and she wanted to make Stanley Gunther aware that he possessed it, too—but she had no words.

As a vehicle of expression the human vocabulary was useless when it came to things of the spirit.

'What can I say?' she wondered, and then a way seemed to be shown to her.

She must forget his calling as he had forgotten it himself. For the moment his priesthood was laid aside; the same weakness which had made him subservient to his wife was now apparent in the frailty of his own faith.

He was just a man crying out for help in his agony and she could reach him only by setting aside all his thoughts of his vocation, remembering only that he was drowning in the depths and she—however strange it might seem—could throw him a life-line.

Drastic methods were needed to save him—as one who would shake a yelling child or slap the face of an hysterical woman.

'I thought you were a Christian,' Mona said provocatively. Stanley Gunther looked at her in astonishment, yet before he could speak she went on :

'As a Christian you believe in after life. Wherever your wife is now, she will understand more fully the purpose of suffering and the difficulties that we encounter here in this world.'

'If it is her understanding that you are worrying about we can assume quite safely that she does or will understand.'

'For you—there are much better and greater things to do than giving way to melancholy.'

'Better and greater things?' Stanley Gunther echoed bitterly. 'I'm a failure.'

'Aren't we all?' Mona asked.

She talked on . . . speaking with a sincerity which came from the depths of her being; thinking at times more of herself than the man she was trying to comfort, yet noting almost dispassionately how the danger of collapse had passed.

Stanley Gunther had stiffened both physically and mentally, he was listening to what she said, and the blue look had faded from his lips. Finally, as her voice died away, he said quietly :

'You make me ashamed of myself.'

'Nonsense,' Mona replied. 'There is only one thing you need regret.'

'What's that?'

'Having wasted opportunities in the past. I'm going to be very frank with you, Vicar. I remember years ago what fun it used to be in Little Cobble because you were always arranging some sort of amusement for us all.'

'There used to be dances, children's parties, cricket matches, and even skating parties when there was enough frost.'

'There was always some very worthy cause behind all these entertainments but I'm afraid we forgot about that and just enjoyed ourselves and found a great deal of happiness and a feeling of real comradeship in joining together to make those things a success.'

'They were fun, weren't they?' Stanley Gunther said wistfully.

'Why don't you start them again?' Mona asked. 'Wouldn't such simple pleasures unite this village again—disperse some of the antagonisms, the quarrels, the hatreds which have grown up in the last few years?'

At first she thought he was going to be shocked at her suggesting entertainments at such a moment, and then he held out his hand.

'I understand all you are trying to express,' he said. 'I can only say "thank you" and promise that everything you have said has some meaning for me.'

Mona put her hand in his, then feeling slightly embarrassed she jumped up and rang the bell.

'I'm going to ask for something to eat,' she said. 'I'm sure you didn't have a proper breakfast.'

'They brought me some but I couldn't touch anything.'

'Well, you're going to have some now. Our hostess, I hear, is in bed, so we will see what the house can provide.'

Ten minutes later, Arthur and Michael came into the study to find the Vicar making a good breakfast while Mona sat and chatted to him. The Doctor gave her a quick glance of approval.

The Vicar already looked better. He still showed signs of the night's strain, but the look of despair had gone, and in its place was one of resignation and hope.

'What about letting the Major drive you home, Vicar?' the Doctor asked. 'I've got a patient the other side of the county whom I must see before luncheon.'

'If it isn't any trouble?'

'None at all,' Michael replied.

'Well, I'll say good-bye to you then,' Arthur Howlett said. 'I will be in to see you, Vicar, some time during the afternoon. I don't suppose you'll be going out?'

'Oh, no.'

'Good. Well, expect me when you see me. Good-bye, Mona.'

He pressed her shoulder in passing, and Mona knew that he was grateful for her help.

Michael drove slowly down to the Vicarage and only for a moment as they neared the house did the Vicar seem to shrink from all that must remind him so forcibly of his wife. Mona, sitting beside him in the back of the car, slipped her hand into his.

'I know what you are feeling,' she said very quietly, 'but remember it is like a sort of nightmare—one comes through it somehow.'

She was thinking as she spoke of her last contact with death—that moment when, quite without reason or warning, she had known that Lionel was dead.

She had been walking down the street looking into the shop windows and, although at the back of her mind there had been that little nagging worry about him, she had never for one moment anticipated that the operation would be anything but successful.

Lionel had been in pain at various times during the past two or three months and then the last night he had been with her he had told her he had decided to have an operation for appendicitis.

They both thought it quite a trivial matter—Mona had had her appendix out when she was sixteen and could remember it being only a tiresome time of convalescence during which she must take things easy.

'It's a nuisance,' Lionel had said, 'but I might as well get it over. Things are fairly slack at the moment and the doctors seem to think that the sooner it's done the better.'

Mona had hated the thought of him being in hospital where she could not see him, but he promised to telephone her as soon as he was well enough and she had been content with that.

In Washington, as everywhere else, they had to be terribly careful not to be seen together or to get their names connected in any way whatsoever, but it was a joy to have an apartment of her own instead of living in some second-rate hotel.

Lionel would come to her whenever he could get an opportunity and the night before his operation they had been together until the early hours of the morning.

It was three days later that Mona suddenly knew what had happened. She could not explain how she was so certain that Lionel was dead; she had no vision, no spirit stood beside her, no voices brought her the news—it was just a sudden and complete conviction, so strong that she broke their strictest rule by going into the nearest drug store and telephoning the hospital.

She could remember as if it was engraved on her mind that moment of putting the nickels into the machine, waiting while the porter put through her call to the nurse, thinking that if Lionel were alive he would be annoyed at what she was doing.

It was some moments before the nurse came and she left her heart beating in terrified apprehension.

Perhaps she was crazy . . . perhaps it was just one of those ridiculous premonitions to which all women in love are subject and which, in nine cases out of ten, prove false.

Then the nurse had told her. She had heard the smooth voice hesitate, heard the sentence which began—'I regret to tell you . . .'—and had known that her instinct was right —utterly and devastatingly right.

After that everything was a little blurred.

She remembered having one very strong drink at the counter and then another; she remembered walking home through the streets, losing her way, walking miles further than she need, too dazed and bewildered to remember where she was going or even to recall her own address.

At last she reached home and, many hours later, became conscious of the fact that she was lying on the floor of her bedroom. It was dark save for the golden glimmer of the street lights coming through the uncurtained windows. Mona had sat up slowly and felt for her handkerchief.

Her face was wet with tears but she had no recollection of crying. She was trembling, and in a curious detached way wondered why.

'Lionel is dead'—the words kept repeating themselves over and over again in her mind and yet they meant nothing. She could not grasp it, she was numb with a misery which was beyond the power of pain or suffering.

For her, this was the end of everything.

For the Vicar it was different, she thought. He had lost not someone he loved, but someone he might have hated. Even so, death was frightening, the moment when one came face to face with the Great Unknown and realised how limited was man's comprehension of the meaning of life in this world and the next.

'What happens after death?' Mona queried as she went into the Vicarage

It was impossible to imagine Mavis Gunther in any traditional Heaven. The house was drab and cheerless and seemed peculiarly lifeless without the woman who had dominated it for so long.

'Will you be all right?' Michael asked, as the Vicar thanked him.

'Absolutely,' Stanley Gunther replied. 'I'm going to have a bath and shave and then I think I shall sleep. I feel there will be a lot to do later on—at present I am so tired I can hardly think.'

'That's splendid, then,' Michael said. 'I'll come in and see you this evening, Vicar, and if you can get a sleep in the meantime it will do you all the good in the world. Good-bye.'

'Good-bye, Merrill—and thank you, Lady Carsdale.'

Stanley Gunther took Mona's hand, hesitated, then raised it to his lips. There was something pathetic in his gesture of gratitude, but Mona understood.

There were tears in her eyes as she walked beside Michael down the garden path and back to the car.

'It's nearly lunch-time,' he said. 'What about having some with me at the Park and I'll drive you home afterwards?'

'I'd like some lunch,' Mona replied, 'but I'll walk home.'

She was glad of the invitation. If Jarvis Lecker came over, she thought, it would be better to avoid meeting him. Char, too, could just be left to guess where she was. She knew her mother would not worry unduly—she often stayed out for meals, and it was an understood thing that no one waited.

'You've done a good morning's work,' Michael said, as she got into the car.

'That poor man!' Mona replied. 'I think the trouble is that he's been in prison so long he's half afraid of freedom. Michael, it's an awful thing to say, but I'm glad—really glad—that Mavis Gunther's dead!'

'So am I,' Michael agreed, then cautioned, 'but we mustn't say so in the village.'

'Of course not, but then there's a lot of things one

mustn't say in the village. I wonder why life has to be a series of pretences—for it is that, isn't it?'

Michael thought for a moment.

'Don't you think that everyone's standard is different and the kindest way to go through life is not to disturb those standards, however limited they may be.'

Mona smiled up at him.

'I like you when you are a philosopher, Michael.'

'And I like you in the role of ministering angel.'

Mona looked at him quickly to see if he was laughing at her, but his eyes were tender.

'I felt embarrassed,' she said, 'but I think I did comfort the poor man a little bit.'

'I'm certain of it.'

'The world's topsy-turvy,' Mona said with a sigh. 'It's a funny thing but we all suspect specialists. What I'm trying to say is, that because I look like a "glamour girl" people listen to me when I preach, and if a Hollywood film-star writes a book on farming we are all more likely to read it than one written by you, for instance.'

Michael laughed.

'You're quite safe—I'm not thinking of attempting such a thing.'

'But you see what I mean?' Mona insisted. 'Stanley Gunther listened to me where he'd perhaps have paid no attention to a clergyman.'

'I do see what you mean,' Michael said, 'and I still think I like you in that particular role.'

Mona smiled.

'I'm glad you approve of me sometimes!'

'You know I do,' Michael replied. 'Mona, you remember what I said this morning?'

'Yes.'

'Well, what about marrying me? Don't you think we might be rather happy together.'

He didn't look at her, his eyes were on the road ahead. They were climbing up the hill towards the Park and suddenly Mona knew with a certainty she had never known before exactly what she wanted.

She wanted to say 'yes' to Michael, she wanted to be his wife, to travel through life beside him, secure in the knowledge that she was his—that he would protect her and look after her.

'I suppose this is love,' she thought to herself and knew it was a love which she had never experienced before.

It wasn't exhilarating or exciting, but it was warm and comforting, with a contented quality which seemed to pervade her whole being.

She knew then that life with Michael would mean the fulfilment of all that was best and most perfect in life.

It would be the final blossoming—a consummation and a union which could stand up against all the difficulties and all the troubles of everyday existence.

That was what she had never had before—something to safeguard her against trivialities. She had desired adventures in life, believing that they could give her everything worth having; they had brought her experience of passionate emotion but she had never known the peace of real happiness.

Happiness for mankind lay not in glittering, spectacular thrills but in 'the daily round, the common task' shared with someone beloved.

Mona realised now that she had never shared things with Lionel. They had loved each other passionately, she had played her part in his life, she had been ready to give him more, but he had not demanded it.

For him she had been a precious valuable possession, but she was not a part of him, there was no real union of their separate lives.

They had never shared the simple things. They had never worked in their own garden; they had never spent hours deciding the colour of the walls or the pattern of a sitting-room chintz; they had not walked upstairs together to look at their children asleep in their cots.

'I loved Lionel,' Mona thought, 'but this love is, perhaps, a greater love, more intense, more sincere.'

Then, as Michael waited for her answer, as they swung up the hill and turned in at the great stone gates of the Park, she remembered Char . . . Char and Lionel . . . how could there be a future for her with Michael or any other man?

A feeling of intolerable pain swept over her because she must hurt him; she closed her eyes, then suddenly felt him take her hand and hold it very tightly.

'Don't keep me waiting too long, my darling,' he said gently. 'I want you—now and for always.'

17

'Now I've got to face Char,' Mona thought as she opened the door of the Priory.

Like a heavy cloud her troubles descended upon her again. She had enjoyed being with Michael and his aunt at the Park. They had been unusually gay and there was a new note of gladness in Michael's voice and in his whole bearing.

'He is happy,' Mona thought, and for the moment could not bear to disperse that happiness by telling him what was on her mind.

When she was with Michael, it seemed impossible that anything so sinister and horrible as Char's threats could be a reality, and she almost believed that she herself was imagining the situation.

But now when she returned home she knew that there was

no illusion, that, definite and disturbing, the threat was there, ready to injure if not destroy her mother's peace of mind.

She opened the door of the sitting-room to find Mrs Vale alone, sitting knitting before the fire.

'Oh, here you are, darling!' her mother exclaimed as she looked up with a smile. Mona walked across the room and kissed her.

'You weren't worried, I hope. I had both breakfast and luncheon at the Park. Have you heard the news about Mrs Gunther?'

'Yes, I heard. Poor Vicar! It must have been a terrible shock for him.'

'He'll be grateful to that lorry when he realises that he's free. After all, it's an ill wind that blows nobody any good. Now don't look shocked,' Mona admonished as her mother said nothing. 'You know that if we were honest we would be hanging out flags to celebrate Mavis Gunther's demise. It's the best thing that's happened to Little Cobble for many a long day!'

'It's better not even to think such things,' Mrs Vale said quietly, 'but if you must think them—don't say them.'

'Darling, you're a hypocrite,' Mona teased. Then she asked apprehensively—'Where's Char?'

Her mother folded her knitting and put it away in a bag.

'Mrs Strathwyn has gone back to London.'

Mona stared at her mother as if she could hardly believe her ears.

'Gone back to London!' she stammered. 'But why? . . . when? . . .'

Mrs Vale looked up at her daughter.

'I had a talk with her this morning, and I asked her to go.'

'You asked her to go!' Mona repeated stupidly. 'But Mummy . . . what did she say? . . . what happened?'

Her mother continued to look steadily into her eyes with an expression of tenderness and compassion, and suddenly Mona dropped on her knees beside her chair.

'Tell me,' she said urgently. 'What did she say?'

Very tenderly Mrs Vale put her arm round her daughter's shoulders, then slowly, as if she chose her words with care, she began to speak.

'Listen, my darling. When you were a child I vowed that I would never be an interfering mother. I suffered from one myself. My mother adored us to such an extent that she refused to allow us to live our own lives. She was always wanting us to learn from her experience—an impossibility, as eventually she discovered—and so I resolved that you should be free, and independent.

'Perhaps I made a mistake, perhaps the pendulum swung too far—one day you may be wiser and more sensible with your children—but I did what I believed to be right and I felt I was there in the background, ready should you want my help.

'You've never come to me for help, but now, today, I presumed to take a hand in your affairs. I am old, Mona, and I belong to a different generation, but I think time and years are of little account when one is dealing with one's own children.

'When you have yours you will understand what I mean. One has an instinct about them—one understands many things which lie without and beyond one's own experience.

'Sometimes one fails, of course, but then one should blame oneself and not one's child.

'But suffering and unhappiness are easy to understand, a mother knows it instinctively, however brave, however courageous a child may try to be.

'You've been both, darling, since you came home, but I knew you were miserable and it's been hard to watch in silence.'

'Oh, Mummy!' Mona's voice broke and suddenly she covered her face with her hands. 'What can I say to you?'

'There's nothing to say,' Mrs Vale said gently. 'Nothing that you need tell me unless you wish to. I have always hoped, since you have been grown-up, that you would confide in me, but when you didn't I realised that I must have failed you—that I couldn't have offered you the sort of friendship which could bridge the years and unite a mother and daughter.'

'Oh! it wasn't that,' Mona said hurriedly. 'It wasn't because I didn't want to confide in you, it was because . . .'

She hesitated.

'. . . You weren't certain that I would understand,' her mother interposed. 'Perhaps you were right to think that. To a certain extent it is hard for me to understand how you, with all your loveliness, with all your gifts, with all your charm could choose a life which could only bring you misery and self-reproach. But that's in the past—there's no use in going over it now. What matters is the present.'

'What did Char say to you?'

'Very little. When I asked Mrs Strathwyn what was the hold she had over you, she was too taken aback to give me any coherent reply, and then I asked her if it was about Lionel. There was no need for her to answer that, I saw by her face how surprised she was that I knew.'

'And how did you know?'

Mrs Vale sighed.

'I am old,' she said again, 'but I am not quite idiotic. I knew there must be a reason which kept you abroad, a reason why you never came home. I'm afraid I didn't quite believe the stories that you told me of your various jobs.

'You see, darling, your letters were disjointed, the stories they contained were somewhat erratic. No employer could have behaved quite so generously or any employee be as lucky as you were in your choice of places and amusements.'

'So you were suspicious?' Mona whispered.

'Shall we say anxious,' her mother replied. 'I hate the word suspicious.'

'Go on. I want to know, Mummy, exactly what happened.'

'Well, then it seemed a little strange that you never mentioned Lionel. I knew, of course, where he was, and if you were both in the same place it seemed ridiculous that you should never meet.

'I know how small society is in Cairo and in Vienna—I have been to both places with your father—and after a time I began to wonder if it was deliberate—the omission of Lionel's name from your letters.

'But still I was not absolutely sure until you came home after he had died in America.'

'And then?'

'Then, dear. I saw your face when I mentioned his death. You thought you were acting well to deceive your mother, but mothers are not easily deceived.

'I heard the pain in your voice and I knew, too—however much you might try to hide it from me—that you were very unhappy those first weeks after you returned.

'So when Mrs Strathwyn came, and it was quite obvious that she was unwelcome, I gradually began to put two and two together until it seemed clear that it was for me to help if I could.'

'Oh, Mummy, what must you think of me!'

It was a cry of bitter misery and remorse, and in reply Mrs Vale put her hand very tenderly on her daughter's shining hair.

'What do you expect me to think?' she asked. 'That you've been very foolish?'

'Foolish!' Mona cried. 'I've ruined my life, but now, what is worse, I've ruined yours.'

Mrs Vale laughed. It was a sweet sound.

'You could never do that, my darling. I've still got you, you see, and that's all that really matters. Always remember that one loves a person because of what they are, not for what they do.

'I should love you just the same were you a murderess. I should be sad and sorry, but I couldn't help loving you—you are a part of myself, my own flesh and blood, and I could not forget that.'

Mona was crying now; her face was covered with her hands and the tears were trickling through her fingers. She was crying brokenly and helplessly as she had not cried since Lionel's death.

'Don't darling, don't,' her mother said. 'Everything's all right now you are home and nothing shall hurt you while I am here to prevent it.'

Mona reached for her handkerchief.

'You are making me cry,' she said through her sobs. 'You're being so marvellous, Mummy. I'd no idea that you could be like this.'

'I only wish you'd trusted me.'

'It would have been much easier for me if I had, but I had only one idea—to keep you from knowing what I was doing. You see, I was ashamed.'

'I thought that must be the reason.'

Mona wiped her eyes and sat back on her heels.

'What a shambles I've made of my life! Why couldn't I have been ordinary like other girls, why couldn't I have married someone nice, had a home of my own and, by this time, a large family of children?'

'That's what I'd have liked for you,' her mother said wistfully. 'That's what I've always hoped would happen, but perhaps . . .' She stopped.

'Yes?'

'Perhaps for some people experience is important whatever the price they pay for it. It is difficult for me to put what I mean into words.

'But you have always been different from other girls—at least I have thought so—more intelligent, more alive, asking more of life than a quiet, placid existence.

'Perhaps there's some reason for this, a reason that we, in our human blindness, find it difficult to understand.'

She looked at Mona, then said :

'One thing I can never undertand is how religion can make some people so narrow and others so broad-minded.

'Religion should help us to expand our comprehension of human frailty, not limit it.'

'But still,' Mona insisted, 'you ought to be angry with me, Mummy. You're religious and good; you ought to point out to me how bad, how weak I've been. I feel it is wrong for you to be sympathetic.'

'I'm not sympathetic with your actions, but with you.' Mrs Vale replied, 'I think we all of us earn our own punishment. Haven't you found that already?'

Mona bent forward and kissed her mother on the cheek.

'You are so right, darling, then there is nothing for me to say.'

Then taking her mother's hand, she added : 'Except one thing—one thing I've got to tell you. Michael wants to marry me.'

She saw the expression of joy on her mother's face before she added quickly :

'But I can't—don't you understand how impossible it would be? I couldn't marry him under false pretences, and Michael would never understand if I told him about Lionel.'

'But why should you tell him?'

Mona looked at her mother in surprise.

'You'd want me to leave him in ignorance of what my life has been? I should feel dishonest.'

Mrs Vale sighed.

'That's the conventional attitude. It is the attitude I should have expected my mother to take up, but to my mind it is against all common sense, all knowledge of human psychology.'

'How can you say that?' Mona exclaimed.

'Let us look at it sanely, without emotion,' her mother suggested. 'You want to confess what we both consider your sins to Michael because you think you would be behaving in a dishonest manner were you to leave him in ignorance of your past.

'Now that is the traditional Victorian idea, they had a kind of superstition that it would be unlucky for a woman to act otherwise and finally that having confessed her sins she in some way became absolved from them.'

'What you are doing in reality is lightening your own burden. Nothing is to be gained by bringing up the past— by making Michael, as it were, a partner in your crimes.

Whatever he feels about them they cannot be eradicated.

'All you are doing is sharing your sense of guilt, making Michael an unwilling participator in that which in reality concerns him not at all.

'And what is more,' Mrs Vale went on, 'in your efforts to make Michael a kind of father-confessor you are forgetting the human element. Michael loves you. He loves you because of what you are at this moment.

'Some of the very reasons for his love may lie fundamentally in the fact that you have gained experience.

'It is difficult for any of us to judge what you would have been like had you not loved Lionel but, wrong though your association has been, it has brought you a mellowness, a kindliness and other gentle characteristics which might not have been there had you lived a more conventional and normal life.'

'I see what you mean,' Mona said slowly, 'but still the idea shocks me.'

'It shocks me much more,' her mother retorted, 'to think of the weakness of what you want to do—for it is weakness to my mind—a legacy from the day when men were looked on as superior beings who could sit in judgment on the frailty of the weaker sex.

'What you must ask yourself is whether or not the satisfaction in confessing your past to Michael is worth the risk of destroying his faith. In my opinion there is only one supreme and utter cruelty, and that is the destruction of someone else's faith.

'Men are like children—when they love a woman they believe in her, they trust her. One wouldn't deliberately hurt a child by failing its trust—it's equally easy to fail a man.'

'I wonder if you are right?' Mona questioned. 'It sounds too easy a way out of my difficulties.'

'It won't really be easy,' her mother answered. 'You think that now, but always you will be haunted by fear, the fear that Michael might find out about you, the fear of not living up to the high standard he will expect of you, the fear that in some way you have as yet hardly suspected your experiences may have coarsened you.

'One can never escape from the consequences of an action, and therein lies one's punishment or reward. But, my dear, you must lead your own life—it is yours to make or to mar.

'Only if you love Michael, you will seek the way that is best for him, not for yourself.'

Nanny interrupted their conversation by bringing in tea. She scolded Mona for not having come back to luncheon and made up the fire. The thread of the conversation was lost, but when they were alone again Mona said to her mother :

'I can't believe that Char's really gone—it's like waking up after a nightmare.'

'Poor woman !' Mrs Vale said unexpectedly.

'Can you really be sorry for her?'

'Very sorry. She told me a little of her life-story before she left, and I saw that she was up against difficulties and temptations of which women living a more sheltered existence may never dream.'

'And did Jarvis Lecker come to luncheon?'

'No, Mrs Strathwyn put him off. She spoke to him on the telephone. I'm afraid he was rude to her—she was most upset when they had finished speaking.'

'Char was right,' Mona thought. 'He won't do a thing for her now. I wonder how she will live?'

As if she read her daughter's thoughts, Mrs Vale said : 'She will be all right for the moment—I saw to that.'

Mona almost dropped the teacup she held in her hand.

'You didn't give her money, Mummy !'

'I was sorry for the poor woman. After all, she has no home and no one to whom she can turn.'

'Mummy, you're hopeless !' Mona exclaimed. 'How could you beggar yourself for a woman like that?'

'I could afford the little I gave her,' Mrs Vale replied.

'It's worth anything to get rid of her,' Mona said, 'but

how can I ever be grateful enough for what you've done?'

Her mother smiled.

'By marrying Michael and giving me a large number of grandchildren that I can spoil to my heart's content.'

But, despite all her mother had said, Mona was not satisfied in her own mind. She knew now that she loved Michael and she was sure that they could find happiness together, but she could not bring herself to lay aside the past.

It was easy to point the way forward to other people, to advise Stanley Gunther to turn his face to the sun and to forget the shadows behind him, but the years with Lionel lay upon her own conscience, standing like a barrier between herself and the happiness she dared not grasp.

It was impossible not to see how different in character were the two men who played such supremely important roles in her life.

Mona wondered what would have been the end of her relationship with Lionel if he had not died. Would they have gone on loving one another until her beauty faded and she could no longer attract him.

She shrank from the idea that Lionel might have had no further use for her once her youth had gone, from believing that their love had been based entirely on a physical passion.

Yet she admitted in all honesty that Michael was very different from the man who had captured and held her imagination during those seven years. Somehow she knew indisputably that Michael's love would be impervious to time or change—a love on which she could rely for all eternity.

He had said little and yet she knew without words that he was hers absolutely and completely and she knew, too, that there were depths in his character of which she had no comprehension.

What would he say if she told him about Lionel?

Surely, he would understand, she thought. 'Mummy's wrong—she doesn't realise that our life together must be built on a foundation of truth.'

All through the evening she turned the problem over and

over in her mind until at last she felt that she must make a decision one way or another. When dinner was over her mother went upstairs.

Her cold was still bad and Nanny, fussing round as Mona said, 'like an old hen,' insisted on Mrs Vale having a glass of hot milk and two aspirins in bed.

'I shall go out tomorrow whatever you say,' Mrs Vale threatened; but Nanny got her way and, as the clock struck half-past eight, she said good night.

Mona sat alone in front of the fire. It was very quiet and still; the ticking of the grandfather clock and the gentle crackle of the flames licking the logs were the only sounds to disturb the peace of the room, but the question in her mind gave her no rest.

She could not relax—could not forget—even for a moment.

At last, as though she could bear it no longer, she jumped to her feet. She put on a thick coat, changed her shoes, and started off to walk across the fields.

There was no frost tonight, the moon was veiled in clouds and there was a promise of rain in the cold wind blowing across the open fields. Mona walked on, half reluctant to go forward and yet afraid to go back.

When she came in sight of the Park she walked slower and slower. She could not prepare what she would say to Michael, but she felt driven by a force stronger than herself.

She rang the bell at the front door and then, as she waited for old Bates to come shuffling across the hall to let her in, she wondered if she was crazy. Was she destroying voluntarily and against her mother's advice her last chance of happiness?

'If I lose Michael,' she thought, 'there's nothing left for me.'

She had a sudden vision of the years without him, of growing old alone, of becoming withered and bitter without the comfort of husband or children and the interest which their love could bring her.

The temptation to turn round was strong—to leave before it was too late. . . . But at that moment Bates opened the door, and she went in.

'The Major's in the library, m'lady.'

'Is he alone?'

'I think so, m'lady. Mrs Windlesham is listening to the wireless. There's an opera on tonight and the Major—he can't bear opera.'

'Nor can I,' Mona smiled. 'I'll go and find him, Bates.'

She opened the library door and found Michael sitting alone at his desk. He turned his head wonderingly, then started to his feet with an exclamation of gladness.

'Mona! How lovely to see you! Why didn't you tell me you were coming and I would have fetched you?'

'I wanted to walk.'

'Come and sit down. You must be frozen.'

He helped Mona off with her coat and, as she smoothed her hair in front of the big gilt mirror over the mantelpiece, he said :

'You are looking very lovely. I was thinking of you when you walked in.'

'And I was thinking about you, Michael. That's why I have come . . . I wanted to see you. . . . There's something . . . something I want to tell you.'

Her voice faltered on the words and she dropped her eyes before his, suddenly afraid, suddenly overwhelmingly shy. . . . Then Michael's arms were round her and she heard his voice—excited, triumphant, and thrilling with a note she had never heard before. . . .

'You've made up your mind,' he said exultantly. 'Oh, my darling, there's no need to tell me!—I know what you've come to say.'

He held her close against him and she could feel his heart beating against her breast. She felt his lips on her mouth gentle at first, then growing more demanding, more compelling.

He took her by surprise and for a moment she struggled against him before she went limp in his arms.

226

She was unable to contradict him, unable to explain that he had made a mistake, she could only surrender herself to his kisses and then respond to them because they lit a flame within her which leapt joyously towards him. . . .

She knew an all-enveloping gladness she had never experienced before; she knew, too, that the world was suddenly golden and wonderful with a glory beyond words. . . .

Finally he let her go. She stepped back, flushed and uncertain, her hands touching her burning cheeks, her rumpled hair.

'Darling! My darling!' Michael said, and would have caught her to him again.

When she put out her hands to stop him he caught them to his lips, kissing her fingers and then the palms.

'I love you.'

Mona could not check her reply.

'I love you, too, Michael.'

'I wish I could tell you what it means to me to hear you say that,' he said, his voice low and deep with emotion. 'I didn't believe that I should ever hear you say those words. You've always seemed to me too wonderful, too beautiful in every way to care for a clod-hopper like myself.'

'Don't say such things, they're untrue.'

'They're not. I'm very humble where you are concerned. I never expected you to look at me, although I've been in love with you ever since I was a schoolboy. It will make you laugh now, but I used to dream about you long before you grew up.'

'Oh, Michael!—and I was so unkind to you.'

'Yes, you were horrid,' Michael replied with a grin. 'I used to feel like crying sometimes when you teased me and yet it was better to be teased by you than smiled on by someone else. I adored you, you see, you meant everything that was wonderful, everything that was beautiful, and— my Queen could do no wrong.'

'Oh, Michael!'

Mona remembered why she had come. Her fingers tightened on his hand. She must find courage to tell him, she thought—she must !

He sat down beside her on the sofa, his arms around her, his cheek against hers.

'And now,' he said softly, 'that all my dreams have come true we can plan for the future. I think, deep down within me, I always knew that this moment would come. I believed that you were meant for me—I had faith in that even when everything went wrong—even when you married someone else.'

'But, Michael, you never asked me yourself.'

'I was afraid to. I felt it was such presumption on my part. It was almost sacrilege to ask the wonderful woman I worshipped to share my dull, humdrum life.'

'How silly of you !' Mona said softly.

She was still afraid, and powerless to voice her confession.

'How can I tell him,' she thought desperately, 'while he talks to me like this?'

Then Michael turned her face to his, his hand beneath her chin.

'I will never fail you, my darling,' he said. 'We will build a life together and it shall be worthy of your trust in me. You are mine, my whole life, my whole happiness—we belong to each other for now and all time.'

It was as if he made a vow and, as he bent forward to seek her lips, Mona knew now that there was no going back. 'I can't tell him now,' she thought. 'Mummy is right—it would destroy his faith.'

18

Mona put her suitcase down on the platform and rubbed her aching arm.

It was very cold and still dark; although she knew the road to the station so well she had some difficulty in finding her way even with a torch, and stumbled against tufts of frozen grass and over the edge of the ill-kept path.

Now she looked at her watch. It was six-thirty—the train was due in two minutes.

There was no-one on the platform and the place seemed deserted, but as she heard the rumble of the train in the distance, a cart drove into the yard and someone got out. She hoped it was no-one she knew or who would recognise her, and walked away up the platform.

She had no desire to be seen. She felt guilty now; yet when she made her decision in the early hours of the morning, departure had seemed the only way out of her difficulties.

'I'm a coward,' she told herself severely, admitting her weakness.

It was cowardly to run away from Michael; to leave her mother once again, but she felt she was incapable of standing up to their arguments, to their protestations, or indeed, to their pleadings.

For she knew that they would plead with her; she could well imagine her mother begging her to stay—to take no irrevocable step, but to let things drift and, of course, eventually marry Michael.

If she stayed that was what she would do—marry him— still haunted by the past, with the scars of memory still unhealed.

No, she couldn't do it! Mona had realised that as she had lain tossing sleepless on her bed until, finally, she had made up her mind and risen to write a note to her mother.

It was short and portrayed her feelings most inadequately, but she felt there was nothing else she could say, and her mother, in her wisdom and understanding, would read between the lines.

'*Forgive me, darling,*' *she had written,* '*but I am running away. You were right about Michael. I can't hurt him—can't bring myself to destroy his faith in me; but everything that is decent within me cries out in horror at the idea of marrying him at the moment. Perhaps my feelings will alter with time—perhaps not. But, until they do, I daren't stay here. You will understand that even if you think me foolish. I am going to find some work—war-work—in a somewhat belated effort to prove my loyalty to my country. Bless you, darling; forgive me for any pain this will cause you, and remember me in your prayers.*'

That was all, and before she left the house she had very quietly laid the letter on the mat outside her mother's door so that Nanny, taking in the morning tea, would see it and carry it to her bedside.

Packing hadn't taken Mona very long. She was determined to take as few things as possible and only those that were absolutely necessary; but one thing she included —her red morocco jewel-case. She had made another decision as well during the still watches of the night.

When the grandfather clock in the sitting-room struck six, she tip-toed downstairs and let herself out through the front door. As the chill darkness enveloped her, she had a sudden impulse to turn round and go back.

'Am I crazy?' she asked herself. 'What am I doing this for?'

And then the answer came to her—'For the sake of honour!'

Yes, that was, in truth, the answer. For the sake of honour—her honour—a virtue she had forgotten in the past but which now seemed to demand not only consideration but sacrifice.

The train came speeding into the station and Mona hurried back towards her suitcase. As she picked it up, she saw in the light of an open door the face of the other traveller from Little Cobble. It was Stella Fairlace.

'Good morning, Lady Carsdale.'

'Good morning.'

Mona's reply was brief and not too cordial, as she clambered into the nearest carriage; but Stella followed her in.

There were no other passengers and they each chose a corner seat facing each other.

'It isn't often I see anyone from the village on this train,' Stella said conversationally.

'Do you often travel by yourself?' Mona asked.

'Whenever I go to London,' Stella replied. 'It gets me up so nice and early that I can get everything done before luncheon.'

'Yes, that's useful,' Mona said indifferently; opening her suitcase, she took out a book.

She did not want to read, but at the same time she did not want to talk. She wanted to be alone with her thoughts, to turn her problems over and over again in her mind, to ask herself whether she was doing the right thing or whether she was being so foolish as to throw away her last real chance of happiness.

But Stella was irrepressibly talkative. She was wearing her uniform because, as she explained to Mona, she had to go to the Ministry of Agriculture, and the big, shapeless coat and felt hat obscured a great deal of her attraction, yet it was easy to see that with good dressing she might be very lovely.

She had the radiance of youth and perfect health, and Mona suddenly felt tired and old beside her youthful buoyancy.

'I wonder . . . If I never return,' she thought to herself, 'whether Stella will marry Michael?'

The idea that Jarvis Lecker had put into her mind was still there and she remembered what a handsome couple they had made as she had seen them across the dancing floor.

'The perfect wife for Michael,' she told herself defiantly, and yet she knew that was not true.

Married perfection did not lie in a similarity of looks and strength but often in a contrast of personality.

She and Michael were completely opposite to one another—perhaps that was why their love might be so completely satisfying; together they would make a whole, for in each could be found the missing complement of the other.

Michael! The thought of him made her heart ache. She knew now for the first time how much she was going to miss him.

In a few days he had come to mean something tremendous in her life, yet she felt time was of no consequence, her love was not something which had grown day by day, or even hour by hour, but a thing that had always been there deep down within herself, and that in loving Michael she was merely uncovering an indivisible part of herself.

Michael!—his very name struck some chord within her, and then abruptly she realised Stella was speaking and forced herself to attend.

'If you could tell me,' Stella was saying, 'a place where I could buy a really pretty frock I would be so grateful. I know how awful my clothes are, but I have never been able to afford nice things. Now I've saved enough out of my wages to have at least one smart frock—something well cut and in good material.'

'I will tell you the name of two or three shops,' Mona replied.

As she gave Stella the names and addresses and watched her write them down, her mind was asking the question.

'Why does she suddenly want to be well-dressed? Is it for Michael?—is she already in love with him?'

It would not be surprising if Stella were. After all, she was living at the Park, she saw Michael every day, perhaps for hours at a time.

He was attractive—no-one realised that better than Mona—and, to a girl coming from a quiet country village in Devonshire, where perhaps young men were few and far between, he might well prove irresistible.

Even pride could not keep Mona from asking in a voice which strove to be light :

'Why do you want to be so smart? Have you found a young man in Little Cobble?'

She was ashamed of herself even as she said the words, but it was too late to prevent them from passing her lips. She simply could not remain in ignorance where anything to do with Michael was concerned.

Stella hesitated a moment and then, to Mona's surprise, she blushed—a lovely flood of colour diffusing her cheeks and making her drop her eyes shyly.

'Oh, no,' she answered, but the words faltered and Mona knew they were untrue. There was silence for a moment before Stella bent forward impulsively.

'You've been so kind to me, Lady Carsdale,' she said, 'that I'd like to tell you. I have never confided in anyone —in fact, there's no-one in my life in whom I can confide —but, well, I suppose you've guessed it—I'm in love.'

'And I hope he's in love with you?'

Mona knew that her voice was cold—icy—but she felt as if all the warmth had fled from her body.

'Oh, no,' Stella replied. 'He doesn't know—he has no idea—in fact, I don't think he'd dream of such a thing. But one can't help loving a person, can one?'

Her question was piteous—the cry of a very young girl who was afraid of her own emotions.

'No, of course not,' Mona said slowly. 'These things happen to us—to all of us—but I hope for your sake that the story has a happy ending.'

'I hardly dare think of that, but perhaps one day . . . I like to think so anyway. It gives me something to dream about . . . to work for and . . . don't think I'm being dramatic . . . to live for.'

There was an expression almost of rapture on Stella's face, and again, as if her voice spoke without her own violation, Mona asked through dry lips :

'Can I guess who it is? Is it Major Merrill?'

Stella's quick exclaimation held surprise and also a note of laughter.

'Of course not! I'd never think of Major Merrill like that—he's—well, how shall I put it?—too grand. No, it's . . .' Again she hesitated. 'I know you won't tell anyone . . . I'd be so ashamed . . . but . . . it's Mr Gunther—Stanley. I think I've loved him ever since I first came to Little Cobble. I felt it was hopeless, of course, but now . . . now he's free, perhaps one day he will notice me.'

A warm gladness seemed to envelop Mona. She put out her hand and touched Stella's.

'I hope so. I hope you both find happiness together.'

As if her confidence had released a flood of words which had been held almost to bursting-point, Stella talked on. Her voice was like the smooth murmur a stream. Mona hardly listened. She felt curiously happy and relaxed. She leant back, making suitable ejaculations from time to time to encourage Stella in the telling of her life story. She talked until they arrived at St Pancras and then, as the train steamed into the station, she turned to Mona with shining eyes.

'You've been so terribly kind to me,' she said. 'I feel encouraged and hopeful—I can't thank you enough.'

'But I haven't done anything,' Mona replied. 'I hope, more fervently than I can say, that everything will come right for you—and Mr Gunther. One word of advice—don't stand too much on ceremony.

'The Vicar may feel that he's too old or too uninteresting to dare to approach you himself. You must encourage him —you must help him. He needs it.'

'I'll remember,' Stella said solemnly.

Then they were threading their way through the crowd of passengers surging down the platform. Mona took a taxi and her last glimpse of Stella was of her marching along towards the underground, her chin held high, a smile of confidence on her lovely lips.

Mona drove first of all to a well-known jeweller in Bond

Street. The shop had a branch in Paris and a great deal of the jewellery which Lionel had given her had been purchased there. She asked to see the manager, and producing her jewel-case, opened it for his inspection.

'I want cash for everything you see here.'

He seemed to take her request as a matter of course. He examined each piece with care, asking the opinion of several experts on the emeralds and pearls. Mona sat watching them.

It was strange, but she felt disinterested now in the glorious gems that Lionel had given her.

Once they had meant so much, but now they had sunk into their true perspective, even as her memories of the lover who had given them to her had become no longer poignant or agonising.

Once she had thought that to part with Lionel's presents would have broken all that was left of her heart. Now she knew that such possessions were important only because to her relentless conscience they were a part of that self-erected barrier which stood between Michael and herself.

'An angel with a flaming sword,' she called it, and imagined that the hilt of the sword was studded with the glittering gems of Lionel's choosing.

The manager interrupted her thoughts. He made a little speech about the jewels.

The diamonds had increased in value—the emeralds were saleable, but the right customer had to be found—the pearls were not of great interest now that their cheap, effective, cultured cousins had swept the market.

It was the usual voluble mixture of explanation and excuse which always accompanied the sale of an article for which one had paid a fancy price.

Finally, however, he made an offer of what seemed to her an immense sum, running into many thousands. She accepted it without argument, adding :

'I want it in cash.'

She was told this would take a little while to procure, but she was content to wait. Someone offered her a cigarette.

She sat half oblivious of her surroundings, seeing, not the discreet brown and velvet interior of the jewellers, but the fields lying between the Priory and the Park—those fields over which she had been walking yesterday morning when Michael had come upon her unexpectedly.

How far away other memories seemed in comparison!— thrown into a misty background; utterly eclipsed and over-shadowed by the present—by Michael, and by all that he meant to her. Paris . . . Egypt . . . Buenos Aires . . . New York . . .

Once they had all meant something stupendous; their names alone could bring a throb to her heart, a sudden quickening to her pulses—now they were but milestones vanishing over an indistinct horizon from which she had travelled a long way.

At last the money was ready for her. She asked for an envelope, and taking two fifty-pound notes addressed them to 'Miss Stella Fairlace', at 'The Park'. One sentence was enclosed with it.

'For your trousseau, with my best wishes.'

She arranged that it should be registered and posted, and then into another envelope she collected the rest.

'I hope you will be careful, Lady Carsdale,' the manager cautioned. 'It isn't wise to walk about with such a large sum on you.'

'I shan't have it with me for long,' Mona replied, and getting into a taxi directed him to drive to an address in Piccadilly.

When she got there, she kept the driver waiting while she handed in the envelope at the door.

'For the Save The Children Fund,' she said.

A little while later she had deposited her suitcase in the cloakroom of a quiet hotel while she went to the telephone. She looked through the directory for the name she wanted —that of her father's brother.

She dialled the number and Father Andrew Vale an-swered the telephone himself. A Catholic priest, he had given up his whole life to working in the slums, and devoted himself to serving the poorest and most destitute of England's citizens.

'Uncle Andrew, this is Mona.'

'How are you, my child?'

'I want your advice. I want to do some war work. I am completely untrained, but I want to go where the work is really hard and where I should be most useful.'

'Go and see Mrs Marchant, 1003 Queen Victoria Street,' was the reply, and then with few more words and an abruptness that was characteristic of him, Father Andrew rang off.

Mona did as she was told.

She found Mrs Marchant, a sweet-faced, white-haired woman, sitting in a busy, over-crowded office, where several typewriters were making an almost unbearable noise. Mona told her by whom she had been sent, and instantly a smile of welcome lit up her face.

'We all love Father Andrew.'

'He's my uncle.'

'Then you are more than welcome.'

'I am looking for work,' Mona said. 'That is why my uncle has sent me here. He said you could help me.'

'Indeed we can,' Mrs Marchant replied.

Then she hesitated, Mona felt that her clothes were too smart, that her air of expensive sophistication was alarming.

'I want something which is really hard. Something where I won't have time to think.'

Mrs Marchant seemed to understand.

'I was half afraid to suggest it,' she said, 'but we are greatly in need of helpers for the war nurseries, which we are setting up in all parts of the country.'

'There are two sorts—those which are placed near factories where the workers can leave their children for the day; the others for children who have been evacuated—tiny children who are too young to be billeted on householders and must therefore be sent as a complete unit, with nurses and helpers to look after them.'

237

'These latter, of course, contain a large number of children who are orphans or whose mothers have been killed in air raids.'

'That is the sort of work I'd like,' Mona said. 'I love children, although I'm afraid I don't know very much about them.'

'You soon will,' Mrs Marchant replied. 'I'm afraid the work will be hard. Are you quite sure you are prepared to undertake it?'

'Quite sure,' Mona said firmly.

A few hours later she was in the train travelling towards Fulton-under-Slough, where one of the nurseries had recently been established.

Before she left London, she arranged with Mrs Marchant that her letters to her mother should be forwarded from the London office. She gave no explanation of this strange request, but Mrs Marchant promised that all letters should be readdressed immediately on their arrival.

Sitting in the train, Mona wrote to her mother and tried to explain as gently as she could the reason why she was not giving her the address of her destination.

'You are too soft-hearted, darling,' she wrote. 'I know Michael would get round you. He'd seem so unhappy and so wistful that you'd just be unable to resist him—then he'd come and see me and all my trouble would have been wasted.'

She made no mention of her jewellery—that was too difficult, too embarrassing to explain even to her mother; but she wrote enthusiastically of what lay ahead of her, letting no suspicion of apprehension or anxiety creep into her letter.

Only to herself, as she stared out at the landscape, did she admit a feeling, not only of doubt, but almost of despair. She was gripped by loneliness, torn within herself at the idea of being utterly alone, and having no-one to whom she could turn.

She thought of Michael and felt she was like a person deliberately leaving the warm, cosy intimacy of a fireside to go out ill-clad into the freezing darkness of the night.

'But I am right,' Mona thought to herself. 'I know I am doing the right thing.'

Although it was cold comfort she tried to encourage herself by considering her own nobility of action.

It was hard. Every pulse in her body ached and longed for Michael.

She thought of how closely he had held her the previous evening, his lips on hers, murmuring words with which he had dedicated them both to a life of love and unity.

'Oh, Michael!' Mona cried suddenly out loud.

The tears were pouring down her cheeks, she could not stop them. She covered her face with her hands.

Children, however much they needed her care and her assistance, were but a poor substitute for the home which Michael had offered her, for the protection and the joy of his love, for the babies they might have had together—children of their own, the perfect consequence of a perfect happiness.

Angry with herself for her weakness, Mona wiped her eyes. There was no looking back—she had to go forward.

She had made the plunge—she had been determined to renounce the easier path and make atonement by the hardest and most difficult way. She could not weaken—she would not let herself be defeated by her own frailty.

She powdered her nose just before the train drew in to Fulton-under-Slough. It was raining and the wayside station looked drab and dreary in the fading afternoon light. Mona got out and carrying her own suitcase, made for the station yard.

There was no car or trap to meet her, only a dray loading up with sacks of potatoes. She addressed herself to the old, bearded driver.

'Do you know if there's anyone here from Ivydene?' she asked. 'Or how far it is from the station?'

'Ivydene?' he said. 'It b'ain't far. Be they expectin' ye?'

'I think so,' Mona said, wondering if the telegram Mrs Marchant had sent early in the morning had reached its destination.

The driver took his pipe out of his mouth and shouted across the yard.

'Bill! Where be that lad? Bill!' A sheepish-looking boy, dressed in a tattered coat two or three sizes too large for him, came out from the goods shed.

'B'ain't ye expectin' a lady fer Ivydene?' the drayman asked.

'Yus, Oi be. Sorry, Miss, Oi didn't realise th' train 'ad cum.'

The boy came shuffling across the yard dragging behind him a dilapidated-looking handcart, on which he put Mona's suitcase.

'It be a tidy step,' he said, 'but it won't tike we no more than quarter of th' hour.'

They set out in the twilight. It was raining softly but steadily, and Mona wished she had a mackintosh. Soon she was soaked through and her hair lay damply against her cheeks.

'Not a very good beginning,' she thought to herself.

But she walked on without complaint, side by side with Bill, who was whistling tunelessly through a missing front tooth.

19

'Auntie Mona, look—there's a big pussy in the garden.'

Mona, who was scrubbing the floor, straightened her back and got to her feet.

'Where, darling?' she asked.

The small boy pointed to the end of the garden where a large tabby cat was surrounded by an admiring ring of small children.

'It's a lovely pussy,' Mona said. 'Be very gentle with it or you will frighten it.'

'Will it hurt us?' asked the child.

'Not unless you are unkind to it,' Mona answered. 'Stroke it, but I shouldn't try to pick it up.'

She remembered last week that one of the toddlers had brought in a kitten which he had found in the farmyard, holding it so tightly round its neck that the poor animal was more dead than alive by the time she could rescue it.

They meant well, but they were all town children who had never before had the handling of animals. Some of them were even afraid of the hens and at the sight of cows they clung to her with screams of terror.

It was funny when one thought what they had been through. Most of them had lived in the very worst-bombed areas, and yet it was exceptional to have a child whose nerves were affected.

But some of them had suffered from sleeping permanently in underground shelters. They were pale, with dark shadows under their eyes and their thin white bodies seemed starved for sunshine and air.

On the whole, the standard of health was a high one, but it was almost like a miracle to see how, after only a few weeks in the country, they filled out, became more sturdy and daring and were always ready for a second helping at mealtimes.

When she looked at them, sitting round the long table in the dining-room, Mona thought that they were worth all the backaches, all the weariness and the long hours of fatigue from which she had suffered since she came to Ivy-dene.

The staff of three were undoubtedly run off their feet. Matron was a capable woman who had retired shortly before the war from the charge of a big children's hospital.

Under her was Sister Williams, a trained nurse who had been for many years in private practice and who, while extremely knowledgeable, seemed to Mona to personify the inhibitions of her particular profession.

She liked things 'just so', and she found it difficult to adapt herself to what, of necessity, must often be a patch-work job of expediency.

Matron had been promised two or even three other helpers when she had taken over Ivydene, but the only person who had arrived had been Mona.

Their task was further complicated by the servant problem.

Fulton-under-Slough was a little west-country village where, before the war, the passing of two or three cars was an event of importance.

Now, only five miles away an aerodrome was being constructed and, even nearer, on the outskirts of the village itself, a small factory had been started for the production of precision instruments.

Although a large amount of skilled labour had been imported there was also a demand for local workers, and every girl in the village, and most of the married women who could spare the time, had offered their services.

Domestic help was, therefore, at a premium and the only person Matron could get 'to oblige' was Gladys, a girl whom the neighbours described as 'a softie'.

Gladys was certainly neither quick nor intelligent and although she was willing enough, at times, her mind simply ceased to function.

'She's been in the asylum twice,' Matron told Mona, 'but any pair of hands seems to be better than none. At least she can cook a little.'

But Gladys's 'little' was very little, and soon Mona found herself becoming proficient at every household task. Someone had to do the domestic work, and so they took it in turns.

Sister Williams made such heavy weather about her share that Matron and Mona often preferred to add to their own burden rather than listen to her grumbles.

Sometimes, when Mona crawled upstairs almost too tired to undress, she would wonder if she were living in a dream or whether all this was real.

She thought back over the years when she had lived in luxury—of her flat in Paris, where, the concierge's wife, had looked after her and had been ready at any moment to cook her a meal fit for an epicure; of her apartment in New York, where an old black mammy had hurried in every morning, to keep the place spotless, and always, before she left to go back to Harlem, putting something appetising and delicious in the ice-box for supper.

It was amusing now to think of the hotels she had found uncomfortable, of the beds she had complained about, of the service which she had often described as 'abominable'.

Now in an unheated bedroom, lying on a bed with a hard and lumpy mattress and a shortage of blankets, she wondered if, when peace came, she would ever grumble again.

But even getting up in the freezing cold, cooking the breakfast, washing and dressing a dozen children, and being on one's feet all day, was worth while, because it gave her a greater sense of satisfaction than anything she had ever done in her life.

She was proud of her own capabilities; proud, too, that she could do all that was required of her. She had, of course, fits of depression and moments of desperate loneliness when she felt she could carry on no longer.

And sometimes when a letter, forwarded by Mrs Marchant, came from her mother or from Michael, it was hard not to renounce her self-appointed task, and to take the next train back to Little Cobble.

Michael's letters were pathetic. She knew that although he said very little, he was bewildered, uncertain and afraid. He did not understand what had happened, and his one fear was that he might lose her—that she might never return to him.

He asked her questions. 'Had he been too hasty? Had he demanded too much?'

If he had she must forgive him and attribute it to a happiness which was beyond his control.

'Poor Michael!' Mona whispered as she read these letters, and yet daily the knowledge grew within her that one day they would be able to be happy together and that their happiness would be all the more intense because of this voluntary separation.

Occasionally she allowed herself to answer him, but only occasionally, and then her letters were short and practical, speaking mostly of care and attention on the children at Ivydene.

To her mother she wrote more fully, expressing her thoughts and her feelings, and even hinting at her hopes for the future.

A new intimacy had grown up between mother and daughter that had never been there before.

It was very sweet to Mona to feel that she had someone in whom she could confide, and speak of anything and everything which came into her mind.

Leaning over the window-sill to watch the children, she felt the spring sunshine on her face and raised her eyes to the sky. Their were small, fleecy white clouds against the blue, blown along by a south wind which seemed to carry the promise of summer.

Already the trees were in bud and the crocuses were out in the flower-beds, which the last owner of Ivydene had tended with such care. Now the garden was neglected and, by the summer, was likely to become a wilderness unless someone found time to work in it.

But the children wouldn't care, Mona thought, watching them run after the cat who had escaped from their attentions and jumped out of reach on top of the brick wall.

Their laughter and excited voices rang out and there was no mistaking that they were happy and that the world, so far as they were concerned, was a very wonderful place.

'I'm wasting time,' Mona thought.

She finished scrubbing the kitchen floor and put the brush and bucket away under the sink. Gladys had her points, but cleanliness was not one of them.

As Mona dried her hands on the towel behind the door, she realised how much they had coarsened in the last two months; the short, unvarnished nails and the rough and reddened skin looked very different from the delicate white hands of which she had once been proud.

She thought of the men who had kissed her hands—Lionel and Michael, especially—and with a smile that was half whimsical, half dismayed, she told herself that no-one would want to kiss them now!

There was no time for vanity at Ivydene.

Getting up when it was still dark Mona would pull on her clothes, run a comb through her hair, and hurry downstairs without bothering even to look in a glass.

It was funny how easily one grew to do without face creams and powder, without all the little aids to beauty which had once seemed so indispensable.

'Three months ago I'd have felt naked without lipstick,' she said to Sister Williams.

'We aren't allowed to use cosmetics in my profession,' Sister Williams replied, 'but of course, if one is doing private work it's different. I always think a good appearance is a great help to a woman.'

Mona could not help smiling. Sister Williams was extremely unprepossessing; she had homely features and lank dark hair, and yet she took an immense amount of trouble over herself in contrast to Mona, who always seemed to get dishevelled when she was working.

Sister Williams' caps and aprons were as spotless at the end of the day as they had been when she put them on in the morning.

Although Mona had a real affection for Matron it was difficult to like Sister Williams. Gladys summed up the general feeling about her very aptly.

'Her asks for this, her asks for that, but her never thinks of fetching it for herself.'

But nothing really mattered except the children. When Mona was feeling particularly lonely or miserable she would go into the big play-room on the first floor, and picking up the nearest toddler, hold him closely in her arms.

There was something satisfying and comforting in the soft warmth of a baby and always Mona's misery was lightened and gradually dispersed by the contact.

'Her favourite amongst all the children was little Peter. 'Peterkin,' she called him, and he reminded her in many ways of Gerry Archer.

He was small, fat and fair, and although he was only just two, was beginning to talk quite a lot. The first night he had arrived he had cried bitterly for his mother, saying :

'Mum . . . Mum . . .' over and over again. His mother had been killed a few days earlier.

The wireless that night had reported :

'A lone enemy aircraft crossed the East Coast early this afternoon. Some bombs were dropped and there were a few casualties.'

Peter's mother was one of the few. His father was serving in the Army; he had come down once to see Peterkin and Mona had wondered what sort of life there would be for father and son when the war was over with no woman to make a home for them.

But Peterkin's tragedy was one of many.

There was hardly a child whose family had not suffered in some way throughout the war.

Yet when their bereaved relatives came to visit them Mona was struck by their bravery and courage, and the way they were ready to carry on, somehow to create a new life for those who remained.

It was a cry from Peterkin which arrested her now just as she was going upstairs to tidy the play-room. She hurried into the garden.

'What's the matter?' she asked one of the older children.

'Don't know,' was the reply. 'Peter keeps crying. 'Spect he's got tummy-ache.'

He was standing by himself weeping bitterly, the tears running down his fat cheeks. Mona caught him up in her arms.

'What's the matter, darling?' she questioned.

He buried his face against her shoulder and then she saw the spots behind his ear and on his neck.

She carried him into the house and, pulling up his blue woollen jumper, looked at his chest. There was no doubt about it—Peterkin had chicken-pox.

Sister Williams was out and Matron had been on night duty; they took it in turns for one of them to be up with the children. Mona decided not to disturb her so, taking Peterkin upstairs, she put him into her own bed. Then she rang up the doctor.

'I'll come out this afternoon,' he promised. '. . . No, there's no need to isolate him. If they've been playing about all the morning the others are sure to get it, but don't worry—it's a very mild child's illness and they had all better catch it and get it over.'

'It's easy for him to say that,' Mona thought as she put down the receiver, 'he hasn't got to nurse them.'

She was determined that Peterkin should sleep with her that night. If he felt ill she would be there beside him. She moved a cot up to her room.

He seemed happier and less inclined to weep; she gave him some books to play with and having lit the fire went downstairs to see if Matron was awake.

She was, and Mona told her what she had done.

'I thought you'd want me to tell the doctor,' she said, a little anxiously in case Matron should think her officious.

'Quite right,' was the answer, 'but there's nothing he can do. "Just put the child to bed and keep him warm," is what he'll say.'

'Now we've got to wait three weeks before we're out of quarantine,' Mona said. 'I had it at school and I remember what a boring illness it is—it seems to go on for ever.'

Matron agreed.

'I think it gives me an excuse to write to Miss Marchant and say we really must have someone else to help us.'

'That's a good idea.'

'Gladys is getting more careless every day,' Matron went on. 'What do you think I found she'd done last night?'

'Something silly, I suppose?'

'She'd put all the clothes which had to be aired in front of the kitchen fire and built it half up the chimney. When I pointed out how dangerous it might be, she said that it saved her relighting it in the morning! I ask you—what can you do with a girl like that!'

'Nothing,' Mona said, 'but don't lose her. We shall need all the help we can get if half the children have to be kept in bed.'

Matron sighed.

'Oh, for the good old days in hospital when things ran smoothly! But I'm not complaining. You've been wonderful, Lady Carsdale. I can't think what I'd have done without you.'

'I feel as proud of your saying that as if you'd given me a medal,' Mona replied.

Then running downstairs she went to fetch the children in from the garden and get them ready for lunch.

It was about three in the morning when she woke up with the uneasy feeling that something was wrong.

Her first thought was that of Peterkin, but as she bent over his cot she found that he was fast asleep, his curly head buried comfortably in the pillows, a small fat fist nestling under his chin.

She listened, but she could hear nothing and yet the idea persisted that something had awakened her.

Quietly, so as not to disturb the sleeping child, she put on her dressing-gown and bedroom slippers, and opened the door of her room. Still there was no sound.

Unwilling to think that her instinct had betrayed her, she went softly downstairs. She peeped into the big dormitory on the first floor. The children were asleep and so was Sister Williams, who was on night duty.

She was snoring rhythmically through her slightly aquiline nose, her feet on a stool in front of her, a warm rug tucked round her knees. Mona did not disturb her.

'I'm imagining things,' she concluded, and then as she turned to go upstairs she smelt smoke.

It was only faint but, as she opened the heavy baize door which divided the hall from the kitchen quarters, a great cloud of it rushed out, almost overpowering her.

'This is Gladys's doing,' she thought, as she fought her way, choking and spluttering, towards the kitchen, but it was impossible for her to reach it.

As she went down the stone passage the smoke thickened and she could hear the crackle of flames.

'The whole place is on fire! The children—we must get them out.'

She rushed back the way she had come and, slamming the baize door, ran breathlessly up the stairs. She banged on the door of Matron's room.

'Get up quickly,' she called, 'the house is on fire!'

She rushed back into the dormitory. Sister Williams was still sleeping and it wasted some precious moments before she realised what was happening. Mona shook her roughly.

'Hurry! We'd better wrap the children in blankets and get them outside.'

'Is it as bad as that?' Sister Williams asked, but Matron, hurrying past the door, commanded:

'Get every child into the garden. We don't want to take any risks.'

The children were far too sleepy to be of any help. Mona and Sister Williams wrapped blankets round them, and snatching up the piles of clothes which lay beside every bed and cot ready for the morning, put them into their arms.

'Hold on to those,' they admonished, and carried the children downstairs.

Once outside in the garden, it was easy to see how the flames had got a firm hold on the kitchen quarters. The whole place was a blaze of light and very soon people were arriving from the village.

The A.R.P. wardens produced stirrup-pumps and some-one shouted that they had sent for a fire-engine. Mona had little time to worry about anything except the children.

Only as she was carrying the last of the toddlers down-stairs did she realise that the fire was getting worse, that the hall was full of smoke and that now, coughing and choking, she had to grope rather than see her way to the front door.

She handed the child over to Matron and turned towards the house again. As she did so there was a sudden rending crash and the ceiling of the dining-room collapsed.

'You can't go back now,' one of the men shouted to her as she made for the door.

'I've got to,' she replied. 'There's another child in there.'

She had not forgotten Peterkin, but she had deliberately left him for one of the last, afraid that exposure to the cold might be bad for him and hoping against hope that the alarm was not as serious as it appeared.

Now she realised she had done a very foolish thing. He was two floors up and the fire had got a firm hold over the lower parts of the house.

'The firemen will be along in a moment,' the man argued.

He put a restraining hand on her arm. Mona shook her-self free and rushed through the doorway.

The smoke was dense, and for a moment she felt it must suffocate her. The flames were already licking their way across the baize door and along one side of the hall, but the stairs were still untouched.

She scrambled up them, holding her breath, her smarting eyes tight shut, guiding herself by a hand on the banisters.

She reached her own room to find Peterkin still asleep. Quickly she snatched a blanket off her own bed and picked him up. He gave a little cry and she spoke to reassure him.

'It's all right, darling. You've got to go downstairs and I'm going to cover you up right over your face.'

He didn't understand and she could feel him struggling

250

against the enveloping blanket. She held him tightly to her breast and started on the downward journey.

Now the smoke seemed to grip at her throat; she felt that it was impossible to breathe—impossible to go on. There was another rending crash and she wondered what had fallen; but still she forced herself forward until suddenly, as she reached the foot of the stairs, she felt the flames leap at her, saw their yellow tongues, evil and menacing, surrounding her.

There was only one thing to do—to make a dash for it. She knew where the front door was—straight in front of her and it was open, the draught blowing the flames higher, making them leap and dance like some devilish fantasy.

'Help me, God help me!'

Mona wasn't certain whether she said the words out loud, but she knew that in that moment of her prayer, strength would be given her to save Peterkin's life.

'I must save him,' she thought.

She held the child even closer and put her face into the blanket that enveloped him.

She went forward . . . it was difficult to go quickly . . . she felt a sudden agony of pain in her legs . . . she heard her hair singe and her own voice scream with the torture of it.

Then there was the coolness of the night on her face . . . the burden of Peterkin was being lifted from her arms . . . people were touching her . . . hitting her . . . there came a merciful oblivion and she knew no more.

20

Mona opened her eyes and took in her surroundings. She was in a small white room, and as she moved, a nurse came to the bedside and raised a glass to her lips.

'Are you feeling better?' she asked.

Mona had been vaguely conscious for some time of voices of people, of an agonising pain which seemed too intense to be borne but which faded away into a grey oblivion.

Sometimes she dreamed, and knew that the fantasies which crept through her mind were dreams. Now she remembered reality.

'Peterkin! Is he all right?' Her voice was broken and hysterical.

'The little boy?' the nurse asked, in a clear, pleasant voice. 'Yes, he's quite all right. You saved him.'

'He . . . he wasn't burnt?'

The nurse shook her head.

'No, he was quite all right—all the children were. You were the only person who was hurt.'

Mona closed her eyes; gradually she became aware that one of her hands was bandaged; that something weighty seemed to be holding down her legs; that there were bandages, too, round her head. She opened her eyes again.

'Am I badly hurt?'

'Not too badly,' the nurse replied. 'The scars on the legs will heal and your hair will grow again.'

Mona shut her eyes. Somehow it didn't seem very important. She was glad that her face was untouched, she would have hated to be ugly, for the rest, well—it didn't matter.

As long as Peterkin was all right. She heard the nurse move across the room, and speak to someone in the doorway, then footsteps approached the bed.

'If I keep my eyes closed,' Mona thought, 'they'll think I am asleep.'

She felt tired, a great lassitude encompassed her, yet she was aware of someone standing there and without conscious effort her eyes opened. . . .

Looking down at her was Michael. She was not surprised to see him, somehow it was inevitable. A sudden gladness made her feel as if life itself returned to her body. When she spoke her voice was stronger.

'Hello . . . Michael.'

'Are you better, darling?' His voice was low.

'Much . . . better. How did you get here?'

'Your mother and I have been waiting some days,' he replied. 'We've been rather worried about you.'

'Have . . . you? How . . . silly!'

'Not really. You see—we love you.'

Mona felt a warmth encompass and enfold her. Everything was all right now Michael was there.

Vaguely and hazily she remembered that in the past she had been lonely and afraid. But she had made reparation —yes that is what she had done. Now, as if a golden dawn lay before her, she knew that the world held herself and Michael, united and together.

A happiness beyond anything she had ever known pervaded her whole being and she waited, saying nothing, savouring that moment of joy as though fearful if she spoke or moved it might evade her.

'Your mother will want to see you,' Michael said. 'Shall I go and call her?'

'In a moment,' Mona replied. 'There are . . . things I want to . . . ask you . . . first . . . how long shall I be . . . here?'

'A week or so, then we will take you home.'

'How lovely that word sounds when he says it,' Mona thought.

'Was the house . . . completely . . . burned?' she asked irrelevantly.

'It's quite uninhabitable.'

'What . . . about the . . . children?'

'They are being looked after. As a matter of fact, your mother and I had quite a tussle as to whether they should

253

go to the Park or the Priory. I won. I wanted to make quite certain that I should have you near me when you got well enough to go on working.'

Mona smiled—for a moment it almost seemed as if she would laugh, but the effort was too great.

'Oh . . . Michael !' she said. 'Do you . . . always . . . get your own . . . way ?'

He shook his head, but there was a sudden hope in his eyes and the vision came to her of him crawling towards that machine-gun post—determinedly, doggedly reaching his objective.

The glory and gladness in her own heart seemed almost overpowering. She felt as if she could talk no longer but must give herself up to feeling it, to letting it drift over her in a wave of utter happiness.

Yet before she surrendered, she looked up at Michael.

'There's . . . one other . . . question,' she whispered.

'What is it, darling ?'

Her voice came very softly from between her lips so that he must bend forward to hear what she said.

'Do . . . you still . . . want me ?'

She saw an almost unbelievable gladness transform his face. Then he was on his knees beside her, his face very near hers.

'I love you, my darling, my foolish wonderful little love. How could you risk your life when you belong to me ?'

There was so much adoration in his voice she could only tremble with a sudden ecstasy that was beyond words.

'Michael,' she managed to say brokenly. 'Look after . . . me . . . I've been . . . such an . . . idiot . . . but I love . . . you . . . I know now I love . . . you with . . . all my . . . heart.'

'That's all I want to hear,' he said softly. 'You're mine, my precious, and I'll never let you go again.'

'N . . . never ?' she questioned weakly.

She closed her eyes—it was all too wonderful to be borne.

'Never,' he answered, and she felt his lips touch hers.

He was very gentle, but a flame shot through her, a flame

so vivid, so compelling, she knew it was the leaping flame of life.

'Oh Michael! . . . Michael!' she murmured wonderingly. 'This . . . is . . . love.'

Below are details of another book by
Barbara Cartland that will be of interest:

THE AUDACIOUS ADVENTURESS   30p

'Druscilla, it is!—Valdo. For God's sake open the door.'

It is the raffish, irresistible Marquis of Lynche, an avowed bachelor, who pleads for help. Earlier in the day he had taken refuge from some wild party games in the Schoolroom of the Duchess of Windleham's small daughter. To his surprise he found the Governess was his second cousin Druscilla, whom he had not seen since they were children. She begged him then to leave the Schoolroom and to forget her existence.

But now in the early hours of the morning the Marquis beseeches Druscilla to provide him with an alibi which will convince the Duke of Windleham, who has returned home unexpectedly, that he has not been seen coming from the Duchess's bedchamber.

How the Duke is not deceived by the Marquis's lies and insists on a duel, how the Marquis in desperation swears he was proposing marriage to Druscilla and how he is forced into an immediate and secret marriage is the beginning of this exciting, romantic and unpredictable 126th story by Barbara Cartland.